VIEW
FROM THE TOP

Visit us at www.boldstrokesbooks.com

VIEW

FROM THE TOP

by

Morgan Adams

2024

VIEW FROM THE TOP

ISBN 13: 978-1-63679-604-8

This Trade Paperback Original Is Published By
Bold Strokes Books, Inc.
P.O. Box 249
Valley Falls, NY 12185

First Edition: March 2024

CREDITS
EDITOR: Barbara Ann Wright
PRODUCTION DESIGN: Stacia Seaman
COVER DESIGN BY Tammy Seidick

To my wife, who has always been my biggest fan.

VIEW
FROM THE TOP

CHAPTER ONE

E lizabeth Taylor exhaled deeply, watching as her breath billowed and hung around her head like smoke in the cold New York air. She leaned her head back and lifted a hand to block the sun as it reflected from the glass building onto her face. The building was too tall to see the top, but the Chrysler Building, a few blocks away, wasn't. She inhaled deeply, ignoring the painful, burning effect of the sharp winter air as it slid down her throat and into her lungs. Slowly, she smiled. Even twelve-degree weather couldn't dampen her spirits today. She was here. She had done it.

Ever since she was little, Lizzy had dreamt of this moment. When she was six, her second-grade teacher had given everyone in the class a career assignment. "What do you want to be when you grow up?" The prompt had read. Students were told to write a five-sentence "essay" about their career choice and dress like whatever it was they were going to be. She'd watched from the front row, hands folded as miniature cowboys, astronauts, and princesses had paraded in front of the room to read their essays. When it was her turn, she'd stood, adjusted her father's tie that hung past her knees, and walked proudly to the front of the room and proclaimed that she was going to be a lawyer.

Now, at the age of twenty-four, that was exactly what she had done. She was only a few weeks into being admitted to practice law in the State of New York, and she had just landed her dream job. She had followed the course to a T. She'd even graduated high school early so she could get on to college, where she'd majored in pre-law to ensure that she was well-prepared for law school. After three years of law school at the University of Virginia, she'd graduated *magna cum laude*, and for the first time in her life, she had been proud of herself. She was even prouder when she'd received the acceptance letter from one of the most prestigious firms in New York City: Byron & Browning, LLP.

She repeated the nutshell version of her life in her head, psyching herself up to go into the revolving doors that she now stood awkwardly staring at. She cinched the thin coat tighter around her waist and shivered slightly. She hadn't had time to buy proper winter clothing before moving. She'd been born and raised in Virginia, and while it certainly had a winter, it was nothing compared to New York's frigid temperatures.

Lizzy gave herself an internal boost of confidence before pushing firmly on the glass revolving door. It gave way under her effort and began to turn. Once inside, she paused and smiled. The high ceilings had round modern chandeliers throughout. People pushed past as they made their way to the various elevator banks, all separated based on floors. In the center of the massive lobby was a long security desk with three people sitting behind it. A silver sign reading *Byron & Browning* hung on the wall directly behind them.

The sound of heels and dress shoes on the marble floor mixed steadily with the *beep, beep* of people scanning their ID badges as they made their way past the turnstiles blocking public access to the elevators. It was as if the building itself was working to ensure only those who had earned a right to be there could enter.

She crossed to the short line forming in front of the security table. In front of her, a tall man who looked to be around her age nervously fidgeted with a shiny new briefcase. "First day?" Lizzy asked.

He jumped slightly and turned. He had strawberry- blond hair that was parted deeply on one side and thick-framed glasses. His face had a smattering of freckles that made him look younger than he probably was, and his eyes were a bright, innocent shade of green. He looked down at her and smiled a wide, friendly smile, revealing a slight chip in one of his front teeth. "Yeah," he said, shoving his glasses higher on his nose. "You too?"

She nodded. "I'm in the junior associate program."

"Me too. I'm Jackson McCluskey," he said, extending a hand.

She shook it firmly, ignoring the clamminess of his long fingers. "Elizabeth Taylor."

A familiar grin spread slowly across his face.

Here we go, she thought.

"Wait, your real name is Elizabeth Taylor?"

Lizzy sighed. Being named after one of the most famous actresses in Hollywood had gotten a fair share of raised eyebrows throughout her life. She nodded. "Yeah, pretty cruel, right? My mom's a big fan of classic films. So much so she actually named her only child Elizabeth freaking Taylor. Most people call me Lizzy. You can imagine why."

He laughed and pushed his glasses up again. She smiled politely and motioned over his shoulder to indicate that he was next in line to check in at the security desk. He whipped around, his briefcase flying, and Lizzy jumped back slightly to avoid being sideswiped by it. "McCluskey, Jackson. Going to Byron & Browning," she heard him say, his voice shaking.

"ID," the security guard said blankly without looking up.

Jackson dropped his briefcase and quickly fumbled through his pockets before finally locating his wallet. He pulled out his driver's license, shoving it in the man's face.

Lizzy hid a smirk as she clutched her own ID in her coat pocket that she had already pulled out before getting off the subway a few moments ago. She'd stalked the office on Google Earth weeks ago. She'd known what the lobby looked like before even stepping foot in it today. She had mapped out her subway route, with various alternates in the event one line was shut down. Yesterday, she'd spent the morning actually riding the 1 train from her apartment at 149th Street down to Port Authority, then taking the 7 train over to Grand Central, and switching to the 6 train down to 33rd street. She knew the timing wasn't exact because of the weekend schedule, but it had given her confidence to feel prepared for her first day.

Jackson smiled so big, his eyes nearly disappeared for his security photo. She was up next, and Jackson picked up his briefcase and scooted to the side, waiting for her.

"Same place as him," Lizzy said, handing the man her ID and smiling.

The guard checked the ID with a list of names attached to a clipboard beside his keyboard. He raised a dark eyebrow at her before telling her to step back and smile as he took a photo. After a few seconds, he extended a hand, giving her a tiny, smooth piece of paper that acted as her temporary badge. The small square photo was too blurry to even make out her face, but she beamed at the smudged B&B logo printed on the bottom of it. She made a note to keep it forever.

"Sixtieth floor," the guard said, waving up the next person in the line.

"Thanks," she said excitedly, but he was no longer looking at her.

"I waited for you," Jackson said, stating the obvious, and she thanked him as they went to the elevator bank on the far right.

The building was only sixty stories, so their office would be at the very top. She wondered what their view would be like from way up there. Her heart began to beat faster as she swiped her little white paper over the black square in the gold turnstile. A loud *beep* came out, signifying that she was allowed to enter.

"Looks like we're worthy," Jackson said, laughing awkwardly as he walked through behind her.

She smiled politely as she followed a herd of people waiting for one of the eight elevator doors. They waited for the group in front of them to pile into one of the cars, and Lizzy pushed the button to bring down another. She checked her smartwatch. She was still thirty minutes early, but she had always followed the philosophy that being early was being on time, and being on time was being late.

The next elevator dinged behind them, and they shoved into the car together, pushing the round *60* before the door closed. Her stomach dropped as the elevator shot up to the forty-fifth floor. She bit her cheek while people piled off. By the time they reached the sixtieth, it was only Jackson, herself, and another man who had not yet identified himself.

"You starting too?" she asked as the doors slid open.

"No," he said curtly, shooting her a dirty look and stepping off.

Lizzy looked at Jackson and shrugged before stepping off herself. Her jaw dropped slightly as she looked around. Before her were two large glass doors with a frosty *B&B* printed in the center. The ampersand was split in two by the clear doors, and Jackson reached out, pulling the right door open for her. Butterflies fluttered in her stomach as the smell of leather, freshly printed paper, and cologne filled her nose. *The smell of success*, she told herself, fighting to hold in a smile. She pinched the skin on the inside of her wrist, reminding herself she wasn't dreaming.

As they entered the lobby, she noticed a group of three people around their age who all sat clutching identical black leather folders on their laps. She wasn't the only one who'd decided to arrive early.

"Good morning," the woman behind the tall white desk said as they cautiously entered the room. She had thin, bleached blond hair and wore way too much blush. She appeared to be middle-aged, and Lizzy thought she detected a hint of a Southern accent.

"Morning," Lizzy replied for both her and Jackson. "We're new junior associates, starting today."

"Oh, yes, more juniors," the blonde said, smiling wide. "Here ya go, these are for you." She handed them each a black leather folder that matched the others.

Lizzy stroked her finger along the B&B that was embossed into the leather and smiled. "Thank you."

"Of course, of course, now you two take a seat over there, and someone will be right with you."

Lizzy relaxed slightly at the woman's kindness. Most people she had met so far in New York were rude and unhelpful. Then again, she had only lived here for a month, and anywhere would be impolite compared to the overly small town in Virginia where she'd come from. She told herself she would keep an open mind and that the locals would grow on her with time.

Jackson slid into the seat next to her, and she bit her cheek as she studied the three others: a man who had quite possibly the most beautiful features she'd ever seen. He was probably Jackson's height, based on the length of his arms and legs, and he clenched his jaw silently and stared at his phone the entire time. He wore a gray suit with black wing-tipped shoes and a matching black belt. His silk lavender tie was fashioned into a perfect double Windsor, and his pronounced Adam's apple gave him an even more slender appearance.

Then there was a woman with glasses who was probably even shorter than Lizzy, a hard feat at five-foot-two. She glanced up with small brown eyes and smiled briefly when Lizzy and Jackson sat. Jackson waved, but neither of them said anything. She wore a tweed suit that looked like it was from Jaqueline Kennedy's personal closet, but was more likely some piece of couture fashion.

Finally, there was a man with long blond hair pulled back into a neat, low ponytail. He was tall and lean, and his hands took up nearly half the size of the folder in his lap. He had a steely disposition and seemed generally miserable; his eyebrows turned into a permanent frown in the center of his otherwise flawless forehead. His white skin was tan, even though it was the end of January. His sky-blue eyes stuck out of his otherwise sun-kissed face, and his jaw angled down into an almost unnatural point. He wore a navy blue suit with a white shirt and a light blue tie that matched his eyes. His brown shoes and brown belt were both smooth, polished leather. He reminded Lizzy of a fashion model for preppy clothing.

Lizzy looked at her outfit selection and then around the circle. It was clear that everyone else came from some form of money. Even

Jackson's shoes were polished and shiny compared to her dull, worn, plain black pumps. She picked a stray hair off her faded black pencil skirt and adjusted in the leather seat, trying to ignore the obvious contrast between herself and the rest.

"So," Lizzy said after a few moments of painful silence. "How about that bar exam?"

The woman wearing tweed sighed loudly. "I can't believe how much property law was on it."

"Me too," Jackson chimed in. "I think I'm going to have the rule against perpetuities playing on a loop in my head for the next ten years."

"No interest is good…" Lizzy began.

Jackson smiled, and they continued in unison, "Unless it must vest, if at all, no later than twenty-one years after some life in being at the creation of the interest!"

They laughed, and the woman behind the desk let out a low cough, signaling that they were clearly being too loud.

The man with the blond ponytail snorted and rolled his eyes. "What a bunch of nerds," he said loudly.

Lizzy directed her attention toward him. "Isn't that the point of being a lawyer? I mean, we're all nerds."

"Not all of us," he replied, finally making eye contact.

She was about to reply to his snarky comment, but the sound of heels approaching their circle cut her short.

"Good morning, everyone," a silky voice said over their heads.

They all looked up to the woman with a black folder identical to the ones they were all holding tucked into the crook of her arm. Her long, thick, black hair was pulled into a low ponytail, and she wore a tan dress that hit just above her knee. Her eyes were warm and also black, and Lizzy heard the slight hint of an accent when she spoke.

Lizzy reminded herself not to check out the woman she had just met. But she couldn't help herself. She'd always had a thing for beautiful, powerful women.

"My name is Ana Mendez. I am one of the senior associates here, but you can just call us seniors. Like you, I got my beginning at Byron & Browning as a junior associate, and I've been here for the last five years. If you'll come with me, we'll get started with training and icebreakers in the conference room."

A general sense of dread filled Lizzy as she slowly stood. She wasn't looking forward to this part, regardless of her enthusiasm for being here.

As if sensing the shift in the room, Ana said, "I know, I know, but if I had to do it, you have to do it." She spun on her velvet pumps and pranced off in the direction of a long hallway.

Lizzy followed her. The last thing she wanted was to get lost on her first day just because she was too afraid to look eager. She *was* eager, and that was fine. She'd worked hard for every second of success she was about to experience. She wouldn't try to hide her excitement all because one stupid guy with a ponytail had made her feel small. Lizzy held her head higher, ignoring the low sounds of whispers and snickers coming from behind her.

She turned the corner and followed Ana, trotting a little to catch up. Ana looked over her shoulder and smiled. "I figured you'd be the first to follow."

"Why?" Lizzy said, unbuttoning her coat and shifting the weight of her bag on her shoulder.

"I can always spot the gunner in the group," Ana said, showing a row of perfect white teeth.

Lizzy frowned and bit her lip. They walked the rest of the way in silence, passing an endless row of offices and cubicles. The glass doors and walls allowed a view of the Manhattan skyline to seep into the cubicles in the center of the floor, making the space seem twice its actual size.

As they approached the end of the hall, they passed three large conference rooms on their right and more offices on their left. A mixture of anxiety, fear, and excitement began to mount as she saw the size of the floor they were on. The hallway seemed to go on for miles. Lizzy looked around at the rows of attorneys just like her. Better than her. *No, not better. Equal*, she chided herself internally. She was surrounded by countless support staff racing back and forth between each other's desks and passing in the hallway while the sound of phones ringing and keyboards clicking echoed from the open office doors.

Ana turned into the corner conference room that had glass walls on two of the four sides. Lizzy took a seat at the long black table in the center of the room and was glad that the ponytail guy stayed far away from her. Jackson slid into the seat next to her as she stared wide-eyed out the window. She could see the top of the Empire State Building right in front of her, and she smiled. Ponytail man caught her staring from the end of the table and followed her line of sight before rolling his eyes and letting out a low huff. She ignored him and followed the skyline along the row of windows until her sight was cut off by a frosted door in the corner.

Ana was leaning over the laptop in the center of the table. Her long, thick, black hair tumbled from its low ponytail over her shoulder and onto a perfect amount of cleavage.

Lizzy shook her head and focused. "Hey, Ana, why is that office window frosted like that, but none of the others are?"

"Hmm?" Ana lifted her head and followed Lizzy's finger. "Oh, managing partners get frosted doors on their offices. That one belongs to Darcy."

"Darcy?" She could tell Ana was getting frustrated with the distraction, but she had never been one to let a sleeping dog lie. It was part of what had convinced her to stick with her childhood dream of becoming a lawyer, her constant persistence until she got an answer that satisfied her.

"Yes," Ana said, her accent becoming stronger as her frustration grew. "Darcy Hammond is one of the managing partners in this office. There are five here who oversee the operations of the New York office. We'll go over firm hierarchy later in the day."

Managing partner, what a dream. She could only imagine what the inside of that office must look like. Darcy Hammond would have a view of both the Empire State Building and probably all the way to Central Park from there. She knew one thing for certain: whoever he was, Darcy Hammond was one lucky man.

CHAPTER TWO

Darcy Hammond bit her cheek as she leaned back in her chair, looking out over the Midtown skyline. It was only three thirty, and the sun was already beginning to set. She hated winter. She hated how dark the days always seemed, and she hated how early the sun set. She hated feeling the bitter air invade her innocent lungs as soon as she stepped outside, and most of all, she hated that it kept her trapped indoors.

Her only respite was that once a year, she took a weeklong trip up to Vermont in March for some spring skiing and relaxation. Other than that, she could be found right where she was now: in her office, sitting behind her immaculate, massive, sprawling modern desk.

She sighed and spun her chair around, looking at her daily calendar. She still had two phone calls and a meeting with the other managing partners before she could leave for the day, and then there was—

A knock at the door distracted her train of thought. "Enter," she said coolly.

One of the associates—Hanna? Anna? Amanda?—stuck her head sheepishly inside.

"Yes?" Darcy said over the screen.

The woman stood up straight and cleared her throat. "The new juniors, they're almost done with their training for the day, but did you want to, um…" Darcy could hear a nervous stammer clinging to the words.

"Did I want to what, exactly?" It was cruel. She knew she was expected to introduce herself to the incoming juniors, but she loathed people who minced words. She much preferred people to be direct and come out with whatever it was they wanted. Hannah Banana was wasting her time with all this fluff.

The woman cleared her throat. "Introduce yourself, ma'am."

Finally. She clicked her pen a few times out of annoyance and dropped it on her desk before standing and straightening her dress. "Very well, then, let's get on with it."

The woman looked down as Darcy walked past.

Pity. She had seen this woman before, and she'd heard good things about her. Clearly, the woman wasn't incompetent since she had been put in charge of training the new hires. Why there was such an air of insecurity now eluded Darcy.

She heard the woman let out a sigh of relief as she was finally past her.

Darcy looked over her shoulder briefly. "Shut my door."

The woman nodded rapidly and closed the door behind them. Darcy began making her way to the corner conference room, not waiting for the woman to catch up.

As she approached, she could hear the sound of small talk echoing into the hallway from the open door. She smiled slightly, remembering how she'd felt when she was in their shoes. Granted, her first job wasn't at this firm. No, she would never have gotten a job like this fresh out of law school.

Every milestone Darcy Hammond had ever attained had been through hard work, grit, and determination alone. She wasn't born into a wealthy family like these blue-blooded kids. She was born into a blue-collar household. Her father had raised her on his own, and safe to say, his mechanic's salary had barely covered the cost of her tuition at the small Catholic school she'd attended. But the public schools in Florida where'd she grown up were rated some of the worst in the country, and her father had insisted that his priority was her education. Education, he'd claimed, was the key to success.

As her thoughts trailed to her father, she cleared her throat and steeled herself at the memory. Her first job had been at a tiny securities and investment fraud law firm down in the Financial District. She'd made a whopping forty-five thousand a year; had four roommates in a two-bedroom apartment in Weehawken, New Jersey; hiked two hours one-way via bus and subway system; and worked out of a cubicle surrounded by old, musty papers.

Then, after a few years, she'd upgraded to a midsized firm in Murray Hill, a neighborhood just east of Midtown. Her commute was still two hours one-way, and after being there for three years, she'd finally earned a shared office with a guy who ate way too many beans with his lunches. Inch by inch, she'd climbed up the ladder, her salary and experience growing with each rung.

Now, at the age of thirty-eight, she was a managing partner of Byron & Browning, one of the nation's most prestigious law firms. Not only that, she was the youngest managing partner in the firm's history, and she was the only female managing partner in the entire New York office. She knew that was the real reason why she was the one elected to greet the incoming hires. The firm wanted to promote "diversity and inclusion," and since she had the benefit of being both a woman and a lesbian, it was a double win for them.

She knew it was all bullshit. At the end of the day, the rich white men in charge made the actual decisions. But she got a nice office and hearty salary to compensate for the blatant misogyny that still dictated the legal industry.

She could hear the nameless voices coming from the conference room clearly now. She paused for a moment to mentally prepare herself for the speech she knew she was obligated to give, then walked through the door.

Instantly, the chatter ended. She moved past the faceless people and marched to the head of the table near the screen where the floating B&B logo was displayed. "My name is Darcy Hammond. I'm one of the managing partners here. As such, it is my duty and my privilege to welcome you to Byron & Browning."

The woman with the black hair was now in the room, closing the door. No one said a word after Darcy finished speaking, and the room was so quiet, even a pin dropping would make an echo.

Allowing the silence to cling in the air for a moment, she looked around for the first time at the young faces.

There was a brooding young man with a long blond ponytail, a handsome man with a lavender tie, a gangly man with strawberry-blond hair, and a tiny woman wearing a tweed suit. All exactly like the ones she had seen before in her many years at the firm. All came from money. All wore the latest fashion. All came from the top five law schools, no doubt. She had seen so many new associates come and go that by now, she no longer even bothered to ask their names. She knew she would never learn them; after all, why would she need to? She never interacted with juniors after this brief mandatory introduction.

But then her eyes landed on the woman seated closest to her.

She had long blond hair draped gracefully over one shoulder in thick, smooth waves. Her suit was a dull shade of black and was cheaply made; Darcy could tell by the stitching. Her eyes were amber, and they stared directly back at Darcy when she spoke. Darcy glanced at her hands. Short nails but not bitten down. Intentionally kept that way.

She could tell there was something different about this woman by the way she was looking at Darcy. Not with fear or intimidation like most people her age did. How old was she, anyway? She couldn't be more than twenty-six. But somehow, this one was different from the rest. It intrigued Darcy and rattled her slightly, though she made an effort not to show any sign of weakness to the room.

She looked down, collected herself inwardly, and continued. "Here at Byron & Browning, we pride ourselves on diversity and inclusion." The words felt like tar, and she hid a grimace as she continued. "We offer a mentorship program for all new associates. I am sure Ms...." She looked at the dark-haired woman who still stood by the door.

"Ana," the woman responded quickly.

Darcy furrowed a brow. "Ana has filled you in on all of these details, but you will be assigned a mentor before the end of the week. From this point on, you are to reach out to them directly should you need any assistance or have any questions."

The blond woman began scribbling the words as Darcy spoke, and the woman in the tweed suit soon followed while the boy with the strawberry hair stared blankly back at her. The other two kept their heads down.

"You are not to bother any superiors with senseless questions after your training sessions are complete, and on no occasion should you come to me or any other partner with questions about the day-to-day function of the firm. Please consult the paralegals or support staff for those types of questions. Of course, if you have any formal complaints or concerns, please make them to HR. Their information is included in your handbook."

The blond woman turned directly to the section titled *Human Resources.* Darcy felt like a pastor on the pulpit who had just asked the congregation to turn to Luke:2.

"Does anyone have any questions?" She paused only for a second and was about to speak again when a pale hand lifted into the air. She stared at the blonde blankly. "Yes?"

"Lizzy, well, Elizabeth, but you can call me Lizzy, everyone does," the woman rambled.

Darcy continued to stare. She hadn't asked the woman's name.

Frankly, she couldn't care less. The blonde might have been different from her colleagues in certain regards, but at the end of the day, she was just like the rest of them: a mindless drone that would carry out the will of the masses.

The woman cleared her throat and continued, "You mentioned something about diversity? Is there some type of LGBTQ club or membership here?"

Darcy raised an eyebrow. *So she's gay.* Not that it mattered. She had been pushing for a diversity task force for years. If Darcy had her way, the firm would have a dozen groups dedicated to people of color, Asian and Pacific Islanders, LGBTQ+ members, people who identified as women, the list went on and on. When she had presented the idea at one of the partner meetings, it had been laughed at, and the next day, she had gotten a raise for her "ingenuity and progressive attitude." She knew what it really was. Hush money.

"No," she said curtly.

"Oh," the woman said, seemingly unable to hide the disappointment in her voice.

Darcy wanted to tell her to come and find her after this. She wanted to tell her that she knew how it felt to be the only queer person in the straight sea. But she didn't. Instead, she pulled her shoulders back and pressed on. "Anything else? No? In that case, I will leave you to Anya."

"Ana," the blonde corrected without missing a beat.

"Excuse me?" Darcy said, glaring downward.

The other woman looked at the table briefly and began picking at the corner of the piece of paper she had been writing on. "Her... her name is Ana. You said Anya." She looked at Darcy beneath thick, perfectly manicured eyebrows, looking slightly more uncertain than she initially did but still resolute and confident.

Darcy paused for a moment and looked her up and down slowly, taking in every inch. She could hear faint gasps surrounding the room, one of which she was sure came from Anya-Ana herself. Once she completed her visual inventory of the poor woman, Darcy pursed her lips and walked away without another word. She wasn't going to let someone who'd just been admitted get under her skin.

After she left the room, she heard the slow sound of mumbles in the conference room behind her. Once she was safely in the confines of her office, she shut the door and let out a loud breath of relief. Thank God she only had to do that once a year.

She sat at her desk and turned her chair to look out the window again. Four fifteen and there went the sun. She watched as the orange ball made its final descent behind the tall buildings and bit her lip.

Who is that woman anyway? Who does she think she is?

Darcy shook her head. What difference did it make? She would never see her again. She never saw junior associates. But there was something admittedly irresistible about that one. She had the most beautiful eyes Darcy had ever seen. And those lips…

"Oh, for fuck's sake," she said breaking her inner reverie and pushing the speaker button on her phone before dialing two numbers.

"Yes, Ms. Hammond?" her secretary's voice echoed on the other end.

"Veronica, get me the files for all of the new junior associates."

"Right away, Ms. Hammond."

She didn't really care what the woman's name was. She was just curious about her. What harm could come from a little curiosity?

CHAPTER THREE

L izzy twisted the key all the way to the right and pushed until the heavy metal door swung open. Her apartment was in West Harlem, just south of Washington Heights. She'd found the room on Craigslist, of all places, and her mother had warned her that moving in with three complete strangers she'd met on an ad site was a recipe for disaster.

"Haven't you seen enough *Law & Order SVU*?" she'd hollered dramatically. "Be an Alex Cabot, Lizzy. Not a nameless victim. *Think!*"

She could still see her mother tapping furiously on the side of her temple as she'd finished the sentence. But Lizzy had ignored her mother's fearmongering and followed her heart. That choice had led her to the cozy, four-bedroom apartment she was now entering, and she smiled as the smell of Indian food flooded her senses.

"Honey, I'm home," Lizzy announced as she made her way down the long corridor, passing two bedrooms on her right.

She proceeded to cross the tiny living room and drop her bag by the door of her bedroom before walking into the kitchen. Her roommate, Amina, was listening to music with her headphones in and dancing while she cooked.

Lizzy tapped her on the shoulder, and Amina spun around. "Holy shit! You scared me!"

Lizzy laughed. "Smells amazing in here."

"Thanks," Amina pronounced proudly, lifting the lid off a large pot that was boiling on the stove. Lizzy leaned over and inhaled deeply. "It's sambar. My nani's recipe."

Prior to moving to New York, Lizzy's sole source of Indian food had been at a single restaurant in Charlottesville. It was good, but she had only ventured as far as butter chicken and naan. Amina, however, was South Indian, and the food there was completely different. At least once a week over the last month, Lizzy had tried some new dish Amina made, each tastier than the last.

"What up, ladies?" Lizzy heard over her shoulder.

Malia exited her bedroom, removing an earbud from her ear and playing with her phone. She casually leaned against the door frame of her room and finished typing something before making eye contact with Lizzy.

"Not much," Lizzy replied. "Survived the first day."

"Oh shit, that's right," Amina said, stirring the sambar slowly. "Give us the deets. Is the office super fancy? Are the people nice? What do rich lawyers in Midtown even look like?"

"They look white," Malia said, raising an eyebrow and turning her attention back to her phone.

Lizzy shrugged. "Well, some of them are white, yeah, but not all of them, actually. And as far as the office itself, yeah. It's, like, super fancy. I kinda felt like an imposter even walking through the doors." She proceeded to recount most of her day while Malia continued to scroll and pretend to listen, and Amina stirred and bobbed her head.

None of them had ever met before a month ago. They had all responded to the same ad on Craigslist and met with the same Realtor at different times. The first time they'd all met, they'd arranged to meet at a bar down the block called Harlem Pub. It was funny meeting three total strangers and knowing she was about to share a living space with them. It was a bit like college but scarier. Together, they'd made quite the cultural melting pot.

Hoko, the one woman missing from the kitchen, was a marketing agent of some kind from Japan. Amina, whose family was Bengali, worked in customer service at Apple, and Malia, whose family was Haitian, was in school for social and economic justice at NYU. And then there was Lizzy. Although the only diversity she brought to the table was the fact that she was gay AF.

"So," Amina said after Lizzy finished telling them all about the training seminar she'd been in for most of the day. "Give us the real tea. Did you meet any hot ladies? Or better yet, any cute men for me to bring home to Mom and Dad so they get off my back about being single?"

Lizzy's cheeks warmed for a moment as she recalled the day. She had met plenty of attractive people today, that was for sure. First, there was the most obvious choice: Ana. She was Cuban, Lizzy had eventually found out, and her sexy hourglass figure and dark brown eyes had been enough to make Lizzy forget everything she'd learned in the morning session. Much to her chagrin, ponytail man, whose name she eventually learned was Micah Willis, was also very handsome, though she had no interest in dating men anymore. And then there was…

Lizzy felt the blood drain from her chest and puddle between her legs.

"Whoa, okay whoever it is you're thinking about right now, spill." Amina put down the large spoon she was stirring with and propped her head on her chin.

Malia also stopped scrolling and crossed her arms to listen.

"What?" Lizzy protested. "I don't know what you're talking about. I mean, there were a lot of attractive people there today. It's hard to pick is all."

"Mm-hmm," Amina said, pursing her lips. "I don't buy it."

"Don't buy what?" A soft voice chimed in from over Lizzy's shoulder. Hoko entered the kitchen to join the gossip.

"Lizzy has a crush on someone at work and won't tell us who it is."

Hoko grabbed a bottle of water from the fridge and crossed her legs as she sat at the small kitchen table. "Oh! In that case, go on," she said taking a sip of water.

Six eyes now rested on Lizzy. She should have been used to this feeling by now. She'd done moot court in law school, for heaven's sake. This was nothing compared to a hot bench of pretend judges grilling her about appellate court decisions. But none of that mattered now as her head began to swim, and her heart raced. She looked down, trying to avoid all eye contact. "You guys are crazy," she said, turning to walk back to her room.

"You can run, but you can't hide, Elizabeth Taylor," Amina yelled after her.

Lizzy heard the sounds of giggles and mumbling as she closed her bedroom door behind her. She leaned against the back of the door and let out a loud sigh. It had been one hell of a day. The firm was everything she had ever dreamed of. The views, the building, even the people, right down to their expensive shoes and suits.

She looked around her square bedroom and its mismatched furnishings. When she'd found out she was accepted into the junior associate program at Byron & Browning, she'd jumped, cried, and then panicked. She had just found out she'd passed the bar and only had a few weeks to find an apartment and move her entire life to New York, where she knew absolutely no one.

Lizzy would be making a decent salary at her new job but not for at least a month, until the first paycheck rolled in. That meant she had pennies left in her savings to buy furniture and move. So a few weeks ago, she'd spent an entire day driving around in a U-Haul, picking up free furniture on the side of the road and buying used stuff for cheap off Craigslist. Even her mattress had been free, an idea which made her cringe only slightly when she'd fallen onto it half-naked that first night after moving in.

She'd spent the first week organizing and arranging the cheap furniture to make it look as presentable as possible, and now it felt almost like home when she walked in every day.

She slid off her blazer and pencil skirt and flexed her toes, allowing them to breathe after a long day in heels. She pulled on a pair of joggers and an old UVA hoodie from law school and walked to one of the two windows in her bedroom. The bitter air bit deeply into her exposed skin as she flung one of them open, but she didn't care. This was her favorite part of her room.

She dipped one leg out the window and bent, allowing her body to slide out onto the metal fire escape. Large, old-fashioned Christmas lights were wrapped around the railing, and a Pride flag hung over one end of it. The "gay Bat-Signal," she called it. She closed her eyes and listened to the sounds of people talking, cars passing, dogs trotting, and sirens blaring, all only five stories below her feet.

The fire escape was on Broadway. Granted, it was at the very end—or rather, the very beginning—but she hadn't told her mom that part when she'd told her about the apartment. Her mom was so proud to say she had a daughter who worked as an attorney in New York City and lived on Broadway. She didn't have the heart to burst her bubble and tell her just how many blocks from "Broadway" her apartment really was.

She opened her eyes and wrapped her arms tightly around her knees and blew a breath of cold air out. She focused on ignoring the cold that now cut through her thin sweatshirt and thought about her first day at work. She thought about her new friend, Jackson, and the other woman in the group who had eaten lunch with them, Cho. She was polite, but Lizzy didn't foresee them being great friends. She thought about Micah Willis and his ridiculous ponytail. She thought about Ana and her insanely perfect body. And then, without her permission, she thought about—

She shook her head. "Stop it. The woman is basically your boss. And she is way out of your league. Plus, she's kind of a bitch."

But she knew the pep talk meant nothing. Any guard she had melted entirely away the second Darcy Hammond had walked into that conference room today. There was something about her presence that instantly drew Lizzy in. The blatant Claire Underwood vibes that Darcy shot off would be enough to freeze any normal person, but for Lizzy, it only piqued her interest.

She couldn't stop thinking about how absolutely perfect Darcy had looked in her fitted, navy blue dress, or how her long, muscular legs had fit perfectly into her nude pumps. Her hair was, of course, also perfect, tied back in streaks of brown and gray into a low French twist. Even the perfume she wore was enough to drive Lizzy wild. She made a mental note to find out what the heck it was and buy a couple of dozen bottles. There was nothing sexier than a woman in charge, and Darcy Hammond was exactly that. Lizzy imagined she was the type of woman who could walk into a room of men and demand just about anything… and actually get it.

Lizzy bit her lip as the cold broke her from her reverie, but she refused to go inside. No. For now, she would sit here in her little castle in the clouds and look at what she had worked so hard for. She would sit here until she couldn't stand it anymore, and then she would go inside and lay out her outfit for her second day of work. And yes, she would probably daydream about her new, perfect, power-suit-wearing boss while doing it.

CHAPTER FOUR

Darcy watched the burgundy liquid reach the halfway point in her glass and stopped. She didn't need a full glass of wine on a Monday night, but half wouldn't hurt. She swirled her night's selection of cab sav around and took a sip. She used to hate the taste of red wine, but after a trip to Napa a few years ago, she had acquired a taste for the good stuff. Now, when she was at restaurants, she took pride in identifying where the vintage was from, the age, and the types of grapes used. She was almost always wrong, but it was fun to try.

This one was a bit dry for her liking, but she drank it anyway. She needed something to settle her nerves after today. She turned on some music and walked to her couch and sat, wineglass in hand. She rested her head back against the cool leather as Billie Holiday echoed through the large open room.

She loved this apartment. It was in SoHo and as such, was incredibly overpriced, but coming home to a beautiful space was worth the expense, or so she'd told herself when she'd first bought it a few years back. "Apartment" wasn't really a proper term for it; it was by all definitions a loft. It had a large exposed brick wall on one side, and one wall was made of windows that faced south, and if she craned her neck a certain way, she could see the top of the Freedom Tower peeking out behind her southward neighbors' buildings. The building used to be a factory of some sort before the area was gentrified in the late 90s, and she loved that it still had remnants of its former life clinging between each brick.

The historical charm of the room was only enhanced by Darcy's classic leather and mahogany furnishings. The Chesterfield sofa she currently sat on was composed of stretched brown leather and was the most expensive piece of furniture she'd ever purchased. Another indulgence that was worth it in her mind. Black-and-white photographs were housed in black-matted frames throughout the large room, all taken by her on her various solo travels and adventures. Those had all happened back before she'd made partner, of course.

Clean lines and perfect right angles engulfed the loft. Not a single appliance sat on the kitchen counter, and not a piece of bric-a-brac haunted her immaculate and color-coordinated bookshelf. Darcy hated clutter. It made her head hurt. She liked things just like she liked her photographs: black-and-white. Shades of gray annoyed her, and she preferred to know the rules first and foremost. Then she could determine which of those rules she would elect to follow. This philosophy had carried over into her taste for interior design, and the stark contrast of historical charm and modern undertones was woven throughout the place she called home.

She'd gotten in too late to make dinner, so she'd decided to have a liquid diet and go to bed soon. Another day, another late night at the office. When she'd made partner all those years ago, she'd thought for sure the title would come with some reprieve of obligations. Instead, in addition to the double salary, she'd inherited double the work.

As a managing partner, Darcy was responsible for overseeing over one hundred senior associates and around twenty-five of counsels, in addition to the administrative tasks that went along with being a managing partner, including daily meetings, weekly networking events, and of course, the obligatory shoulder-bumping and hand-shaking events for major clients that happened around once a month. She was exhausted at the end of every day, and she barely had time to even spend the insane amount of money she was bringing home.

Relationships were a thing of the distant past too. Sure, she'd dated her fair share of beautiful women. After all, there was no shortage of those in New York, but at the end of the day, she'd never met anyone who really understood what it took to succeed in her industry. The long hours, the missed holidays, the weekend work. But, man, had she had fun trying to find Mrs. Right once upon a time.

Darcy smiled as she remembered the events she used to go to back in her twenties. Somehow, she'd gotten on the list for an "invite-only" party that moved around the city every month. It had a speakeasy vibe to it and was essentially a traveling haven for New York's successful and elite femmes. A feasting ground for an ambitious young attorney such as herself. She remembered sauntering into the events every month and going home with a beautiful new woman. Always blond. Always fit. Always amazing in bed.

But when she'd turned thirty, she knew she needed to double down on work if she wanted to advance in her career. Byron & Browning had just lost one of their managing partners, and she had her eyes on the prize. Five years later, she'd attained the goal. Now, eight years later, here she was. Living her dream. Or so she told herself as she sat alone in her beautiful empty home every night. It was easier this way. No relationships, no complications, no risk of anyone getting hurt. She had always lived by the idea that keeping people at arm's length kept everyone safer, and it had panned out for her pretty damn well. She couldn't remember the last time she'd let anyone get close enough to cause actual damage to her heart.

Darcy let her mind wander to the events of the day. She stood from the leather couch and walked to the front door and pulled out the folders she'd brought home with her. She didn't know why she'd brought *all* of them. Probably to convince herself that what she was doing was acceptable. That she was just being an invested partner, researching to get to know the five new junior associates that had joined that quarter. It had nothing to do with the bold, assertive voice that had corrected her in the meeting today. It had nothing to do with the amber eyes that had seemed to melt into her heart when she'd looked up at Darcy. No, it wasn't about that at all.

Darcy flipped open the first file. A pair of dark eyes stared back at her through a subtle, pearly white smile.

Name: Efe Buhle
Age: 25
Pronouns: He-Him
Law School: Stanford University, Stanford, California
GPA: 4.0
Extracurriculars: Spent summer in Uganda with Amnesty
International

Darcy nodded, only impressed with the Amnesty International bit. She recalled the dark man in the gray suit and purple tie but only briefly. It was nice to know he had some hint of depth, although to be fair, all of the junior associates did some form of extracurriculars to make them stand out from the hundreds of applicants that the firm received every quarter.

She moved on to the next. A familiar face glared cockily back at her, and she rolled her eyes at the ridiculous ponytailed face grinning from the page.

Name: *Micah H. Willis*
Age: *26*
Pronouns: *He-Him*
Law School: *Columbia University, New York, New York*
GPA: *3.1*
Extracurriculars: *None*

Darcy shook her head. Of course Micah Willis would be accepted with a subpar GPA and no extracurriculars. His father was Halcomb Willis, one of the judges in the court where nearly all of their trials were held. The blatant favoritism for white privileged snobs like Micah didn't surprise her anymore, but it still angered her. She flipped the file shut and tossed it to the side.

She opened the next, secretly hoping to see a pair of golden-brown eyes. When she saw a scrawny man with strawberry-blond hair, she sighed and closed it without even reading it and moved to the next until she finally landed on the one she wanted:

Name: *Elizabeth A. Taylor*

Well, that's a fucking cruel name.

Age: *24*

How the hell is she so young?

Pronouns: *She-Her*
Law School: *University of Virginia, Charlottesville, Virginia*
GPA: *4.0*
Extracurriculars: *Trial team, national champion; moot court, regional champion; legal journal editor; worked part-time at law school library; law school softball team, pitcher.*

Jesus, no wonder she's so confident. She's spent the last three years gearing up for this shit.

Darcy looked at the photo. Who knew something so beautiful and innocent-looking could be so full of fire and ambition? She hated to admit it, but it made her even more drawn to this woman with the horrible name. She found herself wondering what the A in her middle name stood for. Whether she was originally from the South or had just gone to school there. What had drawn her to New York? Why did she decide to become a lawyer?

After what seemed like way too long to think about someone fourteen years younger than her, she shut the folder and tossed it on the stack with the rest.

Her curiosity was satisfied now. Tomorrow she would go to the office and never see Elizabeth Taylor again. The poor woman would likely be buried in mounds of paperwork in the basement most of the day anyway. There was no way Darcy and her would ever cross paths again. Of that, she was certain.

CHAPTER FIVE

"S leep well?" Jackson asked perkily.

Lizzy covered her mouth as she finished a large yawn. It was only her second day of work, and she was already exhausted. The adrenaline and excitement of yesterday had caused an almost hungover feeling in her head as she rose this morning. Not to mention the fact that she had *not* slept well at all. The blaring sirens and shouting in the streets below her window had echoed long into the night, and she hadn't learned how to drown them out yet. On top of that, Hoko, who still hadn't adjusted to New York time from Japan, was up late cooking a very strong-smelling food.

By the time she made it to the office this morning, she needed coffee badly.

"Didn't they say there was a kitchen somewhere on this floor or something?" Lizzy asked, ignoring his question.

He stroked his chin. "I think it was a kitchen*ette*, and I think it was that way," he said, eagerly pointing down the long hall of windows.

She could already tell his constant perkiness and need to be right would annoy her without enough caffeination, and she tried to remain silent and not roll her eyes. "I'm just gonna grab a cup of coffee before we start."

It was only seven forty-five. She was early, or rather, on time, again, and they weren't all meeting in the conference room until eight, so there was no need to rush. She covered another yawn as she made her way down the endless row of cubicles and other offices. She looked at her outfit. Her faded gray pantsuit had seen better days, and the pants now hung off her hips a bit more loosely than they had in law school. Weight loss was just a side effect of living off one bag of ramen noodles a day; her first paycheck was coming soon, and man, did she really need it. She had been poor in law school, sure, but she was even poorer right now.

She glanced into one of the offices with a silver nameplate on the door that read *Jonathan P. Lyman, Of Counsel*.

She wondered how long it would be until she got a window office or even an office at all. Ana had told them yesterday that they would be split into one pair of two and one set of three and placed in internal offices soon. She wasn't sure what floor they would even be on. The law firm owned the building, but it leased out the first thirty-nine floors to various tenants. Floors forty to sixty were all attorneys, support staff, bookkeepers, accountants, HR, etc. for Byron & Browning. She just hoped she wouldn't be stuck with Micah Willis and his stupid ponytail.

And then there was the dreaded basement. Yesterday, after the shiny colored books were passed out by HR and the sexual harassment training was complete, they were all taken on a tour to the level marked by a simple *B* on the elevator panel.

Ana had led them through rows of shelves all stacked with banker's boxes and Redwelds. It reminded Lizzy of that scene in *Indiana Jones* where they hid the Ark of the Covenant in an unmarked storage box. The room was lit by eerie overhead lights, smelled like mildew, and ran the entire footprint of the building. She couldn't imagine ever being able to find her way around the massive room, let alone locate a single item she might have needed.

"The firm has moved to a paperless model for all incoming cases," Ana had explained, "but for cases that have index numbers before 2020, you'll be down here for some things you need. Hard copies of discs, imaging studies, trial exhibits, blueprints, and other things are all housed permanently in the basement or *the bowels*, as we call it."

The nickname had garnered a few awkward chuckles from the group, who'd all seemed to be pondering how much time they would be expected to spend in the sunless dungeon.

Lizzy shuddered, remembering her brief time in the bowels as she rounded the corner to what she assumed to be the kitchenette. "Oh," she said as she stopped dead in her tracks.

Bending over and leaning into the refrigerator was a pair of long, muscular legs beneath a black dress. The dress hit just above the knees, and Lizzy could see the outline of the stranger's quads peeking out from the hemline. She tilted her head slightly and studied the curve and roundness of the woman's backside.

Could this firm get any better? There were literally hot women everywhere. Lizzy cleared her throat, preparing to make her move on whoever she was openly admiring. "Need a hand?" she said, leaning casually against the door and crossing her arms. This should be easy. Probably a clerk or paralegal. Maybe she could impress her by saying she was an attorney here.

"That depends," a raspy voice from inside the fridge said. "Do you have almond milk?" The legs began to stand before a familiar perfect head of brunette and silver hair emerged from the other side of the door.

Oh shit.

"Oh, Ms. Dar…I mean Ms. Hammond, I didn't…"

Darcy tapped her finger impatiently on the refrigerator door. "You're rambling."

Lizzy cleared her throat. "No, I don't have any almond milk."

Darcy sighed and closed the refrigerator and turned to grab a mug of coffee sitting on the counter. "Black it is," she said coolly, taking a sip of the hot liquid and glaring into Lizzy's eyes.

Lizzy's heart began to race, and her mind went blank as Darcy stared intensely over her cup. Steam from the liquid swirled above, dancing playfully around Darcy's piercing green eyes.

Say something, you idiot. Smile or make a joke. Anything. Say anything. Do anything. But she didn't. She just stood there, mouth still open, half words stuttering and rolling around in her brain.

Darcy finished her sip and stroked the handle of the mug methodically with her index finger. It was then that Lizzy saw a single word written in all caps in white across the navy blue background: *YALE.*

Darcy took another sip in silence and began to walk out of the kitchenette, and Lizzy tried hard to not inhale the musky perfume that wafted into her nose as she did. When Darcy was a few feet past, Lizzy turned and said, entirely too loudly, "Yale, huh? We beat you guys in moot court, you know."

Oh God, seriously, Lizzy? Is that the best you've got? "I don't have almond milk" and "my school is better than your school"?

Darcy turned slowly, pivoting on her black suede pump. She let out a soft, disinterested sigh and took a few steps closer. Lizzy focused on breathing. "What makes you think I went to Yale?" she asked, now standing only a few feet away.

Lizzy cleared her throat but spoke boldly this time, gathering back some of her natural confidence. "Your coffee cup," she said, motioning toward it.

Darcy looked down as if noticing it for the first time and smirked. She took a few more steps closer. Too close. Her perfume invaded Lizzy's senses, and she could feel her strength leaving her as Darcy looked down on her. She looked Lizzy up and down for a moment, almost the same way she had in the conference room yesterday, only this time, it was more curiosity and less soul-devouring. She stroked the handle of the mug again. "Well, you know what they say about assumptions."

She leaned in so close, Lizzy could see flecks of blue and gold in her emerald eyes. She lowered her voice to almost a whisper that made the natural rasp in it somehow even sexier. Lizzy gulped, focusing on controlling her heartbeat, as if that was even possible under normal circumstances.

"I didn't go to Yale," Darcy said. "I just use this cup to annoy Stanley." She nodded in the direction of an office door that read *Stanley R. Cohen, Of Counsel*. "It's his." With that, Darcy turned on her heels and was gone down the hall and out of sight, the smell of her perfume still clinging to Lizzy's senses long after her departure.

She stood there for what felt like hours, replaying the entire encounter over and over in her head. She had no idea how much time had passed when she heard Jackson yelling from down the hall and waving her to the conference room where their training was continuing.

Lizzy jolted back to reality and trotted down the hall, feeling her ponytail swishing back and forth.

"Did you get your coffee?" Jackson asked as she joined him at their same seats from yesterday. Ana was already loading a slide that read *Submitting Expenses*.

Lizzy pulled out her legal pad, already half-full with yesterday's notes. Everything had been given to them in handouts, but Lizzy took notes anyway. An old habit she'd picked up back in college and had never been able to drop.

She was focused. She was ready. Ready to learn all about expenses or…whatever else they were learning today. She certainly was *not* going to sit here and daydream about her annoyingly attractive boss. She had already done too much of that alone in bed last night.

"Woo-hoo, earth to Lizzy," Jackson said, waving in front of her face.

"What?" she said, shaking her head and looking at him.

"You okay? I asked if you got your cup of coffee, and you kinda spaced out on us."

"Oh, that. No, I'm good. Looks like I'm more awake than I thought."

CHAPTER SIX

D arcy set the cup of black coffee on the glass coaster on her desk. She smiled softly as she read the white YALE printed on the side. It was true, she always used this mug to annoy Stanley. And when this one was dirty, there was Harold's *Crimson Crew* mug or Hillary's black *Go Big Red* tumbler. There was an endless sea of Ivy League graduates to annoy here at Byron & Browning, and Darcy loved reminding them of just how insignificant their overpriced degrees were.

She hadn't graduated from an Ivy League school. Not even close. No, she'd graduated summa cum laude from Stetson University in Florida. A state most New Yorkers liked to make fun of until it came time to retire with their easy taxes, beautiful weather, and golf courses. Stetson was, by all definitions, an excellent school, and their trial program was one of the best in the country. But it wasn't an Ivy, and it wasn't good enough to land her a job at a fancy firm like Byron & Browning fresh out of law school. She wasn't like the Stanleys or Harolds or Hillarys of the world, and of that, she was proud.

She took a sip of coffee, gagging a little as she swallowed. She hated black coffee. She had no idea how she'd been able to choke so many sips down during that little encounter with Elizabeth Taylor.

Elizabeth Taylor. The woman with the unfortunate name. And the beautiful, long blond hair and brown eyes. The one human she had hoped to avoid today would, of course, be the one she ran into first thing in the morning.

Darcy bit her thumbnail as she recalled Elizabeth's reaction after seeing her in the kitchen. The look on her face had been priceless. Darcy had watched her go from cocky to shocked to literally speechless when she'd realized who it was hanging out of the refrigerator. Darcy hadn't caused that reaction out of someone in a while.

Was it fair of her to torture the poor thing after she'd seen that painful look of realization? No. Was it even mildly appropriate, considering Elizabeth was barely out of law school, and Darcy was one of the most senior people at the firm? Definitely not. Was it the most thrilling thing she had done in months? Absolutely.

She felt a slight blush rushing to her cheeks as she thought about Elizabeth's face. She shouldn't have stood so close. Even if she was one of the highest-ranking attorneys in the firm, if anyone had seen them, it could have been misconstrued as…what, exactly? What were her intentions with their little banter?

She had flirted. For maybe two seconds. With a subordinate. She was fairly confident that the men in this office had done far worse. *Oh, yeah, because that makes sexual harassment totally okay, Darcy.*

A knock on the door snapped her back, and she jumped slightly before collecting herself and telling the person to come in.

Her paralegal, Patty, walked in. Patty was a middle-aged woman with short, curly red hair that she dyed far too regularly. She was divorced and a single mother, and her Long Island accent grated on Darcy's nerves. But if there was one person Darcy would never be short with, it was Patty. She had been with Darcy since her first day at Byron & Browning, and as Darcy began rising in the ranks, she'd made sure she brought Patty right up along with her. There wasn't much Darcy wouldn't do to make sure Patty was well taken care of at this firm.

She came in every day at eight on the dot to give Darcy a rundown of her day. As if Darcy, with her anal-retentive brain, would ever solely rely on another person to convey her agenda.

"Good morning. Today's itinerary for you. You have a—"

"A partner meeting at nine, client calls at ten fifteen, eleven, and eleven thirty, a deposition at noon that should last until four, then another meeting at four thirty, and maybe at some point after that, I get to eat something?"

Patty flashed a wide smile back at her. "On top of it, as always. I know, I know, but I just like to check." Patty walked over, her short thighs rubbing together against her black hose.

The noise made Darcy's arm hairs stand on end, but she ignored it and thanked Patty for the agenda. She took the paper and laid it on her desk.

"Oh, and don't forget you have the *Meadows* trial coming up next month. It's on the trial calendar," Patty added, folding her hands over her stomach.

Darcy rubbed her forehead as she looked at her monthly calendar. "Fuck me, how is it almost March already?"

Patty chuckled. "Don't ask me, time just flies faster and faster every year. That's a pretty big case. Will you be needing a senior on it? I have Ana already preparing the trial authorizations, and I can get a junior started on making exhibits and binders."

"A junior?" Darcy's eyes shot up. "Are they approved for this case?"

Patty nodded. "Didn't you get the memo from Frank this morning?"

Darcy cringed. Frank Bauman was the CEO of Byron & Browning. She didn't have many bosses, but if she did have one, Frank was it. He worked out of the Los Angeles office, which meant he was not at all in touch with the day-to-day operations of any of the firm's offices, let alone one across the country. He was constantly making new policies and protocols that not only made no sense but were impossible to enforce. In sum, he made Darcy's job a lot harder than it needed to be.

"What sage wisdom passes down the pipeline now?" she asked, rubbing her temple.

Patty chuckled. "Apparently, one of the areas that the firm is working on improving is developing junior associates to stay on long-term. Frank has decided to do that by having a junior associate assigned to a partner or an of counsel for one trial a year."

"Oh, you have got to be kidding me." The last thing she needed was to babysit a junior on a trial. She didn't handle many these days, and if she did, they were big. Like, multimillion-dollar big. She usually had at least two seniors doing the legwork and an of counsel second chairing it with her. But a junior associate? It was unheard of.

Patty just shrugged. "Afraid not. But the good news is, you get to choose whoever you want. I believe their exact words were 'ladies first.'"

Darcy ignored the tongue-in-cheek remark from her fellow partners. Instantly, her mind shot to Elizabeth, and she felt her cheeks flush slightly. She looked unintentionally at the mug on her desk and shook her head. "Well, that tracks."

Can this day get any worse?

CHAPTER SEVEN

"Could this day *get* any better?" Lizzy asked, practically bouncing into her new office. She and Cho had been assigned the two-person office while the three men were forced to share the other one. This one had no windows, and there was barely enough room for two desks and a single bookshelf, but it was hers, all hers.

Well, at least half of it.

Cho delicately placed her black leather Chanel shoulder bag on the swivel chair and looked around. "Pretty small, wouldn't you say?"

Lizzy shrugged. "Sure, but it's only for our first few years. Then we start to move up the ranks. And it's window offices after that."

Cho looked passively in her direction. "I won't be here anywhere near that long. My father says all I have to do is a year, and I can get the federal clerkship I really want. Then it's off to be a judge for me. What about you?"

Lizzy nodded. "I mean, I hope I'm still here in two years. Can't imagine where else I'd want to be."

Cho rolled her eyes walked toward the exit. "Way to dream big, Eight."

Lizzy frowned and gritted her teeth. This morning's icebreaker had involved Ana asking everyone to talk about their law school. Lizzy had listened as everyone took turns. Stanford, Harvard, Yale, and Columbia had all rolled off the tongues of her colleagues until finally, it was her turn.

When she'd announced that she'd attended the University of Virginia in Charlottesville, she was met with snickers and eye rolls from everyone but Jackson, who'd just smiled reassuringly at her. Apparently, the fact that her school was *not* a top-five was common knowledge. On top of that, the fact that it was ranked *eighth* in the nation was also common knowledge, and for the rest of the day, everyone but Jackson had insisted on calling her Eight.

Lizzy had always been proud of her alma mater. She had busted her ass in LSAT prep her senior year and gotten high enough to earn her a full ride. She loved her school. She loved the history, the architecture, and the town. She was so proud to be a Wahoo, through and through. But all of that seemed silly now that she was surrounded by top-fivers with Hermès bags and Armani suits.

She ignored Cho and followed her out of the room. The three men were across the hall getting settled into their small, closet-sized office.

"I see you ladies settled in fast," Micah said, exiting the office.

"Not much to have settled," Cho replied, motioning to the barren room.

The small office had two metal desks and two empty bookshelves, and the overhead lighting was a headache waiting to happen. And if one of them ate seafood for lunch, they would be smelling it all week.

"We'll have to bring in a plant or something," Jackson said, sitting at his desk and twirling in the chair.

"It's not going to get enough sunlight, dumbass," Micah snipped back, rolling his eyes.

Jackson looked down and bit his lip, clearly embarrassed.

"Actually, some plants thrive in darker places. Take orchids, for example," Lizzy chimed in defensively. Jackson had been nothing but nice to her since the moment they'd met. She wasn't going to sit by while the "popular kids" bullied him. She went to college early to get out of high school, not to graduate law school and go back to it.

Jackson's face perked up, and he smiled gratefully.

Micah smirked. "What, was Law of Botany a class at your law school down south, Eight?"

She ignored him and clenched her jaw, checking her smartwatch. It was nearly four thirty. They had been told to get settled in their new offices and meet Ana back in the conference room by four forty-five for one final announcement before they would be set free for the day.

She hoped their formal training would be over soon. She might have to share an office with Cho, but she was ready for space from Micah Willis and his incessant attitude. She was ready to start getting her hands on some cases and working with the senior associates. She was ready to meet the support staff and paralegals. She was ready to feel like the lawyer she was.

"We should get going." Lizzy turned and left, heading back in the direction of the conference room.

She was the first one back and took her usual seat at the large table. She flipped open her notepad and began aimlessly reviewing the morning's notes:

Expenses were to be submitted at the end of each month. Any late expenses were at risk of being disputed. Junior associates were permitted a pretax MetroCard that would make her commute significantly cheaper. Each junior would be assigned to work with three to five seniors. Eventually, they would be assigned cases of their own but still work under the supervision of senior associates and of counsels.

Her brain tingled with the major influx of new information, and she tried to contain the mixed feelings of both excitement and anxiety that seemed to orbit her body. She read the list again and again until the sounds of mindless chatter filled the room, and soon, she was surrounded once again by her fellow juniors in training. Jackson took his normal seat by her side and flashed her a reassuring smile as Ana entered the room.

Lizzy homed in on the section of the handbook titled *Interoffice Relationships*. She glanced over her shoulder in the direction of the corner office briefly before continuing to read:

Any employee who becomes romantically involved with a coworker shall disclose the nature of such relationship to human resources within five to ten business days. While not expressly forbidden, romantic relationships between employees are not encouraged, as they often lead to distractions in the workplace. Should your relationship present a conflict of interest for a client, or should it be determined that the relationship has hindered your work product in any way, appropriate measures will be taken.

Lizzy gulped, trying to imagine what repercussions there could even be for dating someone she worked with. In a firm this large, surely, it was inevitable. The idea of the unknown was enough to send a shiver a fear down her spine. She continued to read subsection A of the general rule:

Romantic relationships of any kind between superiors and subordinates are strictly forbidden. Any employee failing to comply with this subsection of the handbook will be terminated immediately.

Lizzy felt her mouth go dry. *Terminated immediately.* Her worst nightmare. She looked over to Ana. "What exactly does this mean?"

"What's that?" Ana replied.

"In the handbook, it mentions superiors are not allowed to date subordinates. I was just wondering if you could, um, clarify that a little more?" She tried to keep the question light and casual, but her fellow juniors were already giving her their undivided attention, and it was hard not to make her voice go up at the end of the sentence.

A soft smile spread across Ana's face. "It's a pretty loose rule as far as attorneys go. Seniors and juniors are allowed to date, if that's what you're asking. The rule is really in place to prevent partners from placing undue pressure on subordinates."

"Ana and Eight sitting in a tree," Micah chimed up from across the table.

Lizzy rolled her eyes, and Ana's cheeks flushed a soft shade of red. "All right, all right," Ana said, reining in the room. "Like I said, it's a pretty loose rule. It's really designed to make sure partners aren't taking advantage of associates. You know, sexual harassment and such."

"So," Lizzy asked, unable to stop herself. "A partner and a junior associate, for example?"

Ana let out a loud laugh. "Yes, that's exactly the type of thing this policy was put in place to prevent. Lucky for you, most of the partners are nearly twice your age and married."

Most of them?

"All right," Ana continued, "I hope you've all found your offices okay. You're lucky to even be on this floor, honestly, but this is where we had the space, so it just worked out. I do have a few brief announcements before I let you go for the day."

Lizzy clicked her pen and leaned over to begin writing.

"First of all, the firm has announced a new program designed to help develop and foster long-lasting careers with juniors such as yourselves. As of now, you will each be working with a managing partner or an of counsel on a trial. You will assist the attorney in everything and anything they need. You will not sit second chair, but you will be present in the courtroom to assist with technology issues, exhibits, and the frequent coffee run."

Lizzy's ears perked up, and she stopped writing, her heart beginning to race as Ana continued to speak.

"You will each be working with a managing partner or an of

counsel. This is an exceptional opportunity. I advise you to work hard and absorb every ounce of experience you can. Most junior associates at big firms don't see the light of day for their first three years, let alone a courtroom."

Oh shit.

This was unbelievable. Her first week at the job, and already, she was being assigned a trial! None of her friends from law school had even seen a courtroom yet, except the prosecutors, who were basically thrown into the fire on day one. It was unheard of for a big law firm like Byron & Browning to let junior associates be seen, let alone be seen representing a client in front of a judge and jury. Lizzy could barely contain her excitement. She wondered who she would be working with and which—

Oh shit.

Her mind jumped to her interaction with Darcy Hammond that morning. Surely, she wouldn't be working with the tall Adonis she had so smoothly insulted this morning, right? Could fate be so cruel, or rather, so kind?

"Any questions?" Ana asked.

Lizzy's hand shot into the air. "You mentioned we would be working with—"

Ana cut her off. "A managing partner or an of counsel, depending on the trial calendar."

"So," Lizzy continued, "does the partner or, uh, of counsel, get to choose who they want to work with, or is it done at random?"

"I'm not sure. Could be chosen, could be random."

Lizzy breathed a sigh of relief. There was absolutely no chance Darcy would ever choose to work with her. Especially not after their limited interactions had been so…awkward? Intense? She wasn't even sure. And the odds of them getting put together by sheer chance were still manageable.

"What was the second announcement?" Cho chimed in, removing the spotlight from Lizzy.

"Ah, yes, thank you for the reminder," Ana said, her full lips curling back into a heavy smile. "This Friday night, we're going out for happy hour after work. It's a tradition to welcome the new juniors each quarter. We'll all walk over to the Ainsworth after work. It's usually a mixed crowd. Definitely a lot of senior associates and maybe even some of counsels."

Lizzy knew she would regret asking her next question, but she just couldn't stop herself. Try as she might, the question still rolled off her tongue: "Do any of the partners ever go to the happy hour?"

Ana considered the question a moment. "Not since I've been here. It's really a chance for the people you'll be working with on a daily basis to meet you. There's not really a need for partners to show up."

"Relax, you'll get your chance to brownnose the partners," Micah added.

"Shut up, Micah," Jackson said.

"That wasn't why I was asking," Lizzy said, feeling the need to defend herself.

Micah sneered and leaned back in the chair, resting his arms behind his head.

Whatever.

CHAPTER EIGHT

A ll right, Darcy, go ahead. Tell us about your upcoming trial."
Darcy lifted her head and looked around the room where the beady eyes of four older white men stared back at her. She had completely zoned out during Mark's presentation on his upcoming trial, and she had no idea it was her turn until Paul kicked her under the table.

She hadn't slept well once again, and the week had dragged on for what seemed like forever. Other than her little run-in with Elizabeth Taylor, the rest of the week had gone by pretty uneventfully. She had her usual meetings, client calls, court conferences, and various administrative tasks, but nothing was exciting or surprising about any of her days.

The academic training for the junior associates must have been at an end because when she passed by the conference room Wednesday morning, it was empty. Not that she had *intentionally* walked that way, and not that she had *intentionally* peeked inside to see if anyone was in there.

She hadn't seen Elizabeth since Tuesday morning and figured it was all for the best. Someone that pretty and feisty was sure to be trouble, and the last thing she needed right now was any sort of trouble. She was in a good place with her life and her career. She wasn't looking to spice things up. Safe was good. Safe was reliable. Safe was what she knew. Safe was what she had worked thirty-eight years to achieve. A safe, sturdy foundation for herself.

"Yes, of course," she said, standing and straightening her blazer. She walked over to the projector, grabbed the small remote lying at the head of the table, and began clicking through her PowerPoint. The words *The Meadows v. Cohen Construction, LLC* flashed across the screen, and she began by presenting the facts of the case:

Their client was the New York Historical Preservation Society doing business as the Meadows, a nonprofit seeking to prevent Cohen Construction from demolishing a historic home to build apartment buildings. Cohen Construction had sued the Meadows, essentially alleging that the Meadows had illegally prevented them from demolishing the building and were in breach of contract. The Meadows counterclaimed, arguing that various historic preservation acts should preclude the demolition of the building.

Margaret Liventhrop, the original owner of the home, was one of Darcy's favorite authors. She had twisted her firm's arm to take the case pro bono, insisting it would be good for the firm's PR and that they could brag about the victory all over their bar association events. The sales pitch had worked, and they'd agreed to take on the case on the condition that Darcy managed it herself and that no other attorney's time would be "wasted" with it.

As she clicked through each slide, she watched the eyes of the men get droopier and droopier. Finally, when she finished the presentation, Paul spoke up: "Looks like a good case for a junior to help you with. Have you picked which one you want yet?" He leaned back and crossed his arms.

Mark chimed in from across the table, "I'd take the Willis boy if I were you. Good to get clout with his father in the early stages of him being here."

Darcy hid her snarl. "I haven't made up my mind yet, but, yes, one of the juniors will be utilized for this trial."

"When is it on?" Paul asked, adjusting his thick black glasses on his long fat nose.

She had just covered the jury selection date and anticipated trial date in her last slide. "As I said, we go out to select a jury the first week of March. The trial should last no more than two weeks, more likely a week and a half. And then I'm off to Vermont."

"Ah, yes, the annual ski trip," Mark said smiling a gap-toothed grin.

Darcy nodded. "Is there anything else, or is the meeting adjourned?"

The men all looked around and gave a collective nod before standing. "Until next week," one said, but Darcy was already half out the door.

She walked as fast as her heels would carry her back to her office, letting out a deep sigh of relief when the door finally closed behind her.

She was glad to be a managing partner, if only for the fact that her door was not see-through. It was frosted, sure, to avoid any allegations of sexual harassment, but no one could really see what she was doing on the other side. And for that, she was grateful because right now, all she wanted to do was take off these shoes and prop her feet up on her desk.

She hated that their meetings were always on Friday afternoons. She hated that she ended every week with blatant toxic masculinity. She constantly had to remind herself that this was what she had worked so hard for. That this was the dream she had envisioned all along.

Her mind wandered to her father. It hadn't always been her dream to be a lawyer. It hadn't always been her dream to be rich. When she was in high school, she'd thought about being a journalist. She'd loved the idea of crusading for truth, exposing the underbelly of society. She'd gotten pretty into advocating against human trafficking for a long time and thought for sure she would spend her life fighting that in some way. Then, when she'd gone to college, she was drawn to history and had decided to become a teacher. But her junior year, her father had gotten sick. Really, really sick.

Medical bills had started pouring in like those free calendars when someone donated to a charity, and insurance wouldn't cover the medication. She'd begun spending more and more weekends at home to help him manage it all. By the time she'd graduated, she'd known she would never be able to take care of him on a teacher's salary. If she'd wanted to provide for her family, and maybe even a family of her own one day, she'd needed a career that made money. Big money.

That was when she'd decided to go to law school. She'd poured her heart into LSAT prep her senior year and only applied to schools in Florida to be close to her dad, even though her score was good enough to get her into any school she wanted.

Her father had never made it to her graduation. He'd died when she was just about to start her third year. She'd seriously considered dropping out, running away, and living in a van somewhere in a national park. But she'd thought of her dad, how proud he would be to see his daughter—the daughter of a mechanic—become a big-time lawyer.

Now, fifteen years later, here she was. Still working endless days to make a dead man proud.

She sighed and looked out the window at the bright lights from the buildings sticking into a canvas sky. It was now past six. She thought about the case she'd just presented at the meeting. The trial date was quickly approaching, and she still hadn't gotten the trial authorizations processed, and she needed to schedule calls with her experts and, of course, make travel arrangements. Most of that Patty could help with, but she couldn't exactly ask Patty to research jury instructions. As much as she hated to admit it, Mark and Paul were right. She needed help.

A knock on her door caused her to spin in her chair. "You heading home, Darce?" Patty asked, shoving her short thick arm into a puffy down coat.

Darcy bit her cheek and thought for a moment. She *could* just go home and work on her case. In fact, that was exactly what she *should* do. But she really didn't feel like going home to an empty apartment tonight. "I don't know. Maybe I'll walk around a bit."

Patty shivered. "Pretty cold for a walk, but you could always join the youngsters at the bar for happy hour."

Darcy raised an eyebrow. She'd completely forgotten it was the happy hour for the juniors tonight. Partners rarely went, but it wasn't unheard of. What could it hurt? Just swinging by, showing face, having a cocktail with some colleagues.

Then again, she really should get home and start prepping for trial. "What bar are they at?"

CHAPTER NINE

K now thyself" was one of Lizzy's favorite quotes from one of her
favorite philosophers, Immanuel Kant. It was a mantra she'd
adopted back in college that she applied to her life on a daily basis.

So when she knew she was on her way to being drunk at the firm
happy hour, she *really* knew it. She was only on her second cocktail,
but apparently, a Long Island iced tea really was made stronger the
closer you got to Long Island, and she felt her head begin to swim a bit
more as she sat on her barstool.

The Ainsworth was just a few blocks away from Byron &
Browning and had served as the unofficial firm bar for over five years.
It was insanely crowded, and at least half of the people in it were B&B
associates with a few of counsels sprinkled here and there. They had
broken off into smaller groups almost immediately upon arrival. Micah
had quickly found a tall, skinny blonde and had begun flirting with
her off in a corner. Cho and the other guy in their group, Efe, were
chatting with a few tall guys who looked like they'd just gotten out of a
frat party, just substituting three-piece suits in place of Shep shirts and
madras shorts.

Jackson was next to her, attempting to make small talk, but all she
could focus on was how good Ana's ass looked in her black suit pants.
She decided to work up the courage to actually flirt with her; she just
needed one more of these delicious Long Island iced teas.

Out of the corner of her eye, she saw something unexpected: the
unmistakable flash of brunette hair pulled back into a flawless French
twist. Lizzy shifted and leaned around Jackson to look. She could only
see the back of the woman's head, but the streaks of silver and pulled-
back shoulders confirmed what she already knew.

Darcy Hammond was here.

Keeping her head dipped behind Jackson, she watched as Darcy crossed the room to a seat at the end of the bar. Lizzy looked down quickly as Darcy removed her long black coat and sat. She watched as Darcy looked around, clearly taking inventory. Was she looking for someone? Waiting for someone? She hadn't started socializing, so it was unlikely she was here to chat and make nice with the juniors.

Lizzy took note of the charcoal gray suit and how it hugged every curve of Darcy's body as if it had been made for her. Heck, maybe it was. She must have been richer than God; tailored suits would be a dime a dozen for her.

Lizzy hadn't laid eyes on her since their little Yale mug fiasco a few mornings ago, and she had almost forgotten how truly stunning Darcy was. Almost. Still hidden behind Jackson's shoulder, Lizzy stared for a few seconds as Darcy adjusted her watch, then pulled out her phone and checked it before setting it facedown on the bar. She ordered a drink, and Lizzy watched the bartender as he mixed it.

Bourbon, simple syrup, fresh mint.

Don't tell me the queen of New York is ordering a mint julep, of all things.

The bartender delivered the drink, and Darcy took a large gulp. She grimaced slightly, and Lizzy smiled at the brief moment of weakness from the woman of steel.

She took another sip of her own drink and felt her nerve beginning to come back. She was here, at a bar. They weren't at work. In fact, it was an event designed for small talk and socializing. It was totally fine if she went over and just talked to her. That was allowed; in fact, it was encouraged. Right?

As she leaned forward to begin to stand, a warm hand touched her arm. "There you are," Ana said, her thick red lips pulled back in a flirtatious smile. Lizzy could tell she was tipsy by how friendly she was being. "I was hoping to catch you. How are you liking it here so far?"

Lizzy looked at Ana's hand lingering on her arm and smiled. "It's been good. I mean, the attorney who trained us is like *super* boring, but I can tell she's really trying."

"Hey!" Ana playfully slapped at her stomach as she swayed and began to giggle.

"I'm just messing with you," Lizzy said, grabbing Ana's hand and pulling her closer. She looked over Ana's shoulder, and her heart stopped. Staring directly back at her was Darcy Hammond. She was taking a sip of her drink and just watching her and Ana flirt. Her eyebrow twitched slightly as she set the drink down and pulled out her phone again.

Lizzy tilted her head and stood. Turning to Ana, she wrapped her arms around her waist and rotated their position so Ana's back was against the stool she was just sitting on.

"Do me a favor?" Lizzy said. "Sit here and save my seat for me, will you? I'll...I'll be right back."

Ana nodded and shrugged, instantly turning to another nameless senior associate Lizzy hadn't bothered to speak to.

As Lizzy walked through the crowd, she kept her eyes on Darcy, who continued to stare at her phone. It felt like if Lizzy looked away, she might blink, and Darcy would be gone. Or maybe she would have never been here in the first place. Maybe she was just a figment of Lizzy's imagination. Either way, she wasn't risking it.

When she finally reached the end of the long bar, the familiar perfume that flooded her nose alerted her to the fact that this was very much real. Darcy was here, right now, and only a few feet away. She was really doing this. She slid into a small space to the left of Darcy and smiled. "Hi."

Darcy looked up briefly but didn't make eye contact. "Hi," she replied casually, returning her attention to her phone.

"You know, it's bad for your eyes to stare at a screen in the dark like this."

Darcy smirked, finally looking in her direction. When she did, Lizzy realized just how little space there was between them. Darcy's nose was inches from her face, and she felt her breath being sucked out of her lungs. "You're very outspoken for someone so young, you know that?" Darcy said.

Lizzy nodded. "Believe it or not, I've heard that a few times before."

"You don't say," Darcy replied, seemingly feigning shock as she took another sip of her drink.

"Surprised to see a New Yorker drinking a mint julep. Although I have to say, the bartender totally fucked it up."

Oops. Was she allowed to drop the f-bomb on her boss like that? Was Darcy really her boss? Technically, she worked for like eighty attorneys, Darcy among them, but it wasn't like she could fire her or anything. Right? Could she fire her? Crap, what if she fired her?

Lizzy's heart sank slightly. "Sorry."

"For what? Saying fuck?" Darcy shook her head. "Relax, I'm not your mother. Though I am curious as to how the bartender 'fucked up' my order you seem to know so much about." She turned slightly so she was facing Lizzy, resting her index finger against her temple.

Lizzy swallowed hard and kept her confidence. Maybe she should have taken another sip of her drink before she'd come over here. She glanced at the other end of the bar. None of her friends, or even Ana, had spotted her. They were all too caught up in whatever loud conversations they were having. She cleared her throat. "It's all about the ice. Well, the ice and the cup," Lizzy said, touching Darcy's glass.

She traced the bead of sweat dripping down the side. Her fingers touched Darcy's just barely, and a jolt of energy ran up through her hand and into her heart. She slid the drink out of Darcy's hand before picking it up and swirling it around.

"You see, a proper mint julep has crushed ice and is in a silver cup. And it should be piled on top like a snow cone." Without permission, Lizzy took a sip, feeling the sweet, warm bourbon trickle down her throat. It was the final boost of courage she needed.

"And let me guess, it's meant to be served on the first Saturday in May?"

Lizzy smiled, setting the glass on the bar. "Derby Day is the traditional day for a proper mint julep, yes." *Holy shit, I'm flirting with Darcy Hammond. Holy shit. Holy shit.* Lizzy straightened her shoulders and leaned casually against the bar.

Darcy's legs were crossed but facing toward her, and the tip of her heel grazed the back of Lizzy's leg where the space between them had entirely closed. Lizzy's breath hitched at the slight contact. Darcy simply smiled back at her.

That fucking look. The things I would do to wipe that smirk off her perfect, flawless face.

"How did you know what drink I ordered?" Darcy asked, taking another sip from the exact same spot Lizzy's lips had just touched.

She paused, deciding how much honesty she was ready to reveal. "I watched the bartender make it."

Darcy smiled and shook her head. "That's funny. I didn't think anyone noticed me even come in. It's a pretty packed scene." She looked at the bodies that were still multiplying by the minute.

"Who were you looking for when you came in?" Lizzy asked.

Darcy hesitated for a moment and looked down. "Nobody," she

replied, but there was an air of uncertainty behind her voice, and Lizzy homed in on it instantly.

Looking for nobody, huh? She had the perfect pickup line in her back pocket now, but she didn't know how it would land. Was she really about to use this cheesy line on her friggin boss at a firm function after her first week of work? "Well in that case, 'I'm Nobody, who are you? Are you Nobody too?'" Yes, yes, she *was* using that cheesy line on her boss after her first week of work.

Darcy tossed her head back and let out a loud laugh. If the music in the bar hadn't been booming, it would have drawn everyone's attention. Lizzy looked around, slightly insecure. Clearly, this was not the pickup line she should have used.

Darcy continued to chuckle as she took another sip of her drink. "Okay, fine, I'll play along," Darcy said, smiling broadly. She looked around quickly and then leaned in so close, her lips nearly grazed Lizzy's earlobe. She shivered at their proximity but bit her lip hard to hide her reaction. "'Then there's a pair of us. Don't tell! They'd advertise, you know,'" Darcy whispered, quoting Emily Dickinson right back at Lizzy, her voice husky and low.

The comment rendered Lizzy speechless. She had never had such a formidable sparring partner before. It both excited her and scared the shit out of her.

Darcy leaned back and smiled smugly, clearly satisfied with the impact her verbal banter had.

Never one to be outdone, Lizzy adjusted her shoulders. "They teach Emily Dickinson at Yale?" She flashed a flirtatious grin.

Darcy nodded and laughed again. "I really do love pissing off the Ivy Leaguers at this place."

Lizzy shuffled a little closer. Their legs were entirely touching now, barely an inch between them, and the only thing Lizzy could smell was Darcy's perfume and the faint trace of bourbon. "Ever tried something a little more…challenging?" Lizzy said brazenly, grabbing Darcy's drink before taking another slow, intentional sip. Okay, she was definitely tipsy now, but she was totally rolling with it, and Darcy didn't exactly seem put off by her antics.

"Easy, tiger," Darcy said, grabbing her drink and setting it back on the bar. "Don't bite off more than you can chew." She winked as she finished her sentence, and it was enough to send Lizzy over the edge.

She leaned closer, the rush of bourbon coursing through her veins.

She pressed her lips almost on Darcy's ear as she whispered, "Do you want to get out of here?" *Did I just say that out loud? Oh crap. I did. Yup, that was totally out loud. Congrats, Lizzy, you just propositioned your boss.*

But much to Lizzy's surprise, Darcy didn't look repulsed or surprised or even angry as Lizzy slowly pulled away. Instead, she looked like she was…actually considering it? Darcy opened her mouth, but before she could speak, a voice bellowed behind them.

"Well, Darcy Hammond, as I live and breathe. I've never seen you at one of these things. Who dragged you away from that shiny corner office and down here with the peons?" Simon Bellinger, one of the of counsels, turned and introduced himself briefly to Lizzy, who took half a step back from Darcy and politely shook his hand.

Darcy transformed into a totally different person within seconds. The soft, flirtatious eyes Lizzy had been falling into over the last few minutes disappeared. In their place, the cold, steely eyes that had met her Monday in the conference room appeared. Her shoulders tightened, her posture straightened, and her voice went from playful to serious. It was like watching Superman turn back into Clark Kent. "Well, I figured it was about time one of the partners showed their face around here. Good to see this place hasn't changed since the last time I was here."

Simon laughed too loudly, and Darcy flinched. He slapped his knee and stuck his hand out to Lizzy for a second time, as if forgetting she had just introduced herself. "You better watch out for this one," Simon said, smiling at Lizzy. "I had one case with her, and she nearly tore me apart because I was late on one assignment."

"Yes, well, that one assignment was a motion for summary judgment that was due a week prior. We lost the motion on its face and almost got sanctioned for it."

Simon shrugged, his drink sloshing a little over the rim. He was too drunk to notice. "Motion, schmotion, the fact is, she's a vixen, this one, so if I were you, I'd stay sharp and sleep with both eyes open. And whatever you do, don't miss a motion deadline." He winked again and tipped his glass to Darcy before turning and stumbling away.

Lizzy chuckled and turned back to continue her conversation with Darcy but was disappointed to see she was closing her tab. "Leaving already?" Lizzy asked, trying to hide the desperation in her voice.

Darcy signed her name quickly on the credit card receipt and tucked her wallet and phone into her bag. She stood and slipped on the long, black double-breasted coat she had come in wearing. She wrapped a plaid Burberry scarf around her neck a few times before looking at Lizzy. "It's late, Elizabeth."

Lizzy tried to ignore the little prick in her heart at the sound of her full name coming from Darcy's lips. She normally hated when people used her full first name. Only her mother ever called her Elizabeth, and it was usually when she was in trouble. But when Darcy said it, it sounded almost soothing.

Darcy's eyes were cold and aloof once more. Lizzy tried to find something to say. Some words to bring their few moments of intimacy back, but she knew the moment was gone. "Get home safe." Darcy tucked her scarf into her coat, turned, and left.

Lizzy closed her own tab after that and left without saying good-bye to anyone. There was no one else in the bar worth talking to.

CHAPTER TEN

Darcy woke up the next morning feeling hungover. She only had one drink at the Ainsworth and was home by close to ten, but there was still a heavy, cloudy, blurry feeling swirling in her head. What had gotten into her last night? Why had she even gone to that stupid bar in the first place? She never went to events like that. Her work-related events now consisted of wining and dining high-end clients or attending conferences in Austin or Los Angeles. She hadn't been to a simple firm happy hour in years. Yet last night, she had gone out of her way to include it in her agenda.

She shook her head, sitting up in bed. Who was she kidding? She knew exactly why she went there last night, and she knew exactly why she felt so awful this morning.

She had a crush on a way too young junior with long blond hair and great legs. Maybe she had gone there last night to…what? To get it out of her system? To see her hanging out with people her own age? To prove to herself that this woman was just that: a woman fresh out of law school and way too immature for her?

But she hadn't learned that last night at all. In fact, her visit to the bar had the exact opposite effect. Not only was Lizzy intelligent—that Emily Dickinson line was enough to knock Darcy off her feet—but she was bold, assertive, and confident. Okay, yes, maybe she had been a little tipsy, but she *had* been flirting with Ana when Darcy had first sat down. She'd seen them together. Ana had grabbed Lizzy's hand. Lizzy had smiled and flirted back. Darcy had hoped maybe that was what she needed to see. She'd needed to see Lizzy acting her age with someone her own age.

And then something Darcy hadn't expected had happened. Lizzy had approached her. Not only that, but she'd had the balls to flirt with her, and then she'd actually asked if Darcy wanted to leave with her.

Darcy had been taken aback by her proposition at first, but there had been a small part of her that, for a split millisecond, had considered saying yes. She wasn't sure if she should be angry or grateful to Simon for preventing her from answering Lizzy's question.

She rubbed her forehead and climbed out of bed, her soft, white down comforter trailing off the bed behind her. She walked to the espresso maker and slid a small white cup beneath the spout and waited while the dark liquid slowly trickled out of the silver faucet.

Darcy checked the clock on her oven. It was nearly eight a.m. She grabbed the small cup and walked to the window. The city was alive with the sounds of tourists and shoppers shuffling back and forth. Being in SoHo meant there were no high-rises, so she could hear more street chatter than she preferred. But she loved the charm of the neighborhood, and the Harney & Sons right downstairs didn't hurt, either, especially on days when she had a craving for good tea.

After a few moments of sipping the strong liquid, Darcy glanced at a large binder sitting on the island in her kitchen. She could see the white label from here: *The Meadows v. Cohen Construction* was printed in black font across the wide, five-inch binding, and she shuddered at the idea of spending an entire day on trial prep.

She loved that case, she really did, but she just couldn't stand being cooped up inside anymore. It was bad enough that she was stuck in an office—albeit a beautiful one—for fifty hours a week. The weekends were her only time to get outside. To get away. To breathe the fresh air.

"Alexa," she asked, "what's the weather?"

Instantly the robotic, overly friendly voice replied, "Today in New York City, you can expect a high of forty degrees and a low of twenty-two degrees."

Darcy glanced out the window again. It was a clear, sunny day, and the weather was above freezing, a win for January in New York. She decided she would take advantage of the opportunity before the rains of March descended on them.

She hopped up from the couch and went to one of the closets near the front door, pulling out a bike helmet, shirt, and padded pants. She tossed her clip-in shoes in the pile and started to get dressed.

She slipped the black covers over her clip-ins to prevent the wind from getting to her toes and pulled the slim black base layer on beneath her bike shirt before zipping it up. She slid two organic granola bars into the back pockets of her shirt before shoving on her insulated gloves and tucking her ears beneath her wraparound ear warmers. The last thing to complete the ensemble was a pair of oversized bike glasses to keep the wind from ripping into her eyeballs as she rode.

A crisp bike ride on the West Side Highway was just what she needed to clear her mind. No more Elizabeth. No more trial. No more work at all. She would plug in her headphones and shut out the rest of the world.

A few minutes later, she was stepping out of the heated bike storage in the lobby of her building and strutting toward the front door, the clack, clack, clack of her clip-ins echoing in the luxurious lobby. As she left, she gave a passing salute to the security guard at the front desk, who smiled and waved back at her.

She was geared up and ready for a nice, long ride. The cold winter air filled her lungs as she pushed the silver and pink Specialized bike outside and turned west on Thompson Street, heading in the direction of the Hudson River.

CHAPTER ELEVEN

Hey, we're gonna go to brunch with some friends of mine, wanna join?" Amina asked, scrolling through her phone as she sipped a cup of tea, or chai, as she insisted everyone in the apartment call it.

Lizzy zipped her fleece jacket to her neck. "Damn, I'm just going for a bike ride, actually, but next time?"

"A bike ride? Woman, it's, like, negative freezing degrees outside. Where the heck are you riding your piece-of-shit bike?"

"Hey! This bike cost me seventy-five bucks."

Lizzy looked at the solid black, single-speed bike. Its teal rims stood out like a lighthouse in the sea of black. It had some rusty spots here and there, and it squeaked every time she pushed the right pedal, but she had haggled for it with someone on Craigslist and traipsed all the way out to Bushwick to pick it up. In her eyes, it was the most beautiful bike in the world. She hadn't even really had a chance to ride it yet, but it was her first Saturday since starting her new job, and she figured today was the perfect opportunity.

Plus, a ride in the cold winter air was exactly what she needed to forget about what had—or rather, had not—happened between her and Darcy last night.

"I was thinking of heading east, actually. Maybe take this bad boy across the Brooklyn Bridge."

Amina shook her head. "Hope you have something warmer than that. That wind is gonna kick your ass."

Lizzy frowned. She hadn't considered the wind coming off the river when she was dressing. The weather app on her phone said it was forty degrees, and she'd gone with it. Plus, all she had to wear were some leggings under her Adidas soccer pants from high school.

She didn't have leg warmers or base layers, or whatever the heck they called long johns up here. She shrugged. "Guess this will have to do."

Amina gave her a concerned look as Lizzy pushed her bike down the long hallway, past Hoko's room, and out the door. It slammed shut behind her since she wasn't able to catch it, and she hoped she didn't wake Hoko. The poor woman still slept most of the day and stayed awake all night.

Lizzy lifted the bike onto her shoulder and began her descent down the fifth-story walk-up. By the time she got to the bottom, she was already winded, but she braced herself for the cold that she was about to spend the day in. She would ride as far as her legs would take her. Hopefully, all the way to Brooklyn. She hadn't gotten to really see that area since she'd moved here, and she was dying to get across that beautiful big bridge and explore.

She popped in her headphones, pushed play on a random Pump It Up playlist on Spotify, and began pedaling south. The plan was that she would head down the West Side Highway and swing around the bottom of the island before heading north to go east across the bridge. She had no other plans today, so worst-case scenario, she got tired somewhere, hopped on a train, and came home. One of her friends from law school had told her she needed to see Dumbo, so she figured that was as good a heading as any.

Lizzy mounted her bike and rolled down the long hill in the direction of the Hudson River. The air was cold, but the wind when she hit the West Side Highway was colder. It cut through her fleece jacket like knives, and she knew Amina had been right about her being underdressed. She used the pain to push herself to pedal harder and harder and found herself wishing her bike had gears to give her legs a break after just a few miles.

She ignored the burning sensation in her thighs and rode faster, smiling wide and letting the wind brush against her exposed cheek. On her right was the Hudson River. She could see clear to the other side where the Palisades Parkway rose high above the water to greet her. On her left was a sea of skyscrapers. Row after row, building after building, the city poured itself out to her.

She lived here. This was her home. All of these streets, these shops, these little alleys and avenues, they were all hers to explore, to learn, to make her own. She couldn't believe this was her life. The coldness didn't hurt anymore, and she pedaled in a steady, rhythmic beat.

But as she rode farther down the west side, her mind could no longer be distracted by the amazing scenery, and eventually, her thoughts went back to Darcy Hammond in her beautiful, tailored, charcoal gray suit. She thought of her soft, flirtatious smile and wondered how many people ever got to see that side of her. Maybe Lizzy had just been drunk, or maybe she had actually meant something to Darcy. That was the part she wasn't sure about.

Darcy had definitely been flirting with Lizzy, there was no question about that. But what were her intentions? Would she have actually gone home with Lizzy if Simeon or Simon or whatever his name was hadn't interrupted them?

Part of her wanted to approach Darcy next week at work. But the other part thought that was a terrifyingly horrible idea. Maybe it was best to just let it be. It had happened. They'd flirted. It was fun. The end. It didn't have to mean anything.

Lizzy shook her head and pedaled faster, ignoring the nagging feeling that this thing with Darcy was never going to mean anything. Because it already did mean something to Lizzy. She lowered her head to fight against the wind and pushed on. She was making it to Brooklyn today, no matter how cold it was.

CHAPTER TWELVE

Darcy unclipped her helmet and exhaled, wiping the frozen snot from her nose. She had ridden much farther than she'd planned and in the exact opposite direction. *Why the hell am I in Dumbo?*

She approached the door to the coffee shop. She was just popping in to get warm and rest up a bit. Maybe grab a coffee and let her fingers thaw for a while.

She'd started the day by riding to the West Side Highway and turning north as planned. She typically biked all the way up to the George Washington Bridge, then turned and came home. It was about a twenty-mile round trip. But today, the crowded bike paths near Chelsea Piers caused her to about-face and head south.

"Stupid Citi bikes." She'd groaned as she'd U-turned and sent her bike spinning around the bottom of the island and up to the east side. The only problem with the east side, as everyone knew, was that the bike path ended near 33rd Street, and she had to cross over into avenues and streets to keep venturing north. It wasn't possible to ride all the way up the east side of the island like it was on the west side.

By the time she'd reached the rough section where the path had abruptly stopped, she'd decided to venture across the Brooklyn Bridge and into Dumbo. She had no idea why. The bridge was bumpy as hell, and she'd always hated riding across it. Plus, she hadn't been to Dumbo in…actually, she couldn't even remember.

She used to love this part of the city. When she was younger, she'd ride the East River Ferry all day, just for the views of the city. She would hop on at Thirty-Fourth Street and ride all the way down to Wall Street, just to catch a glimpse of the Statue of Liberty. Then she'd get back on and ride up the river, hopping on and off at Dumbo, Williamsburg, and Long Island City. But her favorite stop had always been Dumbo.

She'd walk around, read a book by the carousel, and watch people on awkward first dates. She'd even been part of a women's soccer league that had played on the piers there, and one of her favorite restaurants had been an oyster boat docked nearby.

But that was back when she had been a carefree twenty-nothing, attending wild lesbian parties and sleeping with half of New York's beautiful femmes. She was too old for venturing much beyond the confines of her office and Manhattan now. Or so she had convinced herself.

She had to admit, there was a freeing element to being on this side of the river, where so many fond memories were made for her. Darcy locked her bike to a telephone pole in front of a little coffee shop she used to love. She inhaled through her nose, attempting to stop the river of snot that was now flowing due to the rapid change in temperature as she stepped up to the counter. "Flat white, please," she said, taking another sharp inhale.

The barista nodded and flipped a screen around at her, indicating she could tap her card. She did, but the snot was really pouring now.

"Where's your restroom?" she asked, breathing exclusively through her mouth.

He motioned over his shoulder and pointed down a long, narrow hall. Darcy thanked him and left, grabbing her nose as she walked.

She had known it was going to be a cold ride, even if she was properly dressed, but goddamn it, she hated winter, and this was one of the reasons why. As she reached the safety of the single-occupancy bathroom, she cursed under her breath and blew her nose several times. When she was convinced that it was safe to show her face in public again, she splashed some water on her face and attempted to fix the helmet hair that had turned her smooth, clean locks into a messy, tangled bun.

"Whatever," she said, giving up on looking even remotely presentable. She was just stopping for a quick coffee break to warm up, then it was back to her side of the city. It was already later than she'd planned, and much to her chagrin, she really did need to work on that trial prep at some point this weekend. She finished drying her hands and pulled on the heavy door. She took two steps outside before—

Her feet froze. She couldn't believe her eyes. There, standing less than two feet away, walking into the bathroom she was just leaving, was Elizabeth fucking Taylor.

A look of shock, confusion, and questioning reality spread across

Elizabeth's face. Darcy went to speak, to move, to do anything, but she just stood frozen in disbelief for what felt like ages.

"Darcy?" The words still muddled in Darcy's ears as if Elizabeth was speaking underwater. Her tone was soft, unassuming, and maybe even a little…excited?

The blood slowly drained from Darcy's head, and she began to be able to process thoughts and words more clearly. No. No, she was not happy to see her. She couldn't be. This couldn't be a thing. They couldn't be that stupid adorable couple that fate constantly pulled together. No. Darcy didn't believe in that nonsense. She was logical. She was intelligent. This was just a ridiculous coincidence, or maybe the woman was stalking her or something. Who knew?

"What the hell are you doing here?" Her voice was more accusatory than she'd intended, and Elizabeth recoiled slightly.

"It's a coffee shop," Elizabeth said. "I'm getting coffee."

Darcy looked at the helmet in Elizabeth's hand. "Let me guess, you just happened to ride your bike here too?" *Why am I cross-examining this poor woman right now? She's clearly just as shaken by this as I am. Be nice, Darcy, just be nice, for fuck's sake.*

Elizabeth pulled her shoulders back. Darcy could see the warmth in her eyes leaving, and she hated that it made her heart break slightly. "I'm sorry, is that offensive to you or something?"

Darcy shook her head and looked down. She had no desire to be mean to this beautiful woman that she had literally almost gone home with just last night. Why was she being so cold? She wasn't sure, but something about the way Elizabeth had looked at her last night, the way she'd looked at her just a few seconds ago, unnerved her. It made her feel weak and vulnerable and safe. And she hated it. "Just think it's an odd coincidence is all," she said, crossing her arms.

Elizabeth rolled her eyes. "Jesus, are you really that full of yourself? I wanted to see Dumbo. I wanted to go for a bike ride. I wanted to get out and clear my head. There. Satisfied? Now, if you'll excuse me." She moved to go around and enter the bathroom.

Darcy shifted to the side to let her pass. She ignored the smell of Elizabeth's laundry detergent mixed with sweat. She ignored the desire to grab her and push her into the bathroom. She ignored the desire to reach out and apologize for being such a dick.

When she was safely out of Elizabeth's line of sight, Darcy dropped her head and shook out her hands. She pushed two fingers against her neck. As suspected, her pulse was through the roof. She was shocked, that was all. In fifteen years of living in New York, she had only run into people she knew at gay bars, and that was to be expected in such a tight-knit community. There was that one time she'd gotten on the train and one of her friends had been standing on it, but that was years ago. And what were the odds that the day after she and this woman had been flirting at a bar, she would run into her? In Dumbo, of all places?

"Darcy?" the barista called, and she marched over to the pickup area and grabbed her coffee.

"Thank you." She walked to the exit, her clip-ins clacking all the way. She took one sip of the warm beverage, then threw it in the trash. She needed to get out of here before she did something she would regret. As she unlocked her own bike, she noticed a worn-out black bike with teal rims, rust collecting on the chains and at every nut and bolt. It was rain-rotted; anyone could see that clear as day.

That thing doesn't even look safe enough to get someone down the block. She knew it had to be Elizabeth's. She shook her head and put on her helmet.

As she was mounting her bike, she glanced back. She shoved down the feeling that was already worrying about Elizabeth getting home safely on that death trap. She shoved down the feeling that told her to stand there and wait. She shoved down the feeling that told her to stay and apologize. She shoved all of those things down, hopped on her bike, and pedaled away quickly.

CHAPTER THIRTEEN

How was your weekend?" Jackson asked first thing Monday morning in his usual chipper voice.

"Fine. Yours?" Lizzy replied vaguely. It was a bald-faced lie. There was nothing fine about her weekend, and she knew it. After almost literally running into Darcy at the coffee shop in Dumbo, Lizzy had tried to shrug it off and enjoy her time in the new neighborhood. But try as she might, she just couldn't shake the sound of Darcy's voice, accusatory and annoyed, or the look on her face as she'd come out of the bathroom. She had gone from shocked to downright rude in a matter of seconds.

Lizzy felt like an idiot for even thinking their little flirt session Friday night had meant anything to Darcy. Clearly, she'd been drunk or bored or feeling insecure or something. It was obvious now that Darcy had absolutely no interest in her, romantically or otherwise.

I mean, she didn't have to fuck me, but she could have at least been nice to me, Lizzy told herself as she'd pedaled home later that afternoon.

To make matters worse, one of her tires had gone flat halfway across the bridge, and she'd had to walk her bike all the way to Battery Park and take the red line back home.

It had snowed all day Sunday, and she'd gone to a bar in her neighborhood, hoping to watch the Washington football game. A little piece of home, she'd thought, might make her feel better. But when she'd gotten there, she'd quickly learned the only sports New York cared about were the Jets, Mets, and Nets or, contrarily, the Giants, Yankees, and Knicks. Unfortunately for her, both the Jets and the Giants were playing that day, so she had to stream the game on her cell alone at the end of the bar.

And then there was the weather. She'd always imaged how beautiful it would be to see snow in New York City. She remembered seeing it in movies and on TV, and it had always looked so magical, so romantic. The reality of it, however, was anything but.

The snow had stopped late last night after blanketing the streets with a solid four to five inches. Snowplows had driven by all day until finally, they too had stopped, leaving a wall of black and brown snow acting as an impenetrable barricade between the sidewalks and streets.

By the time she'd made it to work this morning, her shoes were covered in black slush, and considering she didn't have any actual snow boots, she'd been forced to wear her galoshes. They'd kept her feet dry enough but did absolutely nothing to keep them warm.

Jackson stood awkwardly at the door to her tiny office as she removed her soaking-wet rubber shoes and slid them under her desk. Cho wasn't in yet, but she could only imagine what she would say if she saw the bright polka dots. She slipped her icy toes into her usual black pumps and stood.

Jackson was mumbling about his weekend plans, but Lizzy had stopped listening. So far, only she, Jackson, and Efe were in the offices, but Lizzy decided it was a great morning to get a cup of free coffee from the kitchen and start the day fresh.

She reached into her backpack and pulled out the navy blue and orange mug she'd brought with her. The words *Go Hoos!* were written in cursive on one side, and a man riding a horse with a sword raised high above his head was on the other. She wasn't going to let the "Eight" bullies keep her from adding her mug to the prestigious collection in the cupboard. She was proud of her school, and she didn't care who saw it.

Last week, she had been too scared to venture back to the kitchenette after the whole "Yale mug" incident, but this morning, she didn't give a shit. She'd had a rough weekend, and she wanted a damn cup of coffee. If she saw Darcy on the way there or back, that wasn't her problem. As she approached the kitchenette, she felt a fluttery, butterfly feeling in her stomach, but she swallowed hard and told herself to ignore it.

But rounding the corner to the kitchenette, she couldn't hide the feeling of disappointment when she saw it was empty. She paused for a moment, looking around as if Darcy might be waiting to jump out from a cabinet or something.

Jackson popped his head around the corner behind her. "Who ya looking for?"

"Jesus," Lizzy said, jumping back. "You scared me."

He laughed and adjusted his glasses. "My bad."

"It's fine," Lizzy said, releasing a smile and tucking a rogue strand of hair behind her face. She pressed a few buttons on the fancy coffee machine and watched as a beautiful cappuccino with foam poured into her mug.

"Mmm," she said taking a slow sip, letting the hot liquid trickle down her throat. This was just what she needed. New mug, new coffee, new week, new her. She wasn't going to let some woman on a high horse get her down. She took another sip and glanced at her mug. The man riding a horse stared blankly back at her.

Okay, bad analogy.

By the time she and Jackson made it back to their offices, Cho and Micah had both arrived. Cho was leaning on Micah's desk talking with Efe.

"What up, Eight?" Micah said, tilting his head back. His hair was tucked into a low bun today, and she wished she could say the snowy weather had ruined it in some way. But, no. Of course, it still looked perfect, shiny, and flawless, just like the rest of him.

Her own hair, on the other hand, was suffering. Her natural curls were enjoying the wet weather far too much, and while she had taken painstaking efforts to blow it out this morning, once she'd stepped outside, it had all gone to hell. She now had rogue curls popping out all around her face, and she tried to ignore them as they fell into her eyes.

"You do know we kicked your ass in trial team, right?" she said, stepping into her own office.

"Trial team? You would do that shit. Nerd."

Lizzy ignored him and took another sip of the foamy drink. She pulled out her notebook and planner and pretended to be reading something instead of imagining how much she wanted to walk across the hall and punch him in his pretty, privileged face.

"Don't worry about them," Jackson said as he sat at Cho's desk.

"Oh, I don't," she replied and then loudly added, "Some people just peaked in high school."

The giggles and chatter from across the hall grew silent, indicating her comment had landed, and she smirked, taking another victorious sip of cappuccino.

"We better get going," Cho said, entering the room.

Jackson leaped up and motioned for her to sit, but she ignored him and grabbed the notebook off her desk, turned, and left.

Today, they were meeting the individual seniors who would be serving as their mentors. They would be working for a lot of seniors and of counsels, but the firm gave them each one person to act as a mentor along the way. Someone to point them in the right direction, answer questions the paralegals and support staff couldn't, and give them a little insight into how to manage assignments from multiple attorneys.

They hadn't been told who they were being assigned to, but Lizzy hoped it was at least someone nice. She was feeling kinda fragile today with the weather, the homesickness, the bullies at work, and of course, the hot partner who possibly hated her.

She took Cho's lead and scooped up her notebook, clicking her heavy, silver B&B pen as she walked. They were all meeting in the conference room to start the day; then, they'd be breaking up and shadowing their individual mentors for the rest of the week.

Lizzy followed Cho and Jackson into the conference room with Micah and Efe bringing up the rear. She smiled wide as a familiar face was waiting to greet her. Ana wore a deep red dress that cut high across her chest, just under her collarbones. It had a thin black belt that went around her waist and only made it more obvious that she had an incredible hourglass figure. Her suede pumps made her several inches taller than Lizzy, even when they were both in heels, and she wore black pantyhose to complete the ensemble.

Lizzy was flooded with memories from the bar as Ana smiled from across the room. She had been so fixated on all the drama with Darcy that she had completely forgotten Ana flirting with her that night too. Now she felt like a total dumbass for forgetting the fact that such a gorgeous woman had been interested in her. Not only that, but she, unlike Darcy, seemed happy to see her right now.

Ana cleared her throat and began to speak, her subtle accent dripping at the end of each word. "Welcome back, everyone. I know you're sick of hearing my voice, beautiful as it may be, so let me introduce you to your mentors."

Four more people entered the conference room almost creepily on cue and walked up to the front of the room.

Ana lifted the piece of paper she was holding and began reading off names. "Cho Kim, you'll be with Marcus Sweezy." A tall man with brown, curly hair stepped forward and lifted his hand, looking around the room until Cho also lifted her hand and stepped forward. Marcus introduced himself, and they shook hands before leaving the room.

"Micah Willis, you'll be with Seamus O'Hara." Micah stepped forward and shook hands with a man who looked like he could gobble up both Micah and Efe in one bite, he was so wide and muscular.

"Big rugby fan?" Micah smirked, shaking his hand firmly.

"How'd you know that?" the large man asked, raising a confused eyebrow.

"Lucky guess," Micah said, chuckling.

Lizzy rolled her eyes and was glad to see them leave.

Ana continued down her list. "Jackson McClusky, you're with Margaret Duncan."

A mousy-looking woman with bright red glasses stepped forward and shook Jackson's hand nervously. She squeaked out a few words about it being nice to meet him, and he laughed loudly and adjusted his glasses. Lizzy wasn't sure who was in charge of that match, but she could already see heart eyes forming on both their shy faces.

"Efe Buhle, you're with Tamara Landon." A woman with long brown hair stepped forward, and together, they quietly left.

Ana looked around the empty conference room. She looked at her paper dramatically and at Lizzy. "Well, I guess that leaves only one."

"What do you mean? I thought you were done with us after the first week."

Ana shrugged. "I was. But I asked to take you on all for myself."

Lizzy felt her heartbeat quicken at the look Ana gave her. There was definitely more meaning to that sentence than just mentorship. And why shouldn't Lizzy be flattered and interested? Ana was smart, gorgeous, and a hell of a lot closer to her own age than some other people...person...she'd been interested in of late.

Lizzy raised her eyebrows. "Well, in that case, lead the way." She motioned toward the door.

Ana crumpled up the piece of paper and tossed it into the trash, winking at Lizzy as she walked by. Lizzy smiled and followed, taking painstaking efforts to stare at Ana's perfect ass in that dress and *not* at the frosted-over corner office with the door closed down the hall to her right.

CHAPTER FOURTEEN

Darcy wasn't hiding. Yes, she'd had her lunch delivered to her office every day this week. Yes, she had gotten to work at seven every morning and left at eight every night. And, yes, she'd looked both ways before going to the bathroom, but all of that was just because she was so damn busy.

It had absolutely nothing to do with a certain blond junior she had been incredibly rude to last Saturday morning. To her credit, her avoidance act worked flawlessly; she hadn't seen Elizabeth all week.

She bit her lip as she stared at her computer screen. Her eyes were exhausted from so much screen time, and she really wanted to go grab a drink somewhere. She looked at the corner of her screen.

6:39 p.m.

Tapping her desk, she considered the odds that anyone else was in the office right now. It was a Friday night, and most people left by six at the absolute latest. She weighed her options and decided it was worth the risk. Slipping on her camel coat, she threw her bag on her shoulder and cracked open her office door. She stuck her head out, glancing back and forth. All of the individual office lights were off, and she paused for a moment to listen for any signs of life. Satisfied that she was in the clear, she stepped out into the hallway and closed her door, locking it behind her. She let out a loud sigh of relief and walked down the long hallway, passing empty offices on both sides. She was almost to the lobby doors when she noticed a single light coming from one of the inner offices.

One of the associates probably left their light on. She knew the cleaning crew would probably shut it off, but she hated the idea of wasting electricity. She rounded the corner and was about to enter when she saw a shadow coming from inside. She jumped slightly and paused.

"Hello?" she asked, slowly peeking around the corner.

Inside one of the tiny shared offices, she saw the back of a familiar blond head bouncing back and forth. Elizabeth was standing with her back to the door, headphones in, and must not have heard Darcy come up behind her.

Rather than announce her presence, Darcy leaned against the door and bit her lip, watching as Elizabeth danced back and forth, banging invisible drums, her thin hips swaying with some unheard beat. She was barefoot and wore the same faded black pencil skirt and mismatched jacket she'd had on the very first day of work. Darcy knew she shouldn't remember little things like that, but they stuck in her brain.

She tried to keep quiet as she watched the show, but when Elizabeth began singing loudly, she couldn't contain herself anymore. She covered her mouth and attempted to hold in a laugh, but it leaked out, causing Elizabeth to spin around.

"Son of a biscuit," she said, ripping the headphones from her ears.

Darcy let out another laugh. "Did you just say, son of a biscuit?"

Elizabeth blushed and looked down. "My mom never let me cuss growing up, so I kinda adopted my own versions. You know, cheese and rice instead of Jesus Christ, stuff like that." She smiled warmly and looked down again, fidgeting with her headphones that were still playing.

"What are you listening to?" Darcy asked with true curiosity.

Lizzy looked back at her warily. "Nothing you'd have heard of."

Darcy snorted. "Oh, okay let me guess, some 'pretty obscure band' from Brooklyn?"

Elizabeth shook her head, hiding a smile. "No, it's just...okay, fine. It's 'Smells Like Teen Spirit' by Nirvana."

Darcy's jaw dropped. "Oh, come on. You're way too young to even know Nirvana or really any grunge bands, for that matter."

"Excuse me?" Lizzy said, stepping forward. "I'm an old soul, okay."

Darcy nodded, still smiling. "Yes, and I'm just old."

Without missing a beat, Elizabeth said, "Not too old for me," a slow, familiar grin spreading across her face.

Darcy had seen that mischievous look before. It was the same one she'd given at the bar a week ago. The same one she'd given in the kitchen before she had realized who Darcy was. The same one that had made Darcy almost have a major lapse in judgment.

The room hung silent for a few seconds, and it was as if they were both remembering their recent interactions, the fun ones, yes, but also the unpleasant ones over the weekend.

"Listen," Darcy said, taking another step in, "I should apologize for Saturday morning. I was rude and…and unprofessional."

"Unprofessional?" Elizabeth asked, crossing her arms.

Darcy nodded. "Yes. It…it took me aback, seeing you like that, is all." She straightened her shoulders, attempting to return to her formal "partner" state of mind. Elizabeth had disarmed her as usual, dancing around in her bare feet, wiggling her hips, her hair flipping back and forth, looking absolutely adorable. But they were literally at work, and she had to keep her guard up.

"It's fine," Elizabeth said, shrugging. Her confident demeanor disappeared, and a small look of hurt spread into her eyes at the mention of Saturday morning.

Darcy was sorry to see it go, but she didn't know what to say or what she was even allowed to say to make up for it. "What are you still doing here, anyway?" she asked after a few seconds.

"I could ask you the same thing," Elizabeth retorted.

She hated and loved how quick and snarky this woman was. It made her incredibly irresistible and also very annoying all at the same time. Darcy wasn't used to asking questions and not getting straight, immediate answers. Most people were so intimated by her at the office that all she had to do was snap her fingers, and people shuddered to compliance. But Elizabeth didn't seem to have that gene. She saw Darcy's intimidation tactics and always raised the ante with a sharp comeback.

Darcy let out a sigh and shook her head. "Never one for just answering the questions, are you?"

Elizabeth bit her lip and shook her head. "Not when I want information too."

Stop looking at her lips. Darcy cleared her throat. "All right, I'll bite. I had some work to finish up."

Elizabeth nodded, looking as if she was choosing whether or not she wanted to accept the vague answer. "What kind of work?"

Goddamn it, why is she so persistent? Darcy dug her heels in. "Partner work."

It was a low dig and a trump card all at once, and she knew it. Elizabeth let out a slight laugh. "Fine. Play it that way. I take it you're done with all that 'partner work' now?"

Darcy hesitated for a moment but nodded. "For the most part, sure. I mean, what attorney is ever actually *done* with work? But, yes, I'm leaving for the night."

Elizabeth pursed her lips. "And you don't have any fun plans tonight, I assume?"

"Correct again. Yes."

Elizabeth nodded. "Good, you can come grab a drink with me."

Darcy's jaw dropped, and she let out a smile at the realization that she had been caught. *Clever woman.* But what the hell? How did she still possibly want to spend any time around Darcy at this point? She had been hot and cold for the last two weeks, yet still, here Elizabeth was. Like a dog chasing a bone. She was relentless, this one, but Darcy had to admit, she liked it.

"You know I won't take no for an answer," Elizabeth said, taking another step. She was close enough now for Darcy to see the familiar gold specks in her eyes. She could smell the same laundry detergent she'd smelled on Saturday in the coffee shop.

How does she always smell like clean linen? Their proximity alone made her weak in the knees, and Darcy cleared her throat and looked down to break the eye contact, not wanting to show any hint of weakness.

"Come on," Elizabeth continued, "you can even write it off as a mentorship dinner or something like that."

"Oh, now it's dinner?"

Elizabeth smiled a flirtatious grin and shrugged. "It's whatever you want it to be, Darcy."

A warm puddle spread from Darcy's chest and pooled between her legs at the sound of her first name coming from that perfectly formed mouth. She checked the smartwatch on her wrist and sighed. She might regret what she was about to do, but something told her she would regret not doing it more. "One drink," she said firmly.

Elizabeth clapped and raced over to her desk. She bent and picked up a worn-out backpack and shoved a few folders inside. She slid on her black pumps and grabbed a black coat from the back of her chair. "All set," she said resolutely.

"Uh, is that the only coat you wore?" Darcy said, looking at the thin garment. It was way too light for winter weather and had clearly seen better days. Several of the buttons were close to falling off, and it was a dull shade of charcoal, even though it had clearly once been black. It would have been a perfectly fine coat for May or maybe even

April, but it was the dead of winter. It was probably in the teens outside, and Elizabeth wasn't even wearing pants.

She needs a warmer coat, a hat, gloves, my God, anything but what she has in her hands right now.

Elizabeth blushed a little. "It's the only one I have." The confidence was now gone from her voice, and Darcy could sense she had struck an area of insecurity.

She felt the immediate desire to comfort her for some reason. To throw her arms around her and pull her close. To kiss her forehead, her cheek, any part of her. "Just hang on a second," she said, cutting off her own train of thought before it got out of hand. She marched back down the long hallway and unlocked her office. A few seconds later, she returned to find Elizabeth standing in the exact same spot, coat still on her arm, backpack still hanging from her back. Part of her was surprised Elizabeth had actually obeyed for once and not followed her. But the idea of being alone in her office right now, with the lights off…

Darcy shook the daydream and stuck out her hand. "Here," she said. "Wear this one."

Elizabeth hesitated before taking the coat. Their hands grazed, and the breath hitched in Darcy's chest. She cleared her throat and stepped back. Elizabeth held up the long, thick black coat. It was the same one Darcy had worn to the happy hour last week, but she doubted Elizabeth would remember that. It was double-breasted and hit Darcy just below her butt, though on Elizabeth, it would likely fall to her knees.

Elizabeth looked at the label and shot Darcy a skeptical look. "I can't wear this."

"Why not? It's better than the one you have and much warmer. Besides, I'm not wearing black today, so it doesn't even match." Darcy opened her camel coat up, revealing the navy blue pantsuit.

Elizabeth's eyes widened with excitement, and Darcy smiled, inwardly enjoying the attention before zipping it shut again. "I still can't wear it. This thing is cashmere. What if I spill something on it? Or a homeless dude throws something at me?"

Darcy let out a laugh. "Do you often have homeless men throwing things at you?"

Elizabeth nodded. "Uh, yes. Last night, I was walking around Times Square by myself, and this man threw a bottle of water at my head and told me the voices were coming." She shuddered. "Shit freaked me out."

Darcy frowned. "One, you shouldn't be walking alone at night in Times Square. Two, if you get assaulted by a water bottle, I assure you, the coat will be fine. It's just a coat."

Elizabeth bit her lip as she set her own coat on the desk and began to put her arm through Darcy's. "A damn nice coat," she muttered as she finished wrapping it around her small frame.

Darcy laughed softly. The sleeves were just a little too long, and it was probably one size too big, but Elizabeth looked absolutely adorable in it, and now that she was in a true shade of black, not a dull, faded dingy gray, her hair and eyes were sparkling.

"It's definitely warmer than mine, I'll give you that," Elizabeth said, stroking the sleeve.

"Good. Shall we?" Darcy said motioning toward the door. Maybe her little avoidance plan hadn't worked so well after all, she thought as the elevator doors parted, and they stepped inside.

CHAPTER FIFTEEN

This is happening. This is happening.
Lizzy kept telling herself the same sentence over and over again as she walked next to Darcy up Madison Avenue. She stroked the sleeve of Darcy's coat and tried not to focus on the perfume that lingered in the fabric. It was the same coat she had worn to the happy hour last week; Lizzy had known that within seconds. She tried not to think about that night. She tried to clear her mind of the feeling of excitement and potential that coursed through her veins with each step they took. But with each step, she smelled Darcy's smell that was now wrapped around her. And with every inch of skin that it touched—her neck, her wrists, even the tips of her legs—she imagined Darcy's fingers in its stead.

She had no idea what had come over her back in her office. After last Saturday, she'd told herself that Darcy was a thing of the past. That she clearly had no feelings for Lizzy, so she was going to just let go of this ridiculous fantasy. The fact that she'd spent the entire week by Ana's side, not seeing Darcy at all, had certainly helped clear her mind somewhat.

But she'd seen her standing in the doorway of the little office and looking so damn beautiful, and she couldn't help herself. She'd seen the soft, familiar look in Darcy's eyes, just like she had last week in the bar, and she'd pounced instinctively. It was like she was drawn to Darcy in ways she couldn't control.

And what would happen now? Were they going on a date? Was it dinner? Casual drinks? A work-related completely platonic meeting? Lizzy truly had no idea.

She knew what she *wanted* them to be walking to. In fact, she knew exactly what she wanted to be doing to Darcy Hammond tonight.

But she also knew that even though she had agreed to have a drink with Lizzy, there was a slim chance of anything romantic actually happening.

Lizzy sighed, watching her breath billow out of her mouth like a dragon.

"All good?" Darcy asked, apparently hearing her despondence.

Lizzy smiled up at her and nodded. "All great," she said.

Darcy rolled her eyes at the cheesy reply and looked down, but Lizzy saw the thin line of a smile on the side of her face.

They walked about four blocks before Lizzy's feet began stinging from the cold. She usually wore a pair of flats or boots into the office and then changed into her heels. She had no practice walking the streets of New York in heels, and the fact that it was freezing outside and she had elected to wear a pencil skirt and hose today made it that much worse.

But Darcy's pointed maroon heels were about two inches taller than Lizzy's modest, underrated pumps—and probably a few hundred dollars more expensive—and she seemed to be having no issues at all.

"How far can you walk in those things?" Darcy asked, looking at Lizzy's shoes.

"Probably farther than you can in those." Lizzy pointed to the maroon heels defiantly.

Darcy furrowed her brows. "Easy, tiger, it wasn't a challenge. You're never gonna make it in those, though."

Lizzy bit her cheek. Damn it, she was probably right. "Where are we going?"

"Don't worry about it," Darcy replied mysteriously.

The look on her face when she said the last part made Lizzy's heart speed up, and she blew on her hands to avoid blushing. She didn't give a shit where they were going as long as they were going there together and it was warm.

Darcy took a few steps toward the street and leaned out, peering down the avenue. A slew of yellow cars drove by, but she just waited and watched. Finally, one with a white light on the top of the roof came toward them, and she lifted her hand just barely. The car pulled over instantly, and Darcy opened the back door, motioning for Lizzy to get in.

She didn't protest. Her feet were cold, her legs were cold, her hands were cold; hell, even her eyeballs were cold at this point. As warm and cozy as Darcy's coat was, it was still in the twenties outside. She slid across the worn leather seat to the other side of the cab.

Darcy scooted in behind her and leaned over her to speak to the cab driver. "Fifty-Ninth and Fifth," she said quickly, sitting back and shifting around in her camel coat. She adjusted her dark brown leather gloves, pulling them tighter on each finger, and looked out the window as the cab made its way up Madison Avenue.

Lizzy tried to contain her excitement, but the truth was, this was her first time riding in a cab in New York City. She had never visited before moving here last month, and cabs were way above her budget. She leaned back and stared out the window, watching as they passed each street. The numbers grew higher with every block, and she took mental notes of all the sights they passed.

"This is my first time in a cab," she said.

"You're kidding me."

Lizzy shook her head, still staring out the window, mesmerized by the passing lights. She expected Darcy to make fun of her, or at least make a passing jab at her naivete or youth, but she simply let out a soft, "Mmm."

Lizzy leaned her head against the window, feeling the icy weather stick to her forehead. She didn't mind the cold now that she was safe inside the warm cab with Darcy. After about fifteen minutes of rush hour traffic, they reached the streets Darcy had given the driver. She handed the man a large bill and didn't ask for change.

Once they were outside, the cold met them with a vengeance, and Lizzy wrapped her arms around herself and shoved her hands into the armpits of Darcy's coat. She was definitely glad she'd borrowed it. Aside from the delicious smell, and the fact that it had once been pressed against Darcy's body, it was incredibly warm. Much better than her old American Eagle, the one she'd left hanging on her chair back at the office.

"This way," Darcy said, tilting her head across the street.

They trotted across as fast as their heels would allow, and when Lizzy took a few more steps and looked up, she knew exactly where they were going. She'd recognize that building anywhere. Heck, anyone who'd ever seen *Home Alone 2* or *Gossip Girl* would recognize that big beautiful building. Because anyone who knew anything about New York knew the Plaza.

"Holy shit," Lizzy said, stopping in front of the dark green awning.

Darcy proceeded to walk up the red-carpeted steps, never slowing or looking at all unsure of herself. She walked with such confidence that one would think she owned the entire hotel. A man with a little round hat nodded and opened the door for her as she approached, and she turned, motioning for Lizzy to follow.

When they entered the lobby, Lizzy scooted closer to Darcy's side, taking note to stay quiet and follow her lead. Everything she'd ever heard about this place was that a person needed a reservation with the hotel to even come in the doors. Yet, here she was, walking right in and with an incredibly gorgeous woman.

"Two for the Palm Court," Darcy said, approaching a mahogany lectern off to the side of the main lobby.

"Are you a guest here, ma'am?" the woman asked, looking at her iPad.

"No," Darcy replied coolly.

The woman looked up and opened her mouth like she was about to speak. Darcy stared back, unflinching, and the woman looked again at her iPad. "Yes, of course, ma'am, we can seat you right away."

Another man stepped forward and held out his hands. Darcy turned and unzipped her coat before sliding it gently off her shoulders and into the man's arms. Lizzy did her best to follow suit, though she was certain she looked nothing like Darcy while doing it. She blushed as she saw a strand of her hair sticking to the collar of Darcy's coat as he took it away. He returned a moment later and handed Darcy a single ticket. Next, the woman with the iPad handed two menus to another young woman, who led Darcy and Lizzy to their seats.

The Palm Court looked like it was straight out of an Edwardian novel, and Lizzy felt a bit like Jack from *Titanic* when he was invited to have dinner in first class. The chairs were covered in gold fabric, and tall palm trees lined the perimeter of the room. There was a circular bar in the center, and the entire ceiling was made of stained glass, with designs of flowers and vines. A piano player was playing something soft and classical in one of the corners, further adding to the old-world ambiance.

The hostess placed the menus on the table, and Lizzy slid into the chair next to Darcy, even though they were seated at a four-top. If Darcy minded, she didn't say anything.

"I take it you've never been to the Plaza before?" Darcy asked, tilting her head toward Lizzy.

"Uh, nope, nope definitely another first for me," Lizzy said staring at the ornate ceiling above their heads.

"Well, in that case, I'll be gentle," Darcy said, with the familiar flirtatious glimmer in her eye that made Lizzy's head spin.

An older man wearing a black suit and white bow tie came over and greeted them. Darcy reached over and took Lizzy's menu before she could even look at it. "We'll have two of these," Darcy said, pointing to an item.

The server nodded and said, "Very good, ma'am," before disappearing.

"Okay, now *that* was old-school," Lizzy said. "Ordering for me? Not letting me look at the menu? Misogynist much?" Lizzy hadn't actually minded Darcy taking charge like she did. If anything, the power move was a total turn-on. But she wasn't ready to relinquish all control of the evening.

"Oh please, I figured since it's just one drink, we might as well make it count." Darcy winked. "Plus," Darcy continued, "there's nothing wrong with surprising someone with a good drink you know they'll like."

Lizzy crossed her arms and leaned across the table. "What makes you think you know what I like?"

"Oh, let's just call it a lucky guess." Darcy sat back and crossed her arms as if attempting to remain aloof.

Lizzy felt her confidence fading. Tonight felt different than last week in the bar. Last week, she had been so confident approaching Darcy. But last week, there had been music and other people talking and a million distractions, not to mention one too many drinks. Last week had been on her terms. She'd approached Darcy. She'd asked Darcy to leave with her. But here, in the beautiful lighting of the Plaza, there was nothing to hide the fact that it was just the two of them. And this was Darcy's turn. Lizzy didn't have the home field advantage here, and she had a feeling Darcy knew that too.

After a few moments, the server set down two frosty silver cups. Crushed ice was piled like a perfect round snow cone on the top, and a spear of fresh mint was sticking off to one side, while a matching silver straw poked out of the other. It was the most beautiful mint julep Lizzy had ever seen, north, south, east, or west of the Mason-Dixon.

Her mouth hung open as Darcy grinned victoriously.

"Cheers," Darcy said, lifting one of the silver cups before taking a sip from her straw.

Still speechless, Lizzy grabbed the cool cup. It was frosted from the ice, and she left fingerprints on the silver where she touched it. She sipped the sweet, minty beverage and felt a flood of warm bourbon spread from her stomach through her veins. The ingredients were perfectly combined, and she could taste that they'd even used Knob Creek.

"Holy shit, that's good," she said, finally breathing between sips.

Darcy smiled. "I'm glad you like it."

Lizzy took another big swig, feeling the bourbon settle in. "Do you bring all the new juniors here?"

Darcy tossed her head back, her perfect white teeth flashing in contrast with the dim yellow lights of the room, and let out a laugh similar to the one she had last week at the bar when Lizzy had tried to use that Emily Dickinson quote on her. "God, no," she said, still chuckling a little. "No, I've never brought anyone here, actually. It's a special place for me."

"Then why bring me?" Lizzy asked, leaning in closer.

Darcy paused as if carefully considering her answer. She looked like there was something she wanted to say. Some piece of her that she wanted to share. Lizzy kept her eyes locked with Darcy's, waiting for what truth she might reveal.

Instead, Darcy sat back and simply said, "Well, no one else I know likes mint juleps."

CHAPTER SIXTEEN

*K*eep *it together, Darcy. Keep it together.*
    Darcy scolded herself, watching as Elizabeth sucked down the rest of her drink. She was almost finished with hers too, and she could feel the bourbon already loosening her inhibitions.

The worst part was, she wanted another. Not just another drink but another of this, all of this. She wanted more of this night, this feeling, this woman she was with. She didn't know what it was about her, but there was something about the way Elizabeth looked at her that disarmed her. It was like she could peel back the layers Darcy had spent years putting up, all with a single glance.

Darcy knew she was treading on thin ice. She had already compromised too much by even being here with Elizabeth. What she said was true: she'd never brought anyone here. Because the Plaza *was* a special place for her.

When she'd first moved to New York fifteen years ago and was working at a securities firm down on Wall Street, there was a movie playing across the street at the Paris Theatre that she had been dying to see. The theatre itself was tiny, only featuring two movies a night, and it specialized in independent films that one wouldn't normally see in larger theatres.

The movie was about two women in love in the 1950s and was based on one of her favorite books. The fact that it starred one of her favorite actresses as the titular character had sent her into obsession, and every Friday night for the entire month of November, she'd come, sat alone in the theatre, watched the movie, and ended the night with a mint julep at the Plaza. Back then, it wasn't reservations only, and the general public could come and go as they wished. Most didn't know a person could actually sit and eat or drink, but even back then, Darcy had been confident enough to do what most people weren't: she'd asked.

That month was one of the special early memories she had as a New Yorker. It was the first time she'd felt like the city was in some small way hers. Like she had a little safe space carved out for just her, and every Friday, there was a seat waiting for her.

She'd wanted to share that with Elizabeth just now when she'd asked why Darcy had brought her here. She wanted to share a lot of things with Elizabeth. She wanted to do a lot of things with Elizabeth too, but instead, she just bit harder on her cheek and tried not to think about those things.

"Care for another, miss?" the server she hadn't seen asked.

Darcy glanced at Elizabeth. It felt like she was challenging her, daring her almost. It always felt that way with Elizabeth. She wasn't sure how one person could make her feel so safe and yet so exposed all at once.

"Yes. For both of us," she said, locking eyes with Elizabeth.

A triumphant look spread across Elizabeth's face, and Darcy almost hated to give her the victory. The rules of the night had been set by Darcy: just one drink. Darcy had hailed the cab. Darcy had picked the restaurant. But somehow, the tide of power was shifting all of a sudden.

"So," Elizabeth said, folding her hands and scooting closer. "If you didn't go to Yale, where'd you go?"

Darcy chuckled. "Are we really playing that game? We're going to sit here and pretend like the first thing you did after the whole 'Yale mug' incident wasn't run back to your desk and look me up on the firm website?"

Crimson spread across Elizabeth's face, and she cracked a slow smile. "Shit, okay. Yes, I stalked you. But you'd have totally done the same if I was actually on the website."

Darcy tilted her head. "I might have. Then again, maybe not."

"All right, well, in that case, I guess my real question is, how does a woman from Florida end up in New York?"

The server returned with their drinks. They clinked their silver cups quickly, and Darcy took a deep sip. "Probably the same way a woman from Virginia does."

Elizabeth perked up "Oh, okay. So you have stalked me. I knew it. But wait, how…did you google me or something?"

I can google her. Duh. God, why didn't I think of that before lugging those stupid files home? "Let's just say, I did some research on my own."

Elizabeth crossed her arms.

Darcy broke out laughing at her perfectly pursed lips. God, she was cute when she didn't get her way. "All right, don't get your panties in a twist. I looked at your employee file, okay? Happy?"

Elizabeth's arms dropped to her sides. "I'm sorry, what was that? I got distracted when you started talking about my panties."

Darcy rolled her eyes and looked down, mostly to hide the blush that she knew must have crept across her face at the comment. "Are you always this much of a flirt?" she asked bluntly, taking another sip. She was definitely feeling tipsy now.

Elizabeth licked her lips and looked at her cup. "Yup. But not everyone minds it like you do."

Darcy felt her walls slowly start to come back up again, and she leaned back, looking at her drink. The comment stung. It shouldn't have. It wasn't at all offensive. Elizabeth was answering honestly. And the answer to the question was yes, yes, she was a flirt. It was just a game to her. It was all just a game.

"Wait, I didn't mean, I mean no, I mean…"

Darcy waited and watched as Elizabeth fumbled for words. What was she even hoping to hear? "No, Darcy, I only flirt with *you* this way because *you're* special to me"? How ridiculous. She had barely known this woman for two weeks. Besides, Elizabeth was a beautiful, young, single woman. Of course she was going to flirt. Of course she was going to play the field. The logical side of Darcy's brain knew all this. But for some reason, in the emotional side of her brain, the comment made the entire night feel silly.

She was ready to leave. She shouldn't have shared this place with anyone. What the hell had she even been thinking?

Elizabeth was fidgeting with her straw, swirling the loose ice around in the cup. She had stopped speaking and was staring down, her eyes no longer sparkly or confident.

Darcy raised a hand and signaled to the server that they were ready for the check.

"Darcy." Elizabeth's voice was low and soft, not like Darcy had ever heard it before, and she reached across the table and placed a hand on top of hers. Darcy ignored the bolts of electricity that shot through her at the contact as she stared back into Elizabeth's warm eyes. "I didn't mean it like you're taking it," she said with her hand still resting on Darcy's.

Slowly, and painfully, Darcy slid her hand out from under Elizabeth's and placed it in her lap. A look of defeat spread over Elizabeth's face, and she looked down. "It's late," Darcy said, checking her smartwatch.

It was only nine, but Darcy had already crossed a lot of lines tonight. If she stayed any later, she risked crossing more, ones that weren't as easily uncrossed.

The server appeared by her side, delivering a black leather booklet with a gold inscription of a mirrored *P*. Darcy slid her credit card into it and handed it back without even checking the amount.

Elizabeth watched as the server left, then leaned closer across the table again. "Do you always do this?" she asked frankly.

"Do I always do what?"

"Leave when a situation presents itself that you don't know how to work through instantly?"

Darcy opened her mouth to say something, but the server was back to return her card. She flipped open the leather booklet and scribbled her name at the bottom and added a tip to the top. "I don't know what you're talking about," she said. "It's late, I have to get home, and you should too." She stood to leave, and Elizabeth followed her lead, clearly not wanting to make a scene. Once they picked up their coats, she followed Darcy down the red steps and outside. "Where do you live?" Darcy asked when they were both standing at the curb.

"149th and Broadway," Elizabeth answered. "Why?"

"I'm hailing you a cab. It's too late for you to take the subway, and there's not a red line close to here. The orange lines get dangerous at night that far up and—"

"Whoa, whoa, whoa, hold up," Elizabeth said. "Are you seriously going to stand here and pretend that what just happened in there *didn't* happen? Darcy, you're literally doing it right now. You're trying to send me off in a cab just because you don't like a question that I asked." Her voice was elevated, and steam poured out of her mouth from the cold.

"Elizabeth, it's late, I'm just trying to make sure you get home safely," Darcy protested, looking around for a cab.

"Bullshit," Elizabeth said. "Just admit it, Darcy."

Darcy stopped and looked back at her. "Admit what? What are you even talking about right now?"

Elizabeth took another step; her breath was so close that the steam touched the bottom of Darcy's chin as she spoke.

She steeled herself as she looked down. She wasn't going to give in. Elizabeth was a flirt. This meant nothing to her. She was way too young. She was—

"Admit that you're attracted to me," Elizabeth said, staring directly into her eyes.

Darcy looked back, searching for some hint of mischievousness or flirtatiousness. Something to prove that this was all just in fun. That it was just a game. A challenge, even. But there was nothing. Nothing but passion and desire and raw vulnerability stared back at her from the eyes of Elizabeth Taylor.

"Elizabeth, I—"

Before she could think of any more excuses, Elizabeth was up on her tiptoes, kissing her. Darcy felt her lips part instinctively as Elizabeth pressed her soft, full lips to hers. It wasn't like any first kiss she'd had before. This one was like someone had taken a first kiss and plugged it into an electrical outlet. It was wired and charged and illuminating. She felt a flood of warmth rush from her head all the way down to her stomach and into her legs as she kissed Elizabeth back. She bent over farther and wrapped her arms around Elizabeth's waist, pulling at her own coat to bring Elizabeth in closer.

Elizabeth slid a hand beneath Darcy's chin and slowly moved it behind the nape of her neck, pulling her down farther into Elizabeth's arms.

Finally, Darcy pulled back long enough to blink and process what had just happened. Elizabeth let out a slow breath, the steam pouring into Darcy's open mouth.

"Wow," Elizabeth said softly under her breath as she stared.

Darcy smiled and leaned in again, kissing her softly this time before pulling back once more.

"Okay, fine," Darcy said, smirking, "I like you."

CHAPTER SEVENTEEN

Lizzy strutted off the subway with Frank Sinatra's "New York, New York" blaring in her ears. It was a cliché, she knew, but she didn't care. She had spent the entire weekend floating on a cloud.

After Darcy had admitted she liked her, she had stayed true to her word and sent Lizzy home in a cab, putting her number in Lizzy's phone and asking her to text when she got there safely. Lizzy had complied, and they hadn't spoken since.

She considered texting Darcy a cute text the following morning or even asking to see her again over the weekend. But she hadn't. She knew Darcy had been vulnerable with her Friday night, and she probably needed time to process all that. Darcy was probably the type of woman who got suffocated easily, and the last thing Lizzy wanted to do was scare her away.

If she was being really honest with herself, she didn't want to think about Darcy liking her almost as much as she only wanted to think about Darcy liking her. Because for every bolt of joy she felt at the thought, there was a surge of fear that coursed through her. *Termination.* The word from the firm handbook played on a loop in her mind until finally, she forced it out by assuring herself that no one would ever find out. That Darcy knew what she was doing and would… what? Protect her? Lizzy really wasn't sure. She decided to talk more about it with Darcy in person eventually but to just enjoy the ignorant bliss for now.

Saturday, she'd gone to a Rangers game with Amina and some friends. She didn't really care about hockey, but it was her first time at Madison Square Garden, it was something "New Yorkers did," per Amina, and since Amina's friend worked at the Garden, it was free.

Sunday, she'd slid on Darcy's coat and had gone to Serendipity and had one of their famous "Frrrozen Hot Chocolates" before window shopping up and down Fifth Avenue. She was still nervous to wear the cashmere garment and refused to eat anything while wearing it, but she'd left her own coat at the office, and she liked keeping it close to her to remind her that Friday night actually happened.

She'd ended the weekend by standing in line at the Met Opera and snagging a last-minute ticket for *The Magic Flute*. She'd paid twenty-five bucks for a front row, center, orchestra seat, understood no words they sang, and cried because it was so beautiful.

She cinched Darcy's coat tighter as she waited for the elevator in the Byron & Browning lobby, tilting her head so she could smell Darcy's lingering perfume on the collar. She hoped wearing it into the office was okay. She didn't have much of a choice. She'd arrived earlier than she'd ever been and way earlier than any associate would be, hoping to sneak into Darcy's office and leave it for her unnoticed.

The lights were on in the hallway, but the perky blond receptionist, Maggy, wasn't there yet, so Lizzy assumed one of the custodians must have done it early this morning. She bopped her head, singing under her breath as she walked down the long hallway to her small office. Once entering the room, she flipped on the light and dropped her backpack at her desk.

As she suspected, she was the first one in. Jackson's office was still dark, as were the seniors' offices and the of counsels' window-facing ones.

She made her way toward the frosted door she was looking for. The nameplate on the outside of the door read *Darcy E. Hammond, Managing Partner*, and Lizzy smiled briefly before pushing the door open.

"Can I help you?"

The familiar cool voice coming from the other side of the room made Lizzy jump. "Jesus," she said, stepping back and grasping her chest.

Behind a large, glass desk, Darcy sat with both hands folded calmly. She was wearing a fitted black pantsuit with a steely gray tie that was cinched all the way to her throat. Lizzy could see a black stiletto swinging up and down from her crossed leg from under the desk.

She had never looked more powerful, intimidating, or fucking sexy, and Lizzy struggled to find words as she stared blankly back. Darcy sighed and stood, her slender figure becoming even more accentuated as she took several long steps.

"I…I'm sorry, I thought I was the only one here," Lizzy stuttered.

Darcy closed the space between them, and the smell of her made Lizzy's senses cloudy with lust. She stood a few feet away and crossed her arms, a playful gleam in her eye. "So you decided to take the opportunity to sneak into my office, and do what, exactly?"

Lizzy blushed. "Sneak? No, I was just going to give you back your coat."

Darcy nodded suspiciously. "The one you're still wearing, I note?"

"I mean, I wanted to keep it safe."

Darcy continued to stare, her expression impossible to read. Her eyes were warm and piercing all at once, and Lizzy couldn't decide if she should kiss her or run from her office and give two weeks' notice.

"Missed me that much?" Darcy asked, dropping her crossed arms and taking another step.

Lizzy relaxed. "Don't flatter yourself. This was the only coat I had. Someone forced me to leave mine here over the weekend."

"Ah, I see, so this decision was made from pure necessity?" She took another short step and was so close, Lizzy could smell the spearmint gum on her breath.

Lizzy smiled playfully, nodding as Darcy's face continued to move closer.

When her lips were inches away, Darcy whispered, "Are you sure about that?"

Lizzy pressed their lips firmly together. The taste of spearmint and ChapStick flooded her mouth as Darcy's smooth lips explored hers. She parted her lips and let Darcy's tongue graze hers before it exited too quickly.

Darcy pulled back, keeping her lips inches away. "Are you the only one here?"

Lizzy nodded, biting her lip. Darcy seemed to notice and pounced, kissing her harder and pushing her back against the wall. She wrapped her arms around Darcy and pulled her closer. She traced the waist of Darcy's pants before sliding beneath the back of the blazer. She wished she could rip off the puckered, waffled shirt Darcy was wearing but settled for using it to pull her closer.

Darcy unbuttoned her coat on Lizzy's body and slid her hands beneath it, grabbing Lizzy's thigh and squeezing gently before sliding up Lizzy's back and eventually under her chin. She tilted Lizzy's head and placed kisses down her neck.

Lizzy let out a soft moan. Darcy kissed her ear before whispering a low, "Shh," in a husky voice. It was enough to send Lizzy over the edge, and she opened her mouth to let out another moan, but Darcy covered it with her hand.

"Be good, or we'll have to stop."

Lizzy's knees went weak. Hooking up in an office would have gone down as the craziest thing she had ever done. Period. But hooking up with her boss *in* her boss's office moments before everyone else was scheduled to arrive? That was another level of insanity. She grabbed a fistful of Darcy's ass and squeezed.

Darcy stopped kissing. "Easy, tiger, don't start something you can't finish."

"You keep questioning my abilities. It's insulting."

Stepping back, Darcy placed her hand on Lizzy's cheek, stroking it gently. "On the contrary, I have no doubt you're incredibly...capable."

"Then come here," Lizzy said, reaching out.

Darcy smiled and shook her head, looking at her smartwatch. "It's late, Elizabeth."

Lizzy rolled her eyes. "Another thing you love saying to me." She stood straight and finished taking off the coat. "I better give this back to you. It *is* the actual reason I came in here."

"Thank God. I was missing it in my black suit today." She blushed as Lizzy gave her an up-and-down glance.

"Let's talk about this suit," Lizzy said, taking a playful step. She yanked on Darcy's tie, pulling her closer.

"Oh, no, you don't," Darcy said, letting out a soft giggle.

"Ugh, fine." Lizzy pretended to pout. "At least let me take you to dinner this week."

"Elizabeth," Darcy said in a low voice. "I...I do like you. Clearly. But this, us...it can't go anywhere."

Lizzy's heart sank. She had known this was a possibility. But she'd decided the risk was worth taking if it meant getting to kiss the most beautiful woman she'd ever seen. But it still stung. "Why not?" she asked, attempting to remain aloof, but the quiver in her voice betrayed her.

Darcy's eyes looked soft again. "Well, for one, I'm a partner. Not just that, but I'm your boss. Did they skip over the part in the employee handbook that expressly forbids this exact type of situation?"

Lizzy averted her eyes. "They might have mentioned it."

"Then you know as well as I do that if anyone finds out what we did Friday night, and just now, it means termination for both of us. You may be willing to jeopardize your budding career for a fling, but I'm not."

"Okay, okay, I get it," Lizzy said, raising her hand. She didn't need a list of why Darcy was way out of her league to crush her confidence and spirit. "So, you, what? Wanted to kiss me one more time?" She hadn't meant to sound so accusatory or hurt.

"Of course not. Elizabeth, the last thing I want to do is hurt you." She held out her hands. Lizzy didn't want to give in so quickly, but she did, taking her hands and stepping toward her. "I can't believe I'm even saying this," she whispered after a slow, deep exhale. "I want this." She kissed Lizzy on the cheek. "And if you want this too, we can try to… find a gray area in that part of the handbook. A legal loophole, perhaps? But it has to be just physical. It can't be more. And no one can ever know. Do you understand?"

"You want to be fuck buddies? Is that what you're saying?"

Darcy blushed and looked down. "I wouldn't call it that, but sure. I like you. I like kissing you. I like talking to you and spending time with you. I just…I can't do the relationship thing. Dates and flowers and candy, I'm too old for all that nonsense. And I meant what I said about not wanting to risk my career. The second it gets complicated, we end it. As professionals."

"Okay," Lizzy said skeptically. "But how is us fucking not just as bad as us dating?"

Darcy hesitated a moment. "That part isn't exactly about the job. I just don't have the emotional capacity to get involved with someone romantically right now. I'm very busy with this upcoming trial and it just…I can't give you that if that's what you need."

Lizzy nodded. If Darcy wanted to just hook up, fine. Lizzy could do that. She'd just keep her guard up so she didn't get hurt. This wasn't her first journey into fuck-buddy territory, and she wasn't going to make the same mistake twice. During her sophomore year of college, one of her roommates, Lara, had broken up with her boyfriend and decided to find comfort by sneaking into Lizzy's bed when their other roommates had all gone to sleep.

They'd spent an entire semester together, parking in abandoned lots, sneaking into each other's beds, stealing kisses between classes, and leaving each other little notes under their pillows. Then Lara had gone home for Christmas break and gotten back together with her boyfriend. She'd told Lizzy over text on her drive back from Virginia Beach.

Lizzy had been crushed, but she hadn't let it show. They'd stayed "friends" throughout the remainder of the year and never did anything romantic or physical ever again. But the scar was permanent on Lizzy's heart, and she'd learned a valuable lesson: keep her friends close but any friends with benefits far away.

She wasn't looking to relive that experience.

Darcy nodded, seeming impressed. "All right, in that case, there are some terms and conditions we'll need to abide by."

"Should I draw us up a contract then, counselor?"

Darcy relaxed slightly. "That won't be necessary. It's pretty simple. No dates. No presents. No romance. No exclusivity. And most importantly, absolutely no one can know. The firm takes a zero tolerance policy on this type of thing. Not that it's stopped my male colleagues in the past." Darcy rolled her eyes. "Remember, we're not dating, it's just…"

"Sex," Lizzy said bluntly.

Darcy nodded and crossed her arms. "Are you okay with that?"

Lizzy pondered the conditions and nodded, sticking out her hand. "Deal."

And with that, the decision was made. They would be friends with benefits. Nothing else. Sure, it wasn't what Lizzy had hoped for when they'd kissed Friday night. And okay, maybe she had googled several places she wanted to take Darcy on dates around the city over the weekend. And yes, she had imagined them holding hands walking up and down Fifth Avenue. But this was good too. This was what Darcy could handle, and she understood that. Besides, what harm could come of it? They weren't exclusive. Lizzy could still date someone if she wanted. There really was no way this could go wrong.

CHAPTER EIGHTEEN

Darcy had read about this type of thing before, but she still thought she was too young for a midlife crisis. Sure, she was nearing forty, and sure, she was pursuing someone who was almost half her age, but so what? It wasn't like she was cheating on a spouse or blowing her retirement on a red Porsche. She found a younger woman to be attractive. So she had a friend with benefits. What was wrong with that? Technically, the handbook prohibited relationships, and screwing wasn't having a relationship.

She deserved an ounce of happiness in her life, and she refused to feel guilty about it. But there was the issue of her being Elizabeth's boss. Byron & Browning's policy was black-and-white on this issue. If they got caught, they'd both be fired. Was it really worth it? The late nights and weekends she'd worked for years to achieve this position? Why was she so quick to risk it all over a woman she barely knew?

She went back and forth, torturing herself, convincing herself that she had made a terrible mistake. She would argue with herself, taking both sides as if it was a case she was working up. She would make the internal argument that they weren't technically in a relationship and how the handbook didn't mention purely physical relationships. Then, at one point, she convinced herself that she should walk down the hall to Elizabeth's office and tell her their deal was off. Eventually, she gave up and tried to focus on work.

She tried to focus on what Patty was saying when she came into her office, but all she saw as her lips were moving was Elizabeth's body pressed against the wall behind her.

She tried to focus in the partner meeting when Mark rambled on and on about their quarter profit projection. And she tried really, really hard to focus on numerous calls and conferences throughout the rest of her day. But she just couldn't. All she heard was Elizabeth's soft sweet voice and that little moan. All she felt was the touch of her smooth lips as they opened for Darcy's tongue.

It had taken all of her self-control not to take Elizabeth right there against the wall. But even fuck buddies had to take their time. She was incredibly attracted to Elizabeth, that much was obvious, but there was something else that drew her in. Something more. And that was the part that scared her. That was the thing she had been too afraid to admit to when Elizabeth had asked her why they couldn't date.

Because I could fall in love with you, her brain had shouted as Elizabeth had stared with those stupid, beautiful, innocent eyes.

"Get it together, Darcy," she said as she caught herself staring blankly at her computer screen for the tenth time that day. She turned her attention to the one thing she knew would consume her mind: her trial prep for the *Meadows* case.

Clicking open the file, she started to run down her long list of things to do. Trial authorizations were sent last week. Great. Experts had been contacted by Patty, and Darcy was meeting with an architect next week. Perfect. She still had to get up to the house to photograph it and do a site inspection, but that could wait.

She pulled open her calendar and began to map out the potential witnesses based on their availability and how she wanted to present the story to the jury.

"How goes the trial prep?" a male voice said from her open door.

She would have jumped, but she was in the habit of not letting anyone catch her off guard, so she continued to stare at her screen. "It's going," she replied blankly.

Richard Maulson, one of the other partners, stepped into her office uninvited and took a seat at one of the two empty chairs facing her desk. Most of the partners Darcy could tolerate. They were crass and made inappropriate, sexist comments, but Richard—or Dick as she intentionally called him—was just a piece of shit.

Seeing that his visit was not going to be brief, she turned her attention to him and laced her fingers on her desk.

"Listen, Darce," he began, his voice dripping with condescension. "I just wanted to give you a heads-up, I snagged the Willis kid for my *Cysco* trial. I wanted to tell you, man-to-man...if you know what I mean."

Her spine stiffened as he winked, a wide smirk plastered across his wrinkled face. The partners were always making passing comments like that about her sexuality. Letting it slide and ignoring it was just part of her everyday routine now. She gritted her teeth, refusing to show any sort of reaction. "No problem at all, Dick," she said, smiling widely. "Besides, I've already selected the associate I want on my trial, and it isn't Micah Willis."

He tilted his head. "Oh really? And who's that?"

She returned her attention to her computer screen. "Elizabeth Taylor," she said firmly.

She chided herself, hopefully not revealing any form of trepidation as she stared coldly across her desk. She didn't know when she'd decided to make Elizabeth the junior on this trial. Perhaps it had been the second she said it. Or perhaps it had been from the moment she'd walked into that conference room last month. Either way, the decision was made now, and there was no going back.

Richard chuckled. "The Southern belle? Shouldn't be surprised. Birds of a feather flock together."

She knew he meant it to be an insult, but she took it as a compliment. First, Elizabeth was many things, but a Southern belle was *not* one of them. Second, she and Elizabeth did have many things in common, their Southern roots and non–Ivy League education being among them. She wouldn't let someone clouded by privilege sour her opinion. "Is there anything else? I have a meeting to get to."

Taking the not-so-subtle hint, he slapped his knees and rose. "See you at the next meeting, Darce." He adjusted his French cuffs before leaving.

"You too, Dick."

After he left, she stood and began to pace. She shook out her hands and cracked her neck, releasing the tension built up from that brief interaction. She hated how the men in this firm still ruled the roost. Diversity be damned, that glass ceiling was still right there, bearing down on her and Elizabeth and every other female attorney in this firm, hell, in the entire legal profession. The court system was a total boys' club, even in the allegedly progressive city of New York, and she hated that she was contributing to its existence by working in it.

"Everything all right?" a friendly voice said over her shoulder.

Patty was there with a fresh cup of coffee. Darcy couldn't help but smile when she saw the mug. It was navy blue with an orange man riding a horse. The words *Go Hoos!* were written along the side.

"Yeah, just Dick being a dick as usual."

Patty shook her head. "That man gives all men a bad name, I swear."

Darcy nodded and sat. "That for me or have you picked up a new habit?"

After looking at the mug in her hand, Patty jumped slightly. "Oh yes, thought you could use a little pick-me-up. You've been working some long hours lately."

Darcy took the cup, smiling again at the warm handle in her fingers. She liked knowing it was Elizabeth's, knowing she was about to press her lips to the same place Elizabeth's had been pressed countless times. She imagined her curled over her books in the library, studying for the bar exam, taking periodic sips. "My workload should be lightening a little bit. I just told Dick I was bringing on a junior for my *Meadows* trial."

Patty smiled. "Who is the lucky guy or gal?"

Darcy hesitated before finally saying, "Elizabeth Taylor." She was nervous to say her name. She had just said it to Richard two minutes ago, but Patty was different. Patty was like family. She knew Darcy. Knew her face, her voice, her moods. And she always knew when Darcy was attracted to someone, just by the way she talked about them. She hoped she hadn't revealed too much already. She trusted Patty with everything…well, anything but the fact that she was hooking up with a junior.

But if Patty did suspect anything, she didn't let on. She just nodded and smiled before saying, "I think that is an excellent choice."

"What makes you say that?"

Patty shrugged, a slight twinkle in her eye. "I just think it's a good choice." With that, she turned and left Darcy alone, staring at a UVA mug and thinking about its owner, who she was about to spend a lot of time with.

CHAPTER NINETEEN

You get your trial assignment yet, Eight?" Micah Willis piped up from his office across the hall.

Lizzy gritted her teeth, focused on ignoring the lingering nickname. They were the only two in their offices at the moment. Everyone else was working either with their senior or a partner, or down in the bowels hunting for something.

"Nope," Lizzy replied bluntly.

"Well, I did. Richard Maulson asked me to work on some multi-million-dollar contract dispute with him."

She heard him stand, and her shoulders tensed. *Please don't come over here, please don't come over here.* She looked up to see his tanned, perfect face over her computer screen. He leaned casually in the door, his tailored light gray suit bringing out the blond highlights in his smoothed-back hair.

"Pretty ironic, don't you think?" He crossed his arms and cocked his head.

Lizzy let out a sigh. "What's ironic?"

"It's just funny that me, the person who couldn't give two shits about this job, gets stuck with the biggest case the firm has and you, the person who cares, like, way too much, is without a partner to shadow."

Lizzy tilted her head. "Well, no one would ever accuse you of caring too much, I'll give you that."

He let out a laugh, and she was surprised to hear herself laughing with him. She loathed him, but she couldn't disagree with him on this point. She was the only junior to not be assigned to a trial partner yet, and she was starting to get a little worried. On top of that, she hadn't seen or heard from Darcy since their Monday morning make-out session in her office. It was now Friday, and over the last week, the juniors had slowly been picked by either a partner or of counsel that had a case coming up for trial.

She hated feeling like this. Like she was the last kid to be chosen to play dodgeball. She bit her cheek and started to pick at her fingernails.

"You should really try to care a little less," Micah said, uncrossing his arms and standing up straight. "You're way prettier when you're smiling."

Lizzy rolled her eyes, ignoring his efforts at flirting. He flashed one more smile before leaving just as the phone on her desk rang. "This is Lizzy," she said.

"Good afternoon, Ms. Taylor, it's Veronica, Ms. Hammond's paralegal. Are you free to meet with her this afternoon at four thirty?"

Lizzy began frantically searching for her planner. She knew she'd left it somewhere, but her desk was sprawling with papers from cases she was working on with Ana, and she couldn't find it anywhere.

"Ms. Taylor?"

"Yes," Lizzy blurted. She gave up searching. "Yes, I'm free." If she had something then, she'd cancel it or move it or do something with it.

"Very good, I'll let her know."

The line went dead, and Lizzy checked the clock in the corner of her computer screen.

Three fifty-five.

Darcy hadn't exactly given a lot of notice, and Lizzy quickly pulled out her cell phone and flipped the camera to selfie mode to inspect her hair and makeup.

Jesus Christ.

Her eyeliner was smudged from a full day's wear, and her hair was frazzled at the ends from the dry winter air. This would never do. She left her office, pushing past Micah and rounding the corner in the direction of the restroom.

"Whoa, easy," Jackson said as she nearly plowed into him. He was carrying a banker's box full of Redwelds and loose pieces of paper, all evidence of a successful trip to the bowels.

"Sorry," Lizzy said, scooting around him.

"No worries. Oh, hey, before you leave, Margaret and I are going out for drinks after work if you want to join?"

Lizzy paused and smiled. She'd known Margaret and Jackson would hit it off after just a few seconds of watching them in the conference room weeks ago. The fact that Jackson was inadvertently inviting her on a date with him and Margaret seemed to escape his mind. "I think you better go alone," she replied, winking.

His face turned beet red, and he looked down, causing his glasses to slide halfway down his nose. "I guess I should, huh?" he said, adjusting the heavy box in his arms.

"Absolutely," she said reassuringly.

He smiled, turning back in the direction of their offices, and Lizzy proceeded to race down the hall.

Once safely inside the ladies' room, she stared at herself in the mirror and began wiping her fingers under her eyes to fix her mascara and eyeliner. She next spent an unknown amount of time pulling her hair half-up, then into a bun, then into a ponytail, then down again. She slicked the sides, fluffed, and did just about anything and everything she could do to make her hair look good before finally giving up and leaving it almost exactly as it had been.

She checked her cell phone.

Four twenty-six.

Her heart and mind began to race at competing speeds.

Why does she want to see me? Is this business or pleasure? Or maybe both? Would she really risk being caught like that? Maybe she's changed her mind. Maybe she doesn't want to even hook up anymore. Oh God, what if she's firing me? I did kiss her and...oh fuck.

Lizzy left the bathroom and made a beeline to her office, scooping up her legal pad and pen. Letting out a slow exhale, she composed herself before walking down the hall toward Darcy's corner office.

She'd thought that this would have ended by now. The nerves. The butterflies. The anxiety. The glancing around every corner, hoping to see Darcy but being terrified of seeing her at the same time.

It was confirmed: Darcy liked her. Darcy wanted to kiss her. Hell, Darcy wanted to fuck her, for crying out loud. There was no mystery, which meant all of this schoolgirl stuff should be over and done with now. But it wasn't. In fact, knowing all of that only intensified those feelings. Because now there was more than the faint hope that Darcy *might* want to kiss her or touch her or hold her. Now there was a very real possibility of all of those things happening. And that realization was both electrifying and paralyzing.

Nearing the end of the hall, Lizzy cleared her throat before raising her fist and knocking on the frosted glass door. The contact sent a strange echo down the hall, and she flinched at the sound.

"Enter."

Lizzy pushed open the door and smiled when she saw Darcy behind her large glass desk. The sun was setting behind her, and she was wearing a black dress Lizzy had never seen before.

"Hi," Lizzy said, closing the door behind her.

"Good afternoon, Elizabeth," Darcy said formally, clicking her pen. She let out a brief smile before motioning toward the chair across from her desk. "Please, take a seat."

Okay, so we're being formal now. Noted. Lizzy complied, her legal pad resting on her crossed leg. She swallowed hard, trying to still the loud *thump thump thump* in her chest.

"I assume you know why I asked to see you?" Darcy leaned forward and crossed her hands, her long, thin fingers looking distractingly beautiful on the glass.

"I mean, I can think of a few things, but I'd rather hear it from you."

Darcy smiled. "Very well. I think you're smart, and I think you could be a great lawyer. You have grit and determination, and I admire those traits just as much as I admire your intelligence and quick wit." She was oozing compliments, but her voice remained distant and professional.

Lizzy continued to listen, waiting to hear where the speech was going.

"What I'm trying to say is, I'd like you to work on an upcoming trial with me." She paused as if assessing Lizzy's reaction, but Lizzy was too shocked. She couldn't believe her ears. "I know it may seem like odd timing, considering our interlude Monday morning, but you're the one I want helping me on the case." She paused again. "Plus, it would make things less suspicious to the firm. Us spending time together, alone in my office, late nights, all of the logistics that need to align for our little arrangement to work."

Lizzy racked her brain, considering the offer. She had been so worried about not being selected by one of those stupid white men that she had completely forgotten about the most ideal potential. But did Darcy want to work with her just because the "logistics" made sense? Or had Lizzy actually managed to impress her in some other way?

"Are you interested?" Darcy tapped her finger impatiently.

"Yes," Lizzy shouted, lurching forward excitedly.

Darcy laughed slightly, her cold exterior quickly melting. "Okay, then. Patty can bring you up to speed on what you'll need to do on Monday. The trial is in two weeks, so we have a lot to do. It'll be a lot of work, Elizabeth. More work than you've ever done, most likely. It means early mornings and"—her eyes shot to her desk—"and late nights."

"Late nights, huh?" Lizzy asked, crossing her arms. "Probably means we'll be eating meals together, right?"

"I'm sure the occasional meal will be required, yes."

Lizzy bit her lip. "With only weeks to prep, we should probably get a jump start, don't you think?"

"What did you have in mind?" Darcy crossed her arms.

Lizzy leaned forward and grabbed her hands, tracing the lines on the back with her fingertips. "Well, for starters, why don't we get out of here? And maybe I can show you what I have in mind?"

"Elizabeth, it's only five o clock. I can't leave yet, and neither can you." She shot her a reprimanding but playful look and began playing with her hands in return.

"How about later? Dinner? It's not a date if we're talking about a case, right?"

After about ten seconds, Darcy exhaled loudly and let go. "Fine. Dinner at six." She grabbed a piece of stationery and scribbled something down in cursive, sliding it across the table. "Meet me here. I don't want everyone to see us leave together. It would raise too many questions."

Lizzy ignored the slight stab of pain that ran through her heart at Darcy's unwillingness to be seen leaving with her. It was logical. But it still stung. She nodded and stood, clutching the paper, and left. She didn't even make it back to her own office before opening the paper and reading the words scribbled across the page.

"Art Bar," Lizzy said. "Where the hell is that?"

CHAPTER TWENTY

Darcy pulled out her compact before getting out of the cab and checked her makeup one more time. She slicked back a few strands of hair from her face and shut the compact, handing the driver her fare and a tip.

She loved being in the West Village. Like most members of the LGBTQ community living in New York, she could be her most authentic self here. No one would look twice at her holding hands with a woman on Christopher Street, and she had many fond memories of dancing the night away on the second floor of Stonewall just around the corner.

She'd chosen Art Bar not only because it was nowhere near the office, but because she genuinely thought Elizabeth would like it. She probably shouldn't care so much about that, considering they were coworkers who had only recently decided to sleep together, but she did. She didn't want to take Elizabeth to just any bar or restaurant. She wanted to take her somewhere she would enjoy. Somewhere she would remember.

Darcy adjusted her black leather gloves and pulled the coat tight around her. She loved that it still had the trace of coconut from Elizabeth's shampoo. It was faint now, but if Darcy closed her eyes, she could smell it.

As she entered the tiny space, she smiled. Not much had changed since the last time she'd been here. The bar was to the left, and on the right, a row of four half-circle leather booths pressed against the wall, each large enough to seat no more than four. It was dark and lit only by candlelight and had eclectic bright orange checkered wallpaper.

"Reservation for two, Hammond."

The woman with facial piercings checked something on an iPad and nodded. "Right this way."

Darcy followed her toward the back of the long, narrow room, past the bar and the booths, and toward a black curtain. She pulled the curtain back and let Darcy pass through. This room was also familiar, and she was glad to see it was just the atmosphere she wanted.

The walls surrounding the "secret" room were exposed brick, and various pieces of modern art hung on the walls. Instead of traditional tables, there were leather couches, chairs, stools, and coffee tables placed sporadically around the floor.

It was still only lit by candles, and she had to squint to make sure she was in the right spot. It was perfect. Perfect for an intimate, romantic date.

It's not a date.

She slid off her coat and tossed it over the back of a brown leather wingback chair. There was one of similar height next to her, and a small circular table in front of them. She began to study the menu to distract herself from checking her smartwatch every two minutes.

Edamame. She read slowly, emphasizing each syllable in her mind.

Five fifty-five.

Calamari. She focused on each letter, studying the unique font to make the process even slower.

Five fifty-six.

Mango Chicken Wrap. She was running out of ways to make time go faster.

Still five fifty-six.

Dear God, this is going to take forever.

"Hi," a soft voice said.

Darcy jerked her head up. Elizabeth's golden hair was pulled into a smooth ponytail. She must have done it before coming because a few hours ago in the office, her hair was down. She was still wearing her work clothes, a plain gray pantsuit that was too loose in the shoulders and waist, but when Darcy stood and leaned in to kiss her cheek, she was flooded with the sweet, floral smell of freshly applied perfume.

"What scent is that?" she asked as Elizabeth tossed her coat over the back of her chair and sat.

"Miss Dior? I think? I don't know, it's the one Natalie Portman models. That's basically the only reason I bought it."

Darcy laughed. Of course she would pick a perfume based on

the hot model in the commercial. "Natalie Portman, huh? That's your type?" Darcy asked, attempting to remain uninterested and casual. But the eagerness in her voice no doubt betrayed her, and Elizabeth's face perked up.

"What can I say? I like feisty brunettes." Her eyes sparkled with their usual flirtatious glimmer.

Darcy nodded but couldn't think of anything to add.

"And what about you?"

"Me? Oh, I've always been a Blake Lively fan, myself."

It was Elizabeth's turn to laugh. "I meant your perfume. But I'm very glad to hear you like sporty blondes." She winked.

"Oh. It's called Santal 33 by Le Labo. They have a few stores around the city." Darcy returned her eyes to the menu to avoid staring.

"That was one of the first things I noticed about you," Elizabeth said, forcing Darcy's eyes back up. "Well, that and your ass."

Darcy laughed again. "Your brazenness continues to amaze me, Elizabeth."

"Why do you call me that?" she asked, leaning back.

The server appeared and asked if they wanted something to drink.

"Bourbon and ginger," Darcy said instantly. She hadn't made it to the drink section, but she wasn't about to waste time before getting hard liquor into her now.

"Can you do a cosmo?" Elizabeth asked.

The server nodded and disappeared.

Once he was out of sight, Elizabeth leaned forward. "Well?"

"Well?"

"Why do you call me Elizabeth when everyone else calls me Lizzy?"

Darcy considered it a moment. "Elizabeth was my great-grandmother's name. I've always been fond of it. Plus, we both know you only go by Lizzy to avoid people confusing you with the actress."

"Plus, it goes pretty well with the name Darcy, wouldn't you say?"

Darcy shouldn't have been surprised that Elizabeth knew one of her favorite books. After all, she had literally tried to pick Darcy up using a quote from Emily Dickinson a few weeks ago. "Is the lady a fan of *Pride and Prejudice*?" Darcy said, smiling, putting on her best British accent.

Elizabeth smiled wide. "Indeed, I am, Mr. Darcy," she replied in an equally adept accent before returning to her normal voice. "My mom's a big fan of the classics. Or maybe you couldn't tell by the name? She raised me on them. Classic movies, classic books, classical music. People say I'm an old soul, but really, I was just raised by one."

The server returned with their drinks, and they clinked their glasses together before taking a sip. The bourbon slipped down Darcy's throat and into her stomach, and she was glad for the calming effect. She wanted to hear more about Elizabeth's upbringing. She wanted to know her favorite color, her favorite food, her dreams, and her desires. She wanted to know how she'd gotten the small scar on her chin that was only visible when she turned her head to the left. She wanted to know her deepest fears and regrets. She wanted all of it.

She was on the verge of asking about where Elizabeth had grown up when the server returned to take their order.

"What do you think? Split some jalapeño poppers to start?" Elizabeth said confidently.

Darcy nodded. "Sure, but you haven't looked at the menu. How did you know they had those?"

Elizabeth shrugged. "I looked it up online this afternoon. I'll take the turkey burger, thanks."

Darcy shook her head. "I'll do the mango chicken wrap."

"Anyway," Elizabeth said, scooting closer. "Your turn. Favorite book? Favorite movie? Favorite food? Just don't say *Love, Actually* or something like that, and we're golden."

Darcy felt her heart beginning to soften every second they were close together. It was like a block of ice drifting closer and closer to the sun. Her inner walls began to deconstruct as Elizabeth stared back at her. "I think that's more date stuff, don't you?"

The warmth left Elizabeth's eyes, and she sat back. Darcy could have kicked herself for causing such a reaction. Why had she even said it? She was having a great time with a beautiful woman, but her walls came up, even without the work situation complicating things between them. She couldn't help it. Anytime someone got too close to her, the same thing happened. She would deflect, try to keep things casual, and eventually, just leave.

They sat in silence for a few moments, and the server appeared with their appetizers.

Elizabeth tossed one of the jalapeños in her mouth, staring around the room at the various art pieces.

"*The Fountainhead*," Darcy said, defeat ringing in her voice. "My favorite book is *The Fountainhead*."

Elizabeth perked up, and she scooted closer again. "Ayn Rand's great," she said, smiling and grabbing another jalapeño.

Of course she knows Ayn Rand. Darcy took a sip of her drink. *Because just, of course.*

CHAPTER TWENTY-ONE

Lizzy's head spun slightly as she finished her second cosmo. She thought the turkey burger would keep her more levelheaded than she had been with the Long Island iced teas, but apparently, cosmos were *also* made stronger in New York, and she once again felt tipsy around Darcy Hammond.

Curse you, Carrie Bradshaw, for making this drink so iconic.

She and Darcy had just finished a delicious meal, and the conversation was perfectly pleasant, at least after Darcy had made it clear they wouldn't be getting onto too many heartfelt topics. Lizzy abided by the rules for the remainder of the meal and didn't ask too many personal questions. Instead, they discussed objectivism and Ayn Rand in greater depth than she had ever done before.

God, this woman is smart. Lizzy watched as Darcy stirred her second bourbon and ginger.

Lizzy took another sip to ward off her insecurities. They were nearing the end of their drinks now. The plates had been taken away, and they had both said no to dessert, which meant at any moment, the server would be dropping off their check.

Then what? Would the night end? Would she just go home? It was a pretty straight shot to her apartment on the 1 train from here, so that wouldn't be too inconvenient.

But there was the other possibility. The possibility Lizzy secretly wanted to happen.

What if Darcy asked her over? What if she wanted to go somewhere else? To a hotel? Would bringing Lizzy to her apartment be too intimate? Lizzy's mind raced as Darcy set her drink down, only ice and water left in the bottom.

"So," Darcy began, "would you like to come over to my place?" Her green eyes were sparkling, and Lizzy couldn't tell if it was the bourbon or just wild lust talking, but frankly, she didn't care. She absolutely wanted to go back to Darcy's apartment.

She tilted her head and tapped her chin, pretending to contemplate the decision. "Hmm," she said. "I suppose I could swing by for a nightcap.""Great," Darcy said coolly, swirling the small straw in the remainder of her drink. The server appeared right on cue and handed her the check. Lizzy asked her how much it was and if they could split it, but Darcy waved her off. "Consider it trial prep," she said as she slid her credit card onto the wooden slate and handed it off.

A few moments later, they were buttoning their coats. Darcy was wearing the black one Lizzy had borrowed, and she was still in her trusty college peacoat. She seriously needed an upgrade soon.

"Up for a little walk? I'm about ten blocks south." Darcy pointed in the direction of the tall blue tower that loomed eerily over the small, quiet street.

"Sure," Lizzy said, steam gathering around her face. She focused on not shivering as they made their way down Greenwich Avenue. She had worn her usual black pumps, but they were walking at a slower pace this time, and she had grown more accustomed to them over the last week. Plus, she had more alcohol in her this time, which made the walk much less painful than it had been when they went to the Plaza last week.

"You're cold," Darcy said, turning her head toward Lizzy as they walked.

"I'm fine," Lizzy lied.

Darcy shook her head. "We really need to get you a new coat." She wrapped her arm around Elizabeth, pulling her close as they walked. Lizzy could feel the warmth of her skin, even through their coats. They walked in unison, their heels clacking to the same beat on the sidewalk. Darcy's legs were much longer, but she slowed her pace to let Lizzy walk normally.

Lizzy leaned in. She didn't care if it was two degrees outside. If it meant getting to cuddle in Darcy's arms, she'd walk the entire length of Manhattan.

After about fifteen or twenty minutes, they stopped.

"Here we are," Darcy said, turning and entering through one of two glass doors.

The warmth of the lobby flooded Lizzy as they walked inside, their heels echoing loudly on the white marble floor.

"Good evening, Alfonso," Darcy said, nodding to the man behind the security desk.

He gave her a friendly wave and tilted his hat as she passed. The elevator took them to the top floor, and Lizzy's heart began to race as they stepped out.

Darcy walked down the hall and turned left until she reached 5B. *At least we both live on the fifth floor.*

With each passing second, Lizzy's heart beat faster, until the loud clacking of her heels began to fade and only the dull *thump, thump, thump* of her pulse remained. Time seemed to move in slow motion the closer they got. *This is really happening. I'm walking into my boss's apartment after a date—no, not a date—a dinner with her.* A lump began to develop inside her throat, and she found it hard to breathe.

Darcy stuck a key into a large metal door and slid it open before stepping inside. She tilted her head over her shoulder, motioning for Lizzy to come inside. When she entered the room, Lizzy's jaw dropped. It was the most beautiful apartment she'd ever seen. It was a single room with an exposed brick wall, hardwood floors, vaulted ceilings, a wall of windows, and a modern kitchen. A brown leather sofa sat in the center of the living area, facing a large flat-screen TV flanked by two massive, industrial-style bookshelves. It was like something out of a dream.

"Can I hang your coat?" Darcy said, clicking on a few floor lamps that gave the already romantic room an even more sensual ambiance.

Lizzy nodded, slipping off her coat and handing it over.

"I'd give you a tour, but as you can see, everything is pretty much all right here." Darcy motioned to the open room as she hung Lizzy's coat in a closet by the door.

"Darcy, it's stunning. Truly."

"Thank you. It was a little indulgent, but I figured, I work so damn much, what's the point of making money if you're not going to spend it on pretty things, you know?"

Lizzy nodded, but she couldn't relate. She was still struggling to pay her rent, her student loans, and her utilities and eat more than just Taco Bell every month. Adjusting to city living was taking her longer than expected, but she figured she'd reach a balance of earning and spending soon enough.

"Wine?" Darcy was in the kitchen leaning into a wine refrigerator beneath one of the cabinets.

Lizzy focused on how good her ass looked in that black dress and bit her lip. "Sure," was all she could manage. *Keep it together, Taylor.* She exhaled slowly, working on controlling her breathing.

Darcy brought over a glass of red wine and handed it to her. Lizzy took a sip and tried her best to hide her reaction, but she couldn't. It tasted like she was sucking on an oak tree.

Darcy laughed. "Not a red wine fan, I take it?"

Lizzy shook her head. "Sorry. I keep trying it, hoping I'll like it, but it just tastes like…"

"Like a big piece of bark, right?"

"Yes!"

"Don't worry about it." Darcy took the glass and set it on the island in the kitchen. "It took me a trip to Napa to finally start liking wine. I'm sure you'll get there one day."

Lizzy was glad to be rid of the wine, but she wished she still had the glass. Her hands were nervous resting all by themselves at her side, and she wasn't sure what to do with them. So instead of standing there awkwardly, she decided to take a look around.

She walked into Darcy's living area and began to study her collection of records. Billie Holiday, Ella Fitzgerald, Elvis, Frank Sinatra, Dean Martin, and Buddy Holly. The gang was all there. Her mother would love a collection like this, that was for sure.

She continued to explore the bookshelves. Row after row of fiction was followed by tons of historical treatises, biographies, and even some reprints of old journals.

"Looks like someone is a history buff," she said, bending over to read the spine of a slender green book.

"Yeah," Darcy said from across the room. "I always wanted to be a history professor or an archaeologist. Or something like that."

"Why didn't you?" Lizzy stood straight and turned.

Suddenly Darcy was standing only a few feet away. She shrugged, taking a few steps closer and filling the gap. "Life got in the way. My dad got sick and…" She paused as if catching herself from revealing too much. "Anyway, I still enjoy reading about it. But that life is gone now."

Lizzy frowned. "If it's something you really want, you should do it, Darce."

She smiled, reaching out her hands and grabbing Lizzy's. "That's the first time you've called me that."

Lizzy slid her hands up Darcy's arms and around her neck, peering up into her eyes. "Do you like it?"

Leaning down, Darcy pressed her lips against Lizzy's, ignoring the question. Heat spread from Lizzy's mouth to her knees and then up again to her head before finally traveling south and resting between her legs.

"I like it coming from you," Darcy whispered.

Lizzy leaned up on her tiptoes and pulled her face down. Their lips crashed into each other, and they began kissing harder and faster with each second. Lizzy moved her hands around Darcy's back and fidgeted with the gold zipper that ran down the back of her dress.

"May I?" she asked breathlessly.

Darcy nodded. "Please do." Her voice was low and husky, and it made Lizzy wild.

Slowly, she unzipped the back of Darcy's dress, feeling smooth skin beneath her fingertips as she did. When the zipper reached Darcy's ass, she grabbed a handful and squeezed, eliciting a deep moan.

Darcy stepped back and slowly took her dress off, letting it slide off her shoulders and fall to the ground. Lizzy tried to control her face but couldn't. Her mouth opened as she stared at Darcy's perfectly sculpted body. The long, lean legs of a Greek statue were topped by black lace cheekies. Lizzy followed the line of her calves and thighs all the way up to a set of subtle but present abs. A black, see-through bra held up two small, perfect breasts, her pink nipples already standing at attention beneath the thin fabric. The fact that she hadn't taken her black stilettos off yet just sweetened the pot.

"Fuck," Lizzy said, biting her lip. Darcy looked down and flushed crimson. Lizzy grabbed her face and gently kissed her. "You are so beautiful," she said between kisses. She kissed Darcy's neck, her cheeks, her lips, all while sliding a hand down her long, narrow spine. Darcy gasped softly with each new place Lizzy's lips explored.

"Your turn," Darcy said, unbuttoning Lizzy's gray blazer.

Lizzy stepped out of her heels, and Darcy followed suit, closing the height gap between them somewhat but not entirely. Darcy's fingers nimbly worked on the buttons of her shirt as she continued to place kisses down her neck and shoulders. Finally, Darcy slid both shirt and blazer off Lizzy's shoulders.

She was glad she'd worn a cute bra today, even though her basic black 34A from Victoria's Secret paled in comparison to whatever the hell Darcy was wearing. Darcy undid her pants and slid them off. Lizzy blushed as they fell helplessly to the floor, revealing a pair of plain black Calvin Kleins.

Shit. I knew I should have worn better underwear.

If Darcy cared, Lizzy didn't notice because the next thing she did was push Lizzy back toward the king-sized bed resting along one of the walls. When they got to the edge, Lizzy sat, and Darcy stood over her, allowing Lizzy to kiss her long, lean stomach. Lizzy grabbed Darcy's nipples, pinching gently through the thin fabric. Darcy groaned, and Lizzy smiled with pride.

She loved learning Darcy: her body, her wants, her desires. Every inch she touched and kissed was like finding a treasure that had just been waiting to be explored beneath the fancy, tailored suits. This was going to be even more fun than Lizzy originally imagined.

Darcy grabbed a fistful of Lizzy's hair and pulled, gently at first, then harder. Lizzy whimpered with pleasure, taking another handful of Darcy's ass as she did. Darcy returned to kissing her lips and put a hand on her chest, pushing her back onto the bed.

Lizzy scooted all the way back until her head was nestled on a white down pillow. The bed smelled like Darcy's perfume; hell, the entire house smelled like her, and it made Lizzy dizzy with want. Darcy crawled up the bed, kissing along her legs, her stomach, and finally, landing on her nipple. She bit playfully through Lizzy's thin bra, and her body reacted instantly to the contact. Darcy looked up, and Lizzy grabbed the back of her head, pulling her up so she was completely on top.

Instinctively, Lizzy began to move beneath her, wiggling until Darcy's thigh found the place that felt good. Darcy's tongue continued to explore her mouth, and her hand slid around her back to the clasp of Lizzy's bra.

"Is it okay?" Darcy whispered, her fingers on the clasp.

Lizzy nodded, kissing her again as Darcy undid the clasp with one hand. Lizzy reached behind her and undid hers as well, although she required two hands and didn't ask permission. They didn't stop kissing long enough to actually even look at each other's bodies, but Lizzy felt Darcy's hard nipples against her own and knew then that they were almost naked.

Lizzy grabbed Darcy's butt again, and pulled her harder between her legs.

"You really do like my ass," Darcy said, breathless between kisses.

"You have no idea."

Darcy's hand moved from her breast, down her stomach, and to her thighs before finally settling between her legs. Lizzy could feel how wet she was even through her underwear. She hoped Darcy didn't mind.

"Fuck, you're soaked," Darcy said with a growl as she began to massage Lizzy's clit through her underwear.

She tossed her head back as Darcy continued to tease her. It was almost painful now. The buildup, the foreplay, the teasing. She needed Darcy inside her now, or she was going to explode right here.

As if reading her mind, Darcy slid her hand beneath Lizzy's underwear, pressing over her clit, her fingers lingering at her entrance.

"Still okay?" Darcy whispered between breaths.

"I'll be much better once you fuck me," Lizzy said, gripping the back of Darcy's neck and staring into her.

Within seconds, Darcy was inside her. First with only one finger, and soon with two. Lizzy arched her back and gasped. She could feel herself building already as Darcy began to slide in and out, rolling the palm of her hand across Lizzy's clit with each thrust. She couldn't come this soon. She had to make herself last longer.

Keep it together, Taylor. She focused on taking long, deep breaths to slow her rapid climax. But there was nothing she could do now. Darcy was moving in all the right ways. She'd never had a first hookup feel this good, and she'd certainly never had anyone make her come so quickly. After a few more thrusts, Lizzy arched her back even more and dug her nails into Darcy's bare back.

"Come for me, baby," Darcy groaned into her ear.

Lizzy tumbled over the edge and screamed into Darcy's shoulder before finally releasing into her hand. Her entire body felt like Jell-O as she collapsed on the down comforter.

Darcy stayed inside her for a few more seconds before slowly pulling out. She kissed Lizzy's cheek, her neck, even her hair, but all Lizzy could do was lie there paralyzed.

After a few minutes, Lizzy rolled onto her side and brushed a strand of hair behind Darcy's ear and smiled. Darcy stared back, her eyes sparkling, beaming with pride. "Well, someone looks happy with themselves," Lizzy said, propping up on one elbow.

"I could say the same."

In less than a second, Lizzy was on top, pinning Darcy's hands above her head.

Darcy's eyes widened with pleasure, and she bit her lip playfully. "What exactly do you think—"

Before she could finish, Lizzy put a hand over her mouth. "Oh no, you don't," she said firmly. Darcy's eyes flickered with delight as Lizzy leaned over and whispered in her ear. "It's my turn."

CHAPTER TWENTY-TWO

D arcy felt the sunlight burst through her window. She rolled over and reached out toward the other side of the bed, searching for the warmth she'd fallen asleep beside. But all she felt was cool, silky fabric beneath her fingers, and she frowned, opening her eyes slowly. She sat up, pulled the covers around her still-naked body, and looked around the room. Elizabeth was gone.

She shouldn't have been sad. Spending the night was technically a romantic notion, and since they weren't dating, it was only logical that Elizabeth would leave in the night.

At least, that was what Darcy tried to convince herself of as she lay back down alone in bed. The pillow next to her still smelled like coconut from Elizabeth's hair, and she pulled it close, resting her head in the soft down and looking out the large window across the room.

Her mind drifted back to last night, and she felt a smile spread across her face. She pulled the pillow closer and squeezed her legs tight, thinking back to every detail of the night before.

She knew she and Elizabeth had chemistry; that much had been clear from their early interactions, and she supposed she'd assumed the sex would be good. But last night was more than Darcy could have ever imagined. It wasn't just good sex. It was incredible sex. She'd never felt so alive and so connected to someone she barely knew. In fact, she'd never felt so connected to anyone she'd slept with…ever.

Every touch, every whimper, every sigh and breath and moan flooded Darcy's mind, and she wiggled with pleasure. Who was she kidding? She hated that Elizabeth was gone. She wanted her to be here. She wanted them to make coffee and breakfast together. She wanted them to maybe even spend the day together.

You said no dating. You said there were rules. You can't blame her for following them.

She opened her eyes again and sat up, crawling out of bed and slipping into a silky black robe. She'd hoped Elizabeth would get to see her in it this morning, but no matter. There was plenty of time for that.

Walking into the kitchen, she found her cell phone lying on the bar next to the two glasses of red wine and an open bottle. She'd forgotten all about it in the midst of the incredible sexcapades last night, and now the battery was almost dead. Taking a seat at the bar, she unlocked the screen and began to scroll through her notifications.

Her eyes stopped on a single green text alert with the name Elizabeth written across it. She smiled and opened the message.

Elizabeth: *Last night was fun.*

Darcy felt a rush of excitement shoot to her heart as she reread the text. She bit her thumbnail and smiled. She felt like a schoolgirl again. She hadn't been this giddy over someone since her girlfriend her senior year of college, and that was back when she was twenty, for heaven's sake.

Darcy: *Get home safe?*

It seemed like a silly question and maybe one she shouldn't have asked. It wasn't technically any business of hers where Elizabeth had gone after they'd hooked up last night, but she still wanted to know she was safe.

Seconds later, gray bubbles bounced across the screen, indicating that Elizabeth was responding. Darcy stared at them, counting the seconds until another message came through.

Elizabeth: *I did. Sorry for leaving, just didn't think sleepovers were part of the terms and conditions we negotiated.*

She felt her shoulder tighten as she typed out her response.

Darcy: *Not a problem, glad we were able to get so much work done last night.*

She cringed slightly as she hit the send button. She trusted that Elizabeth would keep their situation private. She had just as much to lose as Darcy if they got caught. But talking about sleepovers in writing was too risky for her lawyer brain to accept. She hoped Elizabeth was smart enough to take the hint.

More bubbles appeared and disappeared.

Elizabeth: *I actually just realized I left my trial binder last night. Think I could swing by and pick it up?*

She thought back to last night. Elizabeth didn't have any binder. She didn't even have a bag with her. Safe to say she had taken the hint. Darcy grinned at her sharp mind.

Darcy: *Not at all, I've already started working if you'd like to come over and take what you need.* A feeling of satisfaction began to creep through her at the subtle inuendo.

The bubbles came and disappeared, and Darcy waited for the response to come. But after a few moments of silence, she gave up and started checking her work emails, her legs swinging back and forth, still bare and in desperate need of a shower.

A few seconds later, a loud ding on her cell phone made her jump. She checked the screen, and her eyes shot open wide. The words *Lizzy Taylor wants to share her ride status with you* popped up on her screen, and a little car began moving south from West Harlem toward her loft.

Holy shit, she's on her way right now.

Darcy raced to the bathroom. Her hair looked like a tangled mess. Sex hair. She threw on the shower and flipped the hot water on, letting the steam fill up the bathroom.

She jumped in the shower after plugging her phone into its charger and let the boiling hot water sting her skin. She scrubbed her hair and poured on extra conditioner, hoping it would assist in detangling the rat's nest that had developed in the back of her head. Then she applied a liberal amount of shaving cream and began to remove the overnight stubble from her legs. After scrubbing her entire body with body wash, she jumped out and checked her phone.

Elizabeth's ETA was five minutes. Apparently, there was no traffic on the West Side Highway at nine on a Saturday morning.

Darcy swore under her breath as she ran out of the bathroom and slipped on the black silk robe again. She raced around the loft, scooping up her dirty underwear and bra from the night before and chucking them into the hamper. She scurried into the kitchen and put the two wineglasses into the dishwasher before racing back into the bathroom to begin brushing out her hair, a process that proved much more difficult than originally anticipated.

She desperately wanted to apply fresh makeup, as the shower had removed all traces of eyeliner and mascara, and her face looked like she had only slept a few hours. Which, okay, she had. But by the time she got her hair untangled and back in control, there was a loud buzz at the door.

Shit, shit, shit.

She ran to the large metal sliding door and pushed the electronic dial pad beside it. "Yes?" she said, her voice cool and collected, unlike the rest of her right now.

The morning security guard's face popped up on the small screen. "Visitor for you, ma'am. She says her name is…Dominique Francon?"

Darcy smiled at the joke. Dominique Francon was the female protagonist in her favorite book. Only Elizabeth would know something like that, of course. "Thank you, Lorenzo, you may let her up."

Darcy ran back into the bathroom one last time and flipped her hair to one side. It was still wet from the shower, but it was better than the mess it had been a few minutes ago.

The sound of the elevator door opening on her floor made her head shoot around, and she walked slowly to the front door as a soft knock sounded twice on the other side of it.

Elizabeth was standing on the other side. A slow smile spread across her face, and her eyes opened wide as she stared Darcy up and down. "Well, fuck, just *this* was worth the overpriced Uber down here."

"Get in here," Darcy said, grabbing her by the coat, yanking her into the warm loft.

As soon as the door was shut, Elizabeth pressed her hungry mouth against Darcy's. She wrapped her arms around Elizabeth, the cold from outside still clinging to the thin lining of her coat, and began quickly unfastening the buttons.

"Just rip it," Elizabeth said, desperation in her voice.

Without hesitation, Darcy grabbed both sides of the worn-out peacoat and yanked it open, sending large brown buttons spilling helplessly onto the floor.

Elizabeth slid the coat off and let it fall. She pressed Darcy back against the bar in the kitchen, sliding her hands beneath the thin silk robe. Darcy threw her head back as Elizabeth explored her back, her stomach, and finally, her breasts. Elizabeth parted the robe and covered her nipple with her mouth, looking up as she bit down.

Darcy let out a low hiss from the mixture of pain and pleasure and grabbed a fistful of Elizabeth's hair, yanking her up to kiss her.

"Get up here," Elizabeth said, motioning to the bar Darcy was pressed against.

Last night, Darcy had been the one in charge, but today, it was clear who the dominant one was. Today, Elizabeth was confident, bold, and assertive, and she had no problem telling Darcy exactly what to do. It was enough to make Darcy soak through the new black underwear she'd slid on beneath the robe.

She obeyed and jumped onto the counter, spreading her legs for Elizabeth to stand between. Elizabeth stepped forward, kissing her neck and grabbing a handful of Darcy's backside. She removed Darcy's robe, letting it lie in a pile on the bar.

Darcy was completely naked now, except for her underwear, and Elizabeth was still almost completely dressed. Darcy reached up to take off her shirt but was met with a firm "No."

"I want to fuck you like this," Elizabeth said, her voice low and husky.

Darcy grabbed her face and stared into her eyes. They were filled with passion and desire, but she could still see the warmth hiding behind all that, and she kissed her long and deep. "Do it, baby," Darcy whispered in her ear, grabbing her hips and pulling her closer.

Elizabeth moved her hand between Darcy's legs. Within seconds, she pushed Darcy's panties to the side and without pausing to ask, shoved two long fingers inside.

Darcy let out a loud moan at the sudden force and leaned back, her body now fully spread out for Elizabeth to enjoy.

Elizabeth thrust harder and faster, her fingers curling and stroking Darcy's G-spot. She felt herself begin to build. She sat up, wrapping her legs around Elizabeth so she had nowhere to go but farther inside.

Gripping the back of Elizabeth's neck, Darcy managed to groan out, "I'm gonna come. Fuck, I'm gonna come." And with one final thrust, her body released itself into Elizabeth's hand. She leaned forward, collapsing onto Elizabeth's still-clothed shoulders, trembling and twitching from the power of the orgasm.

Elizabeth kissed her cheek and brushed her wet hair behind her ear, looking into her eyes. A sly, cocky grin began to crawl across her face. "Does that count as trial prep too?"

CHAPTER TWENTY-THREE

The rest of the morning was a blur. Lizzy and Darcy had moved from having sex in the kitchen to having sex on most surfaces of the large, expensively furnished loft. The couch, the bed, hell, even one of the windows had all been marked by their insatiable desire for one another.

Around four, Darcy said she had to get some actual work done. Lizzy asked if it was for their trial together, hoping to find some excuse to stay even longer, but Darcy said no and promised they would really start working on the trial on Monday.

"Try not to get in much trouble without me until then," Darcy said with a wink as she kissed Lizzy good-bye.

Lizzy was trying really hard not to fall for this woman. That was why she'd decided to leave in the middle of the night. The idea of waking up next to Darcy just felt too…too right. Too perfect. When she was with Darcy, it was like something out of a cheesy Hallmark movie. She got these little stars in her eyes, and all she could think about was touching Darcy, kissing her, pleasing her.

No, it was best that she not expose herself to that. That was why, when she did return that morning, she told herself it was just for more incredible sex. Her feelings were just hormones in action. This was fine.

But the second she left the beautiful loft, a slow, dull ache began to grow inside her chest. *Jesus, Taylor, pull yourself together. It was just sex.*

Really, really, really good sex. Okay, fine, it was the best sex of her life. Whatever.

She skipped the song on her playlist, some sappy love song she used to like, and flipped to a more upbeat rap song she knew every single word to. As the 1 train screeched to a halt at 145th Street, she exited and wrapped the borrowed coat around her body.

It was one of Darcy's. Not the black fancy one. This one was a green, military-style jacket that Lizzy would have actually worn herself. It fit her better than the black one too. It still smelled like Darcy, and she ignored the swell in her chest that hit her with each heartbeat as the cold wind made the smell smack her in the face.

"Here," Darcy had said, pulling the coat out of the closet. "It's not the warmest, but it goes with your cute little outfit."

Lizzy had looked at her jeans and brown combat boots before Darcy had helped her slip the jacket on before kissing her long and hard one last time.

"Keep this safe for me," she had said, patting Lizzy's chest. It wasn't clear if she was referring to Lizzy's heart or the borrowed jacket, but Lizzy didn't ask for clarification.

Darcy had offered to call an Uber, but Lizzy had declined. She liked riding trains most days. It gave her a chance to clear her mind and avoid the traffic and mayhem overhead. Plus, she'd spent a shit ton of money on the Uber ride down to Darcy's, and she refused to let Darcy pay for any more than she already had.

The borrowed coat proved warmer than anticipated, and by the time she reached her fifth-floor walkup, she was sweating. She was accosted by Amina almost as soon as she opened the door.

"Oh. My. God. You so got laid." Amina scurried over, a wide, unabashed smile plastered on her face.

"What are you talking about? I was just…out for a walk."

"Oh, okay, and what? These tangled knots in your hair just happened from the wind? Please, I know an afterglow when I see it." She grabbed at Lizzy's messily done bun, but Lizzy dodged her grasp. Her face heated, but Amina pressed on. "So, spill the beans." She sat on the couch and rested her head in her folded hands like a child in school.

"No, I…I mean, okay, fine. Yes, yes, I had sex. There, happy?"

Amina clapped her hands and did a gleeful wiggle with her butt. "And who is the lucky lady? I need deets. None of your usual vague BS. I'm single, I'm horny, and I'm bored. Go."

Lizzy cringed. "It's someone I work with."

Amina shrieked and bounced up and down on the couch. "Oh my God, oh my God, okay, let me guess. Is it that hot girl you talk about all the time? Anna?"

Lizzy shook her head. "It's *Ana*, but no, it wasn't her."

Amina nodded and scratched her chin like Sherlock Holmes following a lead. She wasn't going to let this go. "Hmm, oh God, don't tell me it's that awful woman you share an office with? Wait, was it *in* your office?" Amina's voice rose, and she bit her nails as her eyes grew wide.

Lizzy laughed. "Cho? God no, I'd rather die celibate. It's no one I've mentioned before. She's just…" Lizzy felt the truth on the tip of her tongue. She wanted to tell Amina and anyone else who would listen all about Darcy. She wanted to shout from the mountaintops how she had somehow ended up spending the night and most of the day with the smartest, sexiest, most beautiful, successful, charming, and brilliant woman in all of New York.

But Darcy's "terms and conditions" flashed through her mind.

No one can know. She heard the words echoing through her ears in Darcy's harsh, husky voice. Did she really mean no one? Surely, she was referring to officemates or people in common. Maybe it would be okay if she just told her roommate.

Lizzy contemplated the words for a moment but chickened out. "She's just a rando I met at a happy hour a few weeks ago. She works on another floor, so we never see each other. I don't even know her last name, to be honest."

Seeming satisfied, Amina leaned back. "Well, well, look at you with the casual fling. I gotta say, I'm shocked."

Lizzy raised an eyebrow. "What do you mean?"

Amina shrugged, standing. "I don't know. You just never really struck me as the woman who did casual, you know?"

Lizzy bit her lip and looked down. *That's because I'm not the kind of woman who does casual. Not usually anyway.*

"Anyway, I'm glad one of us is getting some action," Amina said. "Thanks for letting me live vicariously through you." She walked to the kitchen, putting her earbuds back into her ears.

Lizzy walked into her bedroom and shut the door. It was freezing, and she instantly missed the warmth of Darcy's loft. She walked to one of her two windows and shoved the pieces of cardboard she had taped over the seals back into place.

Their apartment had been refurbished just prior to them moving in, which meant brand-new wooden floors, new appliances, and new bathrooms. The single-pane windows, however, had not been updated, and she could see her curtains blowing even with the windows closed most days. Being up on a hill on Broadway facing the Hudson River certainly didn't help, but she knew in the summer, the fire escape would make the room worth the miserable winter.

Lizzy slid off Darcy's coat and hung it up along with her faded pants and blazers. She didn't actually have a closet, so all of her clothes were on a metal rack she'd bought from someone on Craigslist in Chinatown.

A loud ping from her cell phone made her jump, and she pulled it out of her pocket. A familiar name popped up on the screen, flooding Lizzy's heart with warmth.

Darcy: *Get home okay?*

Lizzy bit her lip as she texted back. *Do you worry about all your associates getting home safely?*

Darcy: *Well, I wouldn't want to be liable for anything happening to you.*

She tossed her phone on her bed, leaving the message on read. She needed to shower and get some dinner. Tomorrow, she was going with Jackson, Margaret, Ana, and some other seniors to a Broadway show for a matinee. Apparently, Byron & Browning got a handful of free tickets each quarter, and Ana had snatched them up before anyone else could. Lizzy focused on being excited about that. She focused on not missing Darcy, or her big, beautiful, warm loft, or her even more alluring soft, sex-stained bed. She focused on ignoring the slow, sinking feeling in her stomach that told her this was a huge mistake and that she was heading for heartbreak.

❖

The next day, it was pouring down rain. Jackson texted that he and Margaret were going to skip the show and "stay in." They were basically a full-blown couple now, and it was just too cute for Lizzy to handle most days. Ana texted that she was still down if Lizzy was, and considering it was going to be her first Broadway show, and it was free, Lizzy trucked her way down to Forty-Second Street.

Ana was waiting for her under the awning of the playhouse. The words *Moulin Rouge* written in red and gold overhead made it hard to miss, even in the rain. Seeing her, Lizzy instantly felt underdressed. Ana was wearing black leather pants and black Chelsea boots with a deep red, cowl-necked sweater. Somehow, her beautiful, long dark hair remained unaffected by the rain, and she was done up in full makeup.

"Wow," Lizzy said, stepping out of the rain and closing her umbrella. "You look gorgeous."

Ana blushed and looked at herself. "Thank you, so do you."

Lizzy laughed. She was wearing faded blue jeans, the same brown combat boots she had worn to Darcy's yesterday, and a black V-neck T-shirt. She'd almost worn Darcy's military jacket but had decided against it because she had no idea what the thing was made of and didn't want to risk getting it wet. Instead, she wore a leather motorcycle jacket and a gray beanie. Basically, she looked gay AF.

"Um, definitely not, but thanks anyways," Lizzy said, looking at herself and back to Ana.

"Well, I always think you look great," Ana said, grabbing her arm gently.

Lizzy looked around. "Where are your friends?"

"They bailed." Ana sighed. "Said it wasn't worth getting all wet. I ended up scalping their tickets. Shh, don't tell anyone at the firm." She winked playfully.

"Wow, I'm impressed, Mendez. You're quite the hustler."

"I have my moments." She shrugged coyly.

They took their seats in the balcony, and Ana leaned her shoulder against Lizzy's as soon as the lights went down. She also crossed her leg so that her foot was touching the back of Lizzy's calf.

Probably just a coincidence. It's a small space. She's just trying to get comfortable.

The show was phenomenal, and Lizzy cried at the end. She had a feeling she could get addicted to this Broadway thing real fast. It was a good thing her firm got tickets frequently because she knew she would need to come back soon.

After they left the theatre, Ana asked if Lizzy wanted to get a drink at a nearby Cuban place. "Trust me," Ana said. "They have the *best* coconut mojitos. And there's usually live music."

Lizzy bit her cheek contemplating the decision. She really should be getting home; it was a Sunday, and she had a long week of trial prep ahead of her starting tomorrow. But she knew if she went home, she'd just lie there thinking about Darcy. She still hadn't texted her since leaving her message on read yesterday morning, and the last thing she wanted to do was go home and think about how she wished she was back in Soho with the woman she was going to see tomorrow.

"Okay, one drink," Lizzy said.

"Great! It's this way." Ana looped her arm into Lizzy's as they walked a few blocks up Eighth Avenue.

Lizzy could hear the live music pouring out of the small restaurant. "Guantanamera," the band sang as they entered the dark, candlelit space.

Ana spoke to the hostess in Spanish, and they got seated right away, even though there was a line. One mojito, two mojitos, three mojitos later, and holy shit, was Lizzy not thinking about Darcy Hammond anymore. She wasn't thinking about anything except how delicious these drinks tasted.

"Do these things even have alcohol in them?" Lizzy asked, holding up her now empty glass. But she could tell by the way her speech was slurring that yes, yes, they most definitely did have alcohol in them. She just couldn't tell until it was too late.

Ana smiled and leaned over the table. "Dance with me," she said, her dark eyes sparkling.

Lizzy nodded and smiled a goofy, tipsy grin. "'Kay!"

The band played louder, and Ana twirled around, her hips swaying to the rhythm. Other couples joined in dancing in the center of the room, and Lizzy laughed and moved to the beat. An old man grabbed her by the hand and spun her, and she giggled and clapped. The entire restaurant was alive with the strum of the guitars and pounding of the drums as the lyrics of "Chan Chan" echoed through the small space.

Ana pulled her closer so their bodies were pressed against each other as they swayed in unison. Lizzy's head began to rock back and forth, and everything started to spin as Ana twirled her around and caught her in her arms.

Ana's thick hips were in her hands, and Lizzy looked into her dark eyes. The last thing she remembered was feeling Ana's lips press against hers and the steady beat of Cuban music banging in her ears.

CHAPTER TWENTY-FOUR

Darcy bit her lip as she stared at her computer screen. She tapped her finger anxiously on her mouse and read the same line over and over again. "Shit," she said, lifting her cell phone and checking it for the hundredth time.

It was seven forty-five, and she was once again the first one in the office, but she knew Elizabeth would be arriving soon. She was always there early. She opened her phone and flipped to her recent texts to confirm once again that Elizabeth had not texted her back all weekend.

It really was no big deal. She didn't owe Darcy anything. They'd had an amazing night and day together, and if that was all it was, so be it. Maybe she'd changed her mind. Maybe she'd decided this was a one-and-done thing.

Darcy had spent most of the day Sunday working and running through all eight thousand possibilities for why her last message went ignored. But either way, she would feel better when she saw Elizabeth today. They needed to get working on this trial.

She began organizing a list of things she needed Elizabeth to do so that when she saw her this morning, they could focus on work and not be distracted by...other things. She organized it by priority and added small instructions for where Elizabeth could find things she needed, who she could talk to for assistance, and stuff like that. She knew working with a junior on a trial was a lot different than working with a senior. She would be this helpful for any junior helping on a trial, she told herself. But she knew it was a lie. If she had gotten stuck with the Willis guy, she doubted she would have even met with him.

When the list reached over five pages, she paused and checked the clock. It was eight, and still no Elizabeth. Maybe she had gotten a cup of coffee or gotten caught up on another assignment.

Patty opened her door and presented her with her agenda for the day as usual. She rattled through the list, and Darcy nodded, pretending to listen.

When she was finished speaking, Darcy asked, "Could you have Elizabeth meet me in my office for some trial prep?"

Patty looked down. "She's not in yet, I'm afraid."

Darcy checked the clock again. Associates were required to be in the office by eight at the latest, but the unspoken rule was between seven thirty and seven forty-five. "She's late?" Darcy asked stupidly. Obviously, she was late, or she would have been there.

"Looks that way. Should I send her in when she gets here?"

Darcy paused, frowning. "Yes. Yes, please do," she said returning her attention to her computer screen as Patty nodded and left.

Darcy printed the list for Elizabeth and shifted to some of her other tasks for that day. She checked the agenda Patty had handed her. Meetings, calls with clients and experts, a conference, etc. Just a standard day for her, really. She almost wished she had something exciting going on to distract her from this nagging feeling growing in her stomach. She hadn't experienced this feeling since she was in her early twenties, but she knew it all too well: insecurity.

She distracted herself for the next hour by flying through work tasks like she had just done a line of cocaine. She didn't check the clock once. At least, not until she heard a soft *tap, tap* on her door.

Nine eighteen a.m.

"Enter," she said in a steely tone.

Elizabeth's disheveled hair was the first thing to catch her eyes as the door swung sheepishly open. It looked like she had rolled out of bed and run to the office all the way from West Harlem. She stepped into the office and cleared her throat, only making eye contact with Darcy for a moment before looking down. She had a legal pad gripped in her hand, and she was wearing glasses.

"I didn't know you wore glasses," Darcy said as she came closer.

"Slept in my contacts. I'm sorry."

Darcy turned her chair and crossed her arms. "You're sorry for wearing glasses?"

"Yes, I mean no, I mean…" Elizabeth stuttered and continued to look down.

Darcy stood and came around to the other side of the desk, leaning against it, her arms still crossed. "Okay, is there anything else?"

Elizabeth made eye contact briefly and looked out the window past her. "What do you mean?"

What the hell is going on? She's acting like a totally different person. "I don't know. I mean, you're late, and you're normally the first one here, and you look like you didn't get much sleep." She focused on keeping her voice calm and gentle. She fought every instinct she had that told her to cross-examine Elizabeth. She didn't know what she was hiding or not saying, but there was something, that was for sure. But she didn't want to browbeat her.

Elizabeth shrugged. "I'm fine. I'm sorry for being late. Won't happen again."

Darcy squinted and took another step. Elizabeth had dark circles under her eyes, and she wasn't wearing makeup. She really looked like hell. "Are you...are you hungover?" Darcy asked, unable to hide the slight tone of judgment in her voice.

Elizabeth sighed, her shoulders dropping. "Honestly, yeah. Yeah, I am. My head is splitting, I barely remember my night, and I overslept for the first time since I was a freshman in college and I missed my first humanities class."

Darcy's jaw dropped. She didn't know if she should fire her or give her Advil and send her home. But more importantly, this revelation didn't help that seed of insecurity that had begun to grow inside her belly yesterday and this morning. Elizabeth had clearly gone out last night. Had it been on a date? No, she wasn't like that. She would never go from spending an entire day fucking Darcy to going out with someone else. They were casual, sure, but they had basic human respect for one another. Then again, exclusivity hadn't been one of the terms and conditions of their agreement, as Elizabeth had phrased it.

Elizabeth's comment she'd made at the Plaza about being a chronic flirt flashed back to her memory, and she fought away the thought. "I don't know what to say right now. The part of me that's your boss is furious. The part of me that's your—" She caught herself and shifted words. "The part of me that cares about you is kind of worried."

Elizabeth rubbed her hands on her forehead. "Darce," she said, stepping forward, "I'm sorry." She looked up, her eyes tired and soft.

"Okay," Darcy said stepping closer and grabbing her hand. She kissed her forehead and rubbed her cheek gently. "But I can't give you special treatment, Elizabeth. We'd both be in major trouble. I still need you to work on this trial for me today. Okay?"

Elizabeth nodded silently, leaning in. She looked like she was about to burst into tears. Darcy opened her arms, and Elizabeth stepped into them. Darcy held her there for a moment, kissing the top of her head and brushing her hair behind her ear.

"All right," she said, squeezing her shoulders. "Go get a cup of coffee. Maybe in a pretty green Dartmouth mug? Take this list, and get started. We'll meet later on and go over stuff."

Elizabeth took the printed list and glanced it over before looking up at Darcy one more time. "I really am so sorry."

There was something in the way she said it that made Darcy wonder what it was that she was really apologizing for. So she'd gotten drunk and was late to work? It happened. But the guilt she was displaying now was...suspicious.

Darcy ignored her inner saboteur and kissed her softly on the cheek before sending her on her way.

CHAPTER TWENTY-FIVE

Lizzy sipped the hot liquid, letting it bring new life to her second by second. She was grateful all of the other juniors were off performing various assignments. Micah was shadowing his senior at a court conference this morning, Jackson usually worked in Margaret's office now, and Cho and Efe, well, she had no idea where they were, and she really didn't care. She was just grateful to have the space to herself for however long it lasted.

She needed to focus. She needed to remember what the hell had happened last night. She'd gone to drinks with Ana after the show. They'd drank. A lot. They'd danced. A lot. Did they kiss? Her memory flashed back to the feel of Ana's breath on her neck. Yes, they'd definitely kissed. But how had she gotten home? And more importantly, had she gone home alone?

Normally, she could tell when she had just had sex, but she'd had so much of it with Darcy a day ago, it was hard to discern if the familiar soreness was from that or some more…recent activity.

"God, I am a horrible person," she said, burying her head in her hands.

"Hey, you," she heard from the door, and her head shot up.

Ana stood in her doorway looking somewhat tired but otherwise polished and perfect, as usual. Of course, Lizzy would look like garbage after a few mojitos, and Ana would look absolutely stunning.

"Oh, thank God, it's you," Lizzy said.

Ana smiled and stepped inside. "I'm happy to see you too."

"No, not because of that…I mean, I am, I just…wow, okay, let me back up here."

Ana shifted her weight and crossed her arms.

"Ana, I need to know…last night, did we?"

Ana looked over her shoulder and stepped fully inside, sitting on the edge of the desk so close that her thighs were nearly touching Lizzy's arm. Lizzy gulped at their proximity and stared, waiting for an answer. "Did we what? Did we fuck?"

Lizzy dropped her head and nodded. "Yeah. I mean, I just…I need a play-by-play of the night. It's all kind of a blur. We left the show. We went to that Cuban place. Then what?"

Ana shifted, frowning slightly. "Wow, you really don't remember?"

Lizzy shook her head.

"All right, well, we went to the restaurant and ordered some mojitos. You kept talking about how good they tasted and how there couldn't possibly be any alcohol in them. And after three, you got very giggly." She smiled and bit her lip. "It was pretty adorable. Then I asked you to dance, and we did."

Ana paused and scooted slightly closer. "And while we were dancing, we got…closer, and eventually, yeah, we kissed."

Lizzy nodded. "Then what?"

Ana sighed. "I mean, what do you want me to say here, Lizzy? We made out on the dance floor. We paid the check, well, actually, I paid the check."

Lizzy winced. *Gotta get her Venmo.*

"We left. It had stopped raining, so we walked around a bit. We held hands, and we ended up in Central Park on a bench, and we…I don't know, I mean, we kissed some more and…" She paused looking embarrassed. "I asked you to come back to my place, but you kinda fell asleep, so I stuck you in a cab, and you went home. I'm sorry. I had no idea you were that drunk."

Lizzy stood and grabbed her hand. "Don't be sorry, you did nothing wrong. Obviously, a part of me wanted it too, but I—" She was about to let Ana down easy. She was about to tell her that she wasn't looking for anything more than friendship. That she really respected her and thought it would complicate their working relationship. That she hoped they could stay friends and still hang out because she really did love Broadway.

But Lizzy never got to say any of that. Her thoughts were interrupted by the sound of someone's cell phone ringing in the hall right outside her door. Someone's *familiar* cell phone ring. "What the hell?"

She stuck her head out just in time to see a head of brown and silver hair round the corner, the scent of Santal 33 still hanging in the air.

Oh, fuck me.

"Um, just give me one second, will you, Ana?"

Lizzy followed her, leaving Ana standing alone in her office. Darcy's stride was twice the length of Lizzy's, and she tried to make it look casual. Not like she was literally chasing her boss around. Darcy was already in her office with the door closed by the time Lizzy got halfway down the hall.

She entered without knocking and found Darcy pacing in front of the window. "Darce, please—"

"Here," Darcy said, handing Lizzy a cup from Starbucks. "This is why I came to your office."

The knife was dug deeper, and guilt began to overwhelm Lizzy. "I—"

"You're sorry, yes, I gathered that. Your demeanor earlier makes much more sense now." She crossed her arms and stared out the window over the skyline.

"I swear, I didn't. I mean—"

"Just stop, Elizabeth." She could tell Darcy was trying to keep her voice low, but her anger was making it difficult. "Like you said, you wanted it, or it wouldn't have happened, right? And hey, you warned me, you're a chronic flirt. So, really, it is what it is. This was never going to be a serious thing anyway. Just would have been nice if you'd washed me out of your mouth before moving on to someone else."

The words dripped off her shiny white teeth like venom, and Lizzy winced, feeling like she'd just been struck. Darcy was right. They'd spent an entire night and day in each other's arms. Then less than twenty-four hours later, she'd had someone else's tongue down her throat. Someone Darcy had to see every day. She could try to convince herself that this was fine. That they were just friends with benefits. That this was always supposed to be casual. But it was no use. She'd fucked up, and she knew it.

"Darcy—"

"Elizabeth, it's fine. Honestly. We had fun. It was a fling. It's over. From this point on, I'm your boss, you're my subordinate. We will continue to have a professional working relationship, and that will be the end of it." The warm, soft version of Darcy was gone, maybe forever. She was back to the harsh, cold woman Lizzy met in the conference room on her first day.

Lizzy tried to focus on collecting her breath. This wasn't happening. This couldn't be happening. Forty-eight hours ago, she was floating on air, so happy, and now everything was crashing around her. "What about our trial?"

Darcy's eyes flashed. "*My* trial will go on. You will still assist me, as I have no other alternatives at this point, and replacing you would look unprofessional. We will meet in the office and get all of our work done here." The coldness of her voice was enough to make Lizzy shiver, and she held in the tears welling up behind her eyes.

"Is there anything else?" she said, her voice quivering.

"That's all," Darcy said curtly, taking a seat at her desk and staring at her computer screen.

Lizzy turned to leave, but as she reached the door, Darcy's voice chimed up from behind the desk. "Oh, and Elizabeth?"

Lizzy turned.

"I'll need my coat back."

CHAPTER TWENTY-SIX

Darcy entered her loft and threw off her shoes. She marched to the bed and ripped the sheets off, shoving them into the washing machine. She'd meant to wash them yesterday but had decided one more day wrapped in the smell of Elizabeth wouldn't hurt. Now she would rather burn them then touch them again.

She walked to the kitchen and opened a bottle of bourbon, pouring a hearty amount into a small glass. She threw it back and slammed the glass on the counter, enjoying the burning sensation that sizzled down her throat. She was letting herself feel this way for approximately five more minutes. Then she wasn't thinking about Elizabeth Taylor anymore. Pouring another drink, she tapped her finger on the counter.

She'd known something like this was going to happen. It was the entire reason she'd refused to date Elizabeth in the first place. She'd known she was going to get fucked over somehow. This was why she'd set boundaries. And technically, they had both abided by those boundaries. Logically, this shouldn't hurt. Logically, this shouldn't matter. Logically, no rules had been broken.

Then why does it feel like my fucking heart is on fire?

She tapped the glass. Every surface of her home was now covered in memories of Elizabeth. For heaven's sake, they'd had sex on this very counter two days ago.

She couldn't have even waited a full fucking day?

All of the emotions she had been holding in for the entire workday bubbled up inside now. She grabbed the glass and turned, throwing it against the metal door, watching it smash into a million little pieces, clear brown liquid spilling out onto her floor.

"Fuck," she screamed, full Bette Porter style at the top of her lungs.

She slammed her hands on the counter, and for the first time in a very long time, she began to cry.

CHAPTER TWENTY-SEVEN

The next two weeks were the definition of torture. Lizzy talked to Ana one morning and told her that while she was flattered, she didn't think they should get involved since they worked so closely together. It was technically the truth. She just left out the part about being head over heels for their boss.

Ana had seemingly tried not to look upset when Lizzy let her down, but the hurt was written all over her beautiful face, which made Lizzy feel like an even bigger jerk.

That, however, was the least of her worries. Every day at eight a.m., she had a meeting with Darcy to go over trial prep tasks for the day. Patty was present at every meeting like a parental chaperone to ensure Lizzy didn't try to broach the topic of "them" anymore.

They met at five to review the completed tasks. Darcy insisted the door be left open, and she spoke loudly enough for anyone passing by to hear, another warning to Lizzy not to mention anything that wasn't directly related to work.

Darcy hadn't been lying about the amount of work it took to prep a case for trial. On top of her normal caseload with Ana, Lizzy had inherited an insane number of tasks. Authorizations needed to be followed up on, and the records needed to be reviewed and summarized and eventually organized into trial binders. Experts needed to be prepped before even speaking to Darcy so that their meeting would be efficient and run smoothly. Expert witness disclosures needed to be prepared and served, and a trial schedule needed to be laid out based on the parties' availability. The list was endless.

Lizzy would actually have been glad for the hefty distraction from her pointy love triangle if every other page of the documents she was reviewing wasn't smattered with the name Darcy Hammond in the footer.

She spent the entire week drowning in work. She got to the office around seven fifteen every day and didn't leave until close to seven thirty every night. She and Jackson grabbed lunch together twice, but other than that, her entire existence revolved around this tiny office. Cho was growing more annoyed by Lizzy's presence every day, and their exchanges had gone from casual to downright hostile.

"Are you ever going to leave?" Cho had snapped at her that morning as Lizzy spread hundreds of documents all over their shared floor.

"Does it look like I'm here for the fun, Cho?" Lizzy snapped back, staring from the floor.

Cho simply rolled her eyes and left.

Micah had made his presence known once or twice as well but only to stick his head in and make some joke about her still being "an eight" even if she was on trial with the "only ten in the office." That had burned a hole inside her for more than one reason, and it took all the strength she had not to punch him in his perfectly angled nose.

She checked the clock on her computer screen. It was almost five o'clock. Time for her afternoon meeting with Darcy. It was Friday night. Two weeks ago, they'd been at Art Bar. They'd gone back to Darcy's apartment. They'd spent most of the night and the next day together. She closed her eyes, forcing herself to forget. But she couldn't help but wonder if she was the only one fighting back shared memories tonight.

Lizzy gathered up her things and headed to Darcy's office. As she approached, she noticed the door was slightly ajar, and when she lifted her hand to knock, she overheard a voice from inside: "What exactly are you saying?" Darcy.

A male voice Lizzy had never heard before responded. "Listen, Darcy, this isn't personal. But your numbers are slipping, and the firm needs you to bring in more revenue. You know we've always made… exceptions for you here."

"What exceptions are those, Dick? Buying special pens designed to fit into my delicate lady fingers? I know the numbers. I bring in just as much revenue as all of you. We've been counsel on this case since the answer was filed. We are *not* dropping it now."

"Darcy, a pro bono case by definition doesn't make the firm money."

"This case was approved by all of the partners over two years ago. You included, by the way. Now that it's finally up for trial, you're suggesting I drop it?"

"Don't be dramatic. I'm just suggesting we refer it to another office for the trial, that's all. It's going to cost a fortune to present this thing, and for what? To save some dead woman's house way upstate that no one cares about."

Darcy's voice cut back. "As I said before, we will *not* be referring the case to anyone for trial. We will be presenting it. And we will win."

Lizzy heard a sneer in the man's voice. "And if we don't?"

There was a long pause. "If we don't win, you can all fucking fire me."

Lizzy's jaw dropped. *Holy shit. She just put her job on the line for this thing.*

The man guffawed. "All right, Darcy, but when this comes back to bite you in the ass, don't say I didn't warn you."

The sound of footsteps made Lizzy jump, and she started walking casually in the other direction as a man exited the office. Once he passed, she turned around and headed back. She stuck her head in and saw Darcy at her desk, her head in her hands as she massaged her temples.

"Bad time?" Lizzy asked.

Darcy's head shot up, and she let out a loud sigh. "Elizabeth. No, actually your timing is perfect." Her voice was softer than it had been in their other meetings lately, and Lizzy felt her shoulders relax slightly as she walked across the large room and sat in her usual seat across from Darcy's desk.

She was wearing the same dress she had been wearing during their little Yale mug encounter back when Lizzy had first started working there. That felt like a lifetime ago now, even though it had only been about a month. So much had happened between them since. Yet here they sat across a cold glass table, nothing more than coworkers. Colleagues. Strangers.

Darcy's eyes were foggy and had dark circles around them. Her hair was pulled back into its typical immaculate French twist, but she looked tired. Worn out, even.

"I need you to set up a site visit next week," Darcy continued, handing her a sheet of paper. "Here's the contact information for the client. I'll need a full tour with someone who has historical knowledge of the house and the author who lived there. I want to know everything. When it was built, how it impacts the community, the number of visitors each year, all of the books the author ever wrote, who she voted for. I want to know what the woman ate for breakfast, for fuck's sake." Darcy rubbed her temples. "You'll need to bring a camera, so talk to IT about getting you one and—"

"Hold up," Lizzy said. "Me? Am I…am I coming with you?"

Darcy nodded. "Of course. You need to be familiar with the house too. It's too much information for me to take in alone, and I'll need someone to record our interviews, photograph the sites, and have some questions for me to follow up on. And of course, if you have any questions, feel free to ask them yourself as we do the tour."

Lizzy tried to contain her excitement. An entire day out of the office alone with Darcy? It could be amazing, or it could be terrifying, but for now, she was really hoping for amazing. "Will I need to book a hotel?" There was a hopeful tone in her voice that she couldn't avoid, and she looked up from her legal pad, biting her lip.

Darcy shot her a warning look before saying, "No, that won't be necessary. It's only a two-hour drive."

Lizzy's shoulders sank slightly.

"The appointment needs to be for next week, preferably Wednesday or earlier."

Lizzy nodded, scribbling.

"That's all," Darcy finished, sounding exhausted for the first time since Lizzy had met her.

Taking the hint, Lizzy stood silently and started to leave. "Hey, Darce?" she said, pausing at the door.

Darcy lifted her tired eyes.

"We're going to win this," Lizzy said resolutely. "I promise." She raced back to her office and checked the clock. At five fifteen on a Friday, she knew the chance of getting someone on the phone in a small town like New Paltz, New York, was slim, but she punched in the number Darcy had just given her and crossed her fingers.

"Thank you for calling the Meadows, this is Allison speaking, how may I help you?"

Yes!

This was going to work. They were going to win this trial. Lizzy would make sure of that. There was no way Darcy was losing her job just because that sexist prick—Dick or whatever his name was—who didn't understand passion or history or anything but money.

By the time Lizzy hung up, she and Darcy had an appointment

with the historian at the house for Tuesday morning. She tried to hide her enthusiasm, but the truth was, she couldn't wait.

She ran back to Darcy's office. She wanted to show her how committed she was to winning this trial. She wanted to give her some encouragement or some form of a high note to end the week on. Maybe she would be bold enough to even suggest they order Chinese delivered to the office for dinner.

But when Lizzy reached the corner office, Darcy was already gathering her coat and heading toward her door.

"Oh, you're leaving?" Lizzy said, unable to hide the disappointment in her voice.

"I have plans tonight," Darcy said, looking down as she slid past, shutting the door and locking it behind her.

It was as symbolic as a closed door could be. Lizzy wasn't invited inside after hours. Not into Darcy's office or into her heart. So much for thinking about what had happened between them exactly two weeks ago. No. Darcy had plans. Maybe even a date. But that was none of her business. Even a few weeks ago, it wouldn't have been her business. The door was closed and locked. Lizzy saw that now more than ever before.

She nodded, biting her tongue before asking more. "All right, well, enjoy your night."

"You too, Elizabeth," Darcy said coldly, turning and walking away from her.

CHAPTER TWENTY-EIGHT

Darcy sank into the plush cushion of the dark gray sofa. She tried to cross her legs, but the sofa was too soft, and it made her dress hike up her thigh. She straightened her back and scooted to the edge, trying to find a comfortable position. She was still adjusting and shifting when the therapist walked in the door.

"Good evening, Darcy," the tall blonde said as she took a seat in a chair across the room.

The room was small and lit by a single lamp looming over a brown nameplate with the words *Danielle Blankenship, LC* inscribed on it. A white noise machine was playing by the door to ensure confidentiality, and the only other form of light came from a single window looking out over Chinatown. The neon lights outside bounced around the white walls like in an old bordello. She had no idea why she'd chosen this location, other than the fact that this therapist was highly recommended online, and she knew there was no chance of running into anyone she knew in this neighborhood.

"Good evening," Darcy replied, crossing her hands over her knees. She hadn't been to therapy in years. She'd gone when she was little, back when her parents had divorced. She supposed everyone wanted to make sure she wasn't going to have a mental breakdown or something like most kids would have had when their mom had abandoned them and moved to Europe to "find herself."

But it hadn't broken her. In fact, the divorce had just made her and her dad closer, and it had made Darcy the fiercely independent woman she was today. She really should thank her mother for getting out of her way at such a young age.

But after everything happening with work and Elizabeth, she felt like it might be a good time to head back and do a check-in of sorts on her emotional health scales.

"It says here you're a managing partner at Byron & Browning, LLP. Can you tell me a little more about that? Sounds like a very big job for someone so young."

She nodded. "I'm responsible for overseeing a large number of senior associates, of counsels, and a few junior associates. I'm actually the youngest partner in the firm's history," she added proudly.

"Wow, that's very impressive. Did you always want to be a lawyer?"

She shook her head. "No, actually, in college, I wanted to do something with history. It's been a passion of mine for a long time. My father was a big history buff, and we used to spend our weekends visiting old houses in Florida, Georgia, and South Carolina. We'd take a trip up to St. Augustine every year too. We loved it."

Danielle began scribbling notes. "So what changed?"

Darcy adjusted in her seat. She hated this part of the conversation. Whenever her life story reached this specific part, she tried to skip over it as fast as she could. "My father got sick. Bills had to be paid. I saw the importance of having a job that paid well, and I altered my career course accordingly." She knew she sounded like she was in the military or something with such a rigid response, but it was the best she could do.

Danielle continued to scribble and nod. "And where is your father now?"

Darcy paused, looking down. "He died in my third year of law school. Lung cancer."

"I'm sorry to hear that," Danielle said crossing her legs and leaning in. "It sounds like you're pretty used to taking care of people, huh?"

"What do you mean?"

"Well, you took care of yourself when your mother left. You took care of your father when he got sick. And now part of your job is to oversee other attorneys, and in a way, you take care of them too."

Darcy bobbed her head. She had never thought of it that way before. "I suppose that's true." She let out a slight chuckle at the revelation and bit her lip.

"Are you in a relationship currently?"

Instantly, her mind flashed to Elizabeth. She shook her head and cleared her throat. "No, um, no. There was someone recently, but we... it didn't work out."

Danielle nodded again and continued to scribble. "Can you share a little with me about this person? Who are they? Why didn't it work out?"

Darcy sat back, considering the compound question before her. Like she was arguing before an appellate judge, she took the questions in turn. "She's a colleague of mine, well...technically, she's a subordinate. She's much younger than me. She just started working at my firm barely a month ago and we..."

"You were attracted to each other," Danielle added, helping Darcy along.

She nodded. "Yes. Instantly. It was like something out of a stupid movie. Every chance I had to see her, I took. I went to a ridiculous happy hour just to talk to her. I agreed to go to dinner with her even when I knew it was a horrible idea. I took her to one of my favorite spots in the city, the Plaza, and then..."

"And then, what?"

"She asked me on a date. I said no, of course."

"Why of course?"

Darcy bit her lip. "Well, she's a subordinate, like I said. Our firm policy expressly forbids this type of relationship. We could both be fired on the spot if anyone were to find out. I've already been too foolish with her. I've done too much, said too much. Plus, she's young. Too young. It just...it wasn't going to work." She wanted to get to the part about them sleeping together and then Elizabeth racing off to make out with another woman, but Danielle kept making her pause.

"Well, if you think about it, as a managing partner, isn't everyone a subordinate to you?"

Darcy nodded silently. "Yes, but firm policy—"

"Is she underage, this woman?" Danielle cut her off. "Is that why you're afraid of making this a thing?"

Darcy shook her head. "God, no, she's twenty-four, almost twenty-five, actually. She's an adult, just a very young one."

Danielle nodded. "It sounds to me like there's something more than just the logistics of this situation that made you say no. I mean, you were already willing to take a risk of being fired by sleeping with her. Sounds like that wasn't a problem for you. Think about it for a moment, and if you're ready, share with me why it is you really didn't want to get romantically involved with this person."

Darcy inhaled deeply. This was why she had been hesitant to come here. This pushing and prodding and digging into the deeper issues. She knew she needed to do it, but God, was it painful. Like a deep tissue massage of the heart or something. "I said no because I was afraid I would get hurt. She'd get bored and leave or realize I was just some conquest and move on or brag about it to the wrong person, and I'd lose everything I ever worked for. The repercussions are endless for this type of stupidity."

Danielle sat back, seemingly satisfied. "Well, that sounds very logical, counselor." She paused for a moment. "Why do you assume she'll leave?"

"Because." Darcy exhaled. "It happens. Because that's what my mother did and my father too. Everyone leaves one way or another."

Danielle started scribbling again. "Okay. That's something I can work with."

CHAPTER TWENTY-NINE

Lizzy just knew this was going to be the longest day of her life. Mondays were usually long, for obvious reasons, but this one was the day before she was going to spend an entire day with Darcy out of the office.

She spent most of the morning confirming everything they needed for tomorrow, checking the camera equipment, charging the battery, packing a backup battery, extra memory card, and extra macro lenses. She was very grateful for the Intro to Photography class she'd taken in college because the camera the firm supplied her with was anything but easy and simple. She played with the settings, adjusting the focus and taking practice shots around the office. She wanted to make sure there were no accidents or mistakes tomorrow.

"Look at you, scoring a day out of the office with a dime like Darcy Hammond," Micah said, leaning against the door to her office.

She rolled her eyes and continued to play with the camera. "Don't be jealous, Micah. Green isn't really your color," she said, pointing the lens at him and snapping a picture.

"Fuck, yeah, I'm jealous," he said, snickering. "Darcy Hammond is a smoke bomb. Everyone knows it. Can't believe she's not married. Then again, she plays for your team." He wiggled his eyebrows, and Lizzy shook her head.

"Can we maybe *not* talk about this?" She sighed.

He shrugged and left her office. "Whatever, Eight."

Later that day, Jackson came in for lunch and told her all about how things were going with Margaret. Apparently, they'd spent the entire weekend together watching *Lord of the Rings* and all three *Hobbit* movies. A truer nerd match could not be made, of that she was certain.

"Do you ever struggle with the power dynamic?" Lizzy asked, crunching her Caesar salad.

He slurped his soup and wiped his mouth. "What do you mean?"

She shrugged. "I don't know, she's your senior. You guys work together, like, every day. And she's got more experience than you. Do you ever wonder how it'll look or how it'll affect your work?"

He paused, seemingly considering the question. "Well, I guess on paper, sure. But when I'm with her, it doesn't feel like I'm with my superior, ya know? It just feels—"

"Normal?"

His eyes lit up. "Yeah. Yeah, exactly. Plus, I mean, this is a great job, but it's just a job, you know?" He took another loud slurp. "There are lots of jobs in the world, but there's only one Margaret."

She smiled warmly as he pushed his glasses up his nose. They were covered in steam from his soup, and he let out a goofy laugh that filled the room.

"I know why you're asking all of this, by the way." A slow grin spread across his face.

Her heart began to race. He didn't know about her and Darcy. He couldn't. Nobody knew. They'd only hooked up once in her office, and no one else had been here. Her mind began to replay the last few weeks, trying to remember that morning. Had they been too loud?

"You can talk to me about it if you want," he said, lowering his voice. "I mean, Ana sure has been."

She shook her head. "Ana?"

He nodded. "Yeah, Margaret overheard her a few weeks ago talking to her friend, Stella, about how you guys kissed after the show. Seems like she really likes you. Hey! We should go on a double some night."

Lizzy's shoulders slumped, and her heart sank. She *should* go on a double with Ana. The gorgeous, multilingual, smart, clever woman who was clearly super into her. But all she felt when she thought about her and Ana now was regret and shame. Regret that she had lost any chance of a future with Darcy and shame that she had made Ana a bystander in all of this mess she'd created.

"Oh, yeah, I don't think that's gonna work out," Lizzy added, looking at her salad again.

He waited a few seconds. "If you really like her, you shouldn't give up, you know. Just because she's technically your superior, and you work together, that shouldn't matter. All that really matters is how you both feel when you're with each other. The other stuff will work itself out in the end."

Wiser words had never been spoken, Lizzy thought. If only he was saying them about the right woman.

❖

Lizzy sat across the desk from Darcy for their five o'clock meeting. Patty was gone for the night, but the door was open as usual.

"We're all set for tomorrow," Lizzy said proudly. "I confirmed with the historian and the property manager that we are meeting them both tomorrow at ten a.m. The camera is charged, and I made a list of potential questions for you today." She slid a piece of paper across the large desk.

"That's good work, Elizabeth," Darcy said, looking over the questions. "Really."

Lizzy's heart swelled, and she smiled. Darcy's eyes locked with hers over the page but only for a second before she pointed them back at the paper.

"I'll pick you up tomorrow at eight."

"Oh," Lizzy said. "Do you need my address? Or do you want me to meet you here?"

Darcy set the paper down. "149th and Broadway, right?"

Lizzy blushed, remembering their first kiss outside the Plaza when she had told Darcy where she lived. The first time Darcy had admitted she had feelings for her. What she wouldn't give to go back to that night, back to before she had messed all of this up before it even really began.

She nodded. "You have a good memory."

"It depends on what I need to remember."

Lizzy wasn't sure, but she thought she saw a flirtatious glint in her eye as she finished the sentence. Probably just wishful thinking.

They finished up the meeting, and Lizzy went home on time for once. She needed to pick out an outfit for tomorrow. Maybe jeans and a cute blazer? But they would be walking around outside a lot, and it was freezing. She really needed to get a new coat when she got paid. She'd never gotten one after Darcy had ripped hers open a few weeks ago, so she'd been walking around with missing buttons, and the remaining few were dangling by threads. Maybe her brown combat boots? But Darcy had already seen her wearing those.

Her mind continued to race as she got on the 6 train and headed up toward Grand Central.

CHAPTER THIRTY

Darcy gripped the steering wheel of her black Audi, her fingers sliding over the paddle shifters. It was another one of her little indulgences she'd used to dull the sting of her endless, meaningless career. It was the newest electric model; she'd paid over a hundred thousand dollars to buy the thing and five hundred bucks a month just to park it in the basement of her building. She took it out on weekends when the weather was nice or when she was itching to get out of the city. It was pretty, fast, and a hybrid. What more could a woman want?

She checked the clock on the center console, its blue lights illuminating the otherwise fully black, immaculate interior. Seven fifty-eight. Right on time. She looked at the white brick building she was parked in front of. It was exactly what she'd pictured when Elizabeth had said she lived at 149th and Broadway. West Harlem was a newly gentrified area, with old Dominican roots clinging between the brownstones. There were a good number of restaurants just downstairs, and a fire escape crawled up the wall. Darcy wondered if Elizabeth ever went out and sat on it. She sure would. Her apartment had a rooftop that she used in the summer, but it wasn't private. It wasn't hers.

A quick knock on the window made her jump, and she looked over to see Elizabeth standing by the car, waving to her. She unlocked the door, and Elizabeth slid into the leather seat, the smell of coconut and Miss Dior flooding the compartment.

Darcy tried not to notice how beautiful she looked, but she couldn't help it. Her long hair flowed down her back and around her shoulders in perfectly done waves. Her freshly applied mascara and dark black eyeliner made her amber eyes pop. She wore a navy blue blazer with a baby blue sweater beneath it, dark blue jeans, and brown leather oxford shoes. Her usual black coat was slung over her arm, then tossed into the back seat along with the camera bag with the B&B logo on it. God, Darcy wished she'd get a better coat.

"Coffee?" Elizabeth said, extending a thermos in Darcy's direction.

Darcy took it and smiled. "Thank you," she said, taking a slow sip. It was bland, but she drank it anyway. "Shall we?" she said, shifting the car into drive. The Audi purred out of the parking spot, and Darcy pointed it in the direction of the George Washington Bridge.

They drove in silence for the first hour, and Darcy turned the radio to a classical station. For some reason, it wasn't as awkward as she imagined. There was a certain element of peace to just sitting in silence with Elizabeth. It felt like her mind was at rest. But there was still a twinge of pain that shot to her heart every time she caught a whiff of perfume or saw a strand of hair in her peripheral vision.

As the car sped north, Elizabeth let out a long sigh. "It's beautiful up here," she said, staring out the window.

"Have you never been to the Hudson Valley?"

"No, never. It actually looks a lot like Virginia."

Darcy nodded. "It's all Appalachia, so that makes sense." She paused, considering if she should just let the conversation end there. She decided against it. "I love it up here. Always amazed me that something so peaceful and quaint could exist so close to the hectic chaos of New York City."

"Yeah, when you're in the city, it feels like nothing exists outside of the five boroughs. Like, going to Brooklyn is the farthest you'd ever want to travel."

Darcy smiled. "People who are born and raised in New York City just don't know what a disservice they've been done. There's so much in this country to see, so many different viewpoints to consider and sights to explore."

"Totally! I actually had to convince Ana that—"

As soon as she said the name, her voice caught. Darcy felt the familiar stabbing pain in her heart, and she gripped the wheel harder to focus on anything but the emotional response rising inside her. Nothing had changed. Elizabeth was probably dating Ana by now. The whole office was talking about their little date at the theatre a few weeks ago. Even Patty knew about it, for heaven's sake.

"I'm sorry, I didn't, I mean, I was just saying that because she's lived here her whole life and—"

Darcy waved. "I'd rather we move on," she said with her usual steely tone.

She could see Elizabeth biting her lip as she turned to stare back out the window. Their little interlude of casual conversation was over. It was back to reality now. Back to business. This was a business trip. They were coworkers. The end.

"We're not together," Elizabeth blurted.

Darcy focused on not showing any reaction but was inwardly elated to hear it. "Okay."

"We never were together. It was all just a big misunderstanding. A mistake. I made a huge mistake, and I—"

Darcy lifted a finger. "Elizabeth, please don't assume because we're away from the office that the rules no longer apply. We're colleagues. You're free to date and sleep with whomever you want."

"But we didn't..." She stopped, seemingly giving up on any further self-defense.

They stayed silent for the remainder of the drive, Elizabeth looking out the window, and Darcy switching the stations between classical to jazz until eventually, they lost service.

Finally, after two hours on the winding roads, the small town of New Paltz opened itself up to them. Its quaint main street was covered with rainbow flags hanging from local artists' studios. On both sides of them were bookshops, cafés, places for palm readings and tarot cards, and even a yoga studio.

Darcy had always loved this place. She had spent a lot of time here over the years on her frequent escapes from the city. It had wonderful hiking nearby, and she loved a particular draft at the nearby brewery. Maybe they would stop there on their way back, depending on how the day played out. She wasn't optimistic, given the car ride so far.

Once they passed the town, they made their way down a long winding road that eventually turned to gravel. A single wooden sign with the words *The Meadows* was planted on the side of the road with an arrow pointing left. Darcy turned to follow the signs, and they traveled beneath large trees that hung low.

Then, as if by magic, the trees stopped, and a huge meadow revealed itself. It was the most picturesque thing Darcy had ever seen, and she couldn't believe she'd never been there before.

In the middle of the large empty meadow was a three-story Victorian house. The purple and white paint was chipping from the turret in the front, and there were immediate signs of weathering, but other than that, the house was stunning and in beautiful condition. The mountains lifted up behind it into soft, naked peaks while thick gray clouds gathered overhead.

Darcy pulled the car into a gravel parking lot, and they both stepped out. Darcy stretched her legs. She had picked today's outfit carefully, with the hope of looking good not only for the client but for woman who had hurt her only a couple of weeks ago. Her long, black leather boots hit just below her knee, and she knew her fitted black pants gave her legs a more slender, sleeker appearance than normal. She wore the black coat Elizabeth had once commandeered, though it had been dry-cleaned since to purge it of its coconut smell. Beneath the coat, she had selected a turtleneck that elongated her already lengthy neck. She was pleased when Elizabeth checked her out as she was gathering the camera bag from the back of the car.

A short stout woman wearing bright red glasses with wiry gray hair came trotting out from the house. "You must be Darcy Hammond. I'm Molly Rosenberg, I'm the historian here at the Meadows. Welcome!" She shuffled toward Darcy, smiling wide and extending a round hand.

Darcy smiled back and shook her hand. "Wonderful to meet you. This is my associate, Elizabeth Taylor. I believe you spoke on the phone."

Elizabeth approached with the camera bag slung over her shoulder and shook the woman's hand.

"Yes, yes of course. Quite the persistent one you are, Miss Taylor. I was going to call off work today on account of the weather, but you persuaded me how important this little visit was. I'm afraid our property manager did stay home today, so it's just us."

"The weather?" Darcy said, looking at the sky.

"Haven't you heard? Ulster County is going to get slammed with snow. Any moment now, it should hit. Well, we better hurry along. Come on, I'll give you a tour, and we can talk more in the house."

Darcy looked at her skeptically. She didn't recall seeing anything about snow in the weather forecast, but in all honesty, she had only checked the weather for Manhattan while deciding what to wear. This far north and with the mountains so close, she had no clue what the weather would do. No matter, they would be long gone before the first flake hit.

Darcy followed Elizabeth and Molly into the house. She smiled wide as the smell of mothballs and old wood hit her nose. She loved the smell of old houses. There was something so magical thinking about the lives that were once lived within these very walls, and it took her back to her times with her father, spending their weekends traveling to old Spanish homes around Florida and Southern plantations in Georgia and South Carolina.

"As you know," Molly began, "this home was originally owned by Margaret Liventhrop. The house was built in 1874 as a present from her father. She had expressed an interest in writing from an early age, and he was a progressive man who supported his daughter's education and passions. He also supported her living a free and—oh, how should I say this—modern lifestyle?"

Her voice hung for a moment, and her beady eyes bounced back and forth between Darcy and Elizabeth as if waiting for some realization to strike them.

Darcy had read all of Margaret Liventhrop's novels. She knew that her father had built her the house as a sanctuary from the community, where she could write without any disturbances. She also knew she had lived alone, never married, and died a spinster in this very house. As many times as Darcy had been to New Paltz, she had never stopped here, a decision she was sorely regretting as she looked around.

Molly led them into one of the salons as the tour continued. Elizabeth scribbled notes furiously, stopping to listen and nod along. She bit her lip as she wrote, and Darcy had to look away to avoid smiling at the adorable sight.

"In which room did she write *The Golden Apple*?" Elizabeth asked.

Darcy's eyes shot over to her. How the hell did she even know about that book?

Molly clapped. "I can see someone here knows their authors. Margaret actually wrote mostly from her library that I can take you to right now."

Elizabeth gave Darcy a quick up-and-down glance before winking and following Molly up the stairs.

Keeping this trip strictly professional was going to be a lot harder than she'd initially thought. It looked like Elizabeth had brought her A game, and all Darcy brought was a pair of nice shoes.

CHAPTER THIRTY-ONE

Lizzy did an inward fist pump as she entered the library of Margaret Liventhrop. Of course she had researched the woman before coming here today. Of course she had checked out one of her books from the library the second she'd gotten the trial assignment. And of course she remembered seeing *The Golden Apple* on Darcy's bookshelf in her loft.

And holy shit, was she feeling good about herself right now. Darcy had clearly not expected her to be so well-informed on one of her favorite authors. The look on her face was priceless. She felt so good about herself that she'd actually let herself flirt for a second. It sure didn't look like Darcy had hated it, either.

She listened to Molly talk about the author, the books she wrote, how old she was when she wrote and published each of them, and how she had to publish under a man's name because, hello, 1800s. It was fascinating to Lizzy, but nothing was as fascinating as watching Darcy soak it all in.

She was completely in her element. Her hands were tucked neatly behind her back as if she was a child who had been told not to touch anything. She beamed with smiles at each new room they entered. She was hanging on every word Molly said. Lizzy wished Darcy had decided to do something with history. She was a great lawyer, but Lizzy had never seen her look so happy before this moment.

"In fact," Molly continued, "Margaret often found dresses to be too restricting, so she eventually resigned herself to wearing men's trousers and dress shirts. Well, you can imagine the reaction that got from the local yokels." Molly laughed, her heavy belly jiggling.

"And what can you tell us about her relationship with Judith Levens?" Darcy asked, nearly cooing like a dove in the sacred room.

"I'm very glad you asked, Ms. Hammond. Judith Levens is one of the most unsung heroes we have here at the Meadows. Judith and Margaret were friends who met in their early twenties. Judith was once married to a man, but when he abandoned her and moved to California in the late 1800s, Judith actually moved in here with Margaret. Of course, they told everyone Judith was a boarder, but there is no record of any rent ever being paid." Molly paused for a moment. "There are records, however, demonstrating a very unique relationship between the two women." Her voice lingered awkwardly on the word *unique*, and Lizzy caught on.

"They were lovers," Lizzy said softly.

Molly nodded. "Many historians have denied the accuracy of that statement, but in more recent years, irrefutable evidence has come out about the truth of their romantic relationship."

"Well, that tracks. First, they want to erase the woman's sexuality. Now they want to erase her damn house," Lizzy said, raising her hands.

"Elizabeth," Darcy said, shooting her a dirty look.

Molly interjected. "I'm afraid Elizabeth is quite right, Ms. Hammond. For me personally, it's one of the reasons why this lawsuit is so important. You see, we're just starting to uncover so much about Margaret's personal life. Not just the books she wrote but how she felt, how she chose to live her life, and who she chose to live it with. But without this house here to honor that memory and push forward that discovery, well, I fear it will all be left at the wayside, like so much queer history."

This was ridiculous. How could this greedy corporation, probably run by a bunch of old white dudes, just come in here with their bulldozers and mow this place to the ground? Lizzy wouldn't stand for it. She wouldn't let it happen. If she had to chain herself to the front door, this house was going to live on. Margaret and Judith's house would live on. Their memory would live on.

"We're going to win this trial, Ms. Rosenberg," Lizzy said, her brows furrowed into a deep frown.

The woman's face lit up like a firecracker on the Fourth of July. "Oh, I certainly do hope so," Molly said, beaming with joy.

"Elizabeth," Darcy said with a warning tone to her voice.

Lizzy turned and stared directly at her. "I promise you. We're going to win."

She spent the rest of the tour doing what she was supposed to do:

taking photos, notes, video, and listening. She had said her piece and she had made up her mind. There was no need to keep pushing Darcy. They made their way outside to finish up the tour about two hours later, and Lizzy was struck with an instant wave of cold.

A thick blanket of white covered the road and meadow, and it was still snowing heavily.

"You two better get going," Molly said, climbing into a big truck. "I've got my partner's truck, but I don't reckon you'll make it far in that little thing." She pointed a chubby finger at Darcy's black Audi that was now white with snow.

"Thank you for this," Darcy said, shaking her hand. "It's been incredibly illuminating. I'll see you at the trial, and we'll speak before then to go over your testimony."

Molly pulled out of the driveway, leaving them standing alone in front of the house.

"Can you take a few more of the outside?" Darcy asked, staring back, steam pouring from her mouth.

"Sure, but it's pretty hard to see with all this snow," Lizzy replied, pulling out the camera. She walked around the house and snapped as many as she could.

As she was walking back, she caught a glimpse of Darcy in front of her Audi, and she lifted the lens to her eyes. She snapped at the perfect moment, with snow falling around her long hair. She looked like a model. Lizzy made a mental note to email that one to herself when they got back to the office later today.

When she walked to the car, Darcy began brushing the snow off the windshield and back window. But with every stroke, more snow just piled on harder. "Oh, for fuck's sake," she said. "Get in."

They climbed in, and Darcy dusted off her cashmere coat, thick flakes of snow falling into the clean car. She started her wipers and let the heat begin to melt the windows before slowly pulling out of the driveway. The car slid in a few spots as they reached the normal road, where people were traveling with their hazard lights on. Darcy followed suit. All the cars on the road now inched at a glacial pace. The snow was too thick for anyone to move any faster.

"Darce?" Lizzy said after a few minutes of tense driving. "You think maybe we should pull over somewhere?"

Darcy bit her lip before nodding. "Yeah, I do. I know a place nearby. It's random, but it's safe, and they have food. We can grab lunch and get on the road after the snow slows down." She took a sharp right and turned down another long, windy road. They went on for what felt like ages through the trees before reaching a guard shack made of stone.

A tall man stepped out with a clipboard and leaned over. "Checking in?"

Darcy shook her head. "Just trying to get out of the storm, actually."

The guard paused for a moment. "Normally, we wouldn't allow nonguests, but considering the circumstances, I'll make an exception. Follow the road to the right, then follow the signs that say 'check-in.' Be safe."

Darcy thanked the man and raised the window, driving down the gravel road to the right as instructed. The snow was still so thick, they had to go very slow, but Lizzy could see they were on a mountainside when she looked out her window.

"Where the heck are we?" she asked.

"You'll see," Darcy replied, a slow grin spreading across her face.

Her voice was soft and calm, shocking given the raging storm. She drove cool and collected, like she was pulling into her own driveway as the car rolled down the winding road before turning a corner.

Lizzy's jaw dropped. She could barely make it out through the snow, but a massive stone and wood lodge with a deep red roof was nestled at the bottom of the mountainside. A large frozen lake was to the left of the main building, and she could see barns, cottages, gardens, and fields, all surrounding the beautiful monstrosity. "Holy shit," Lizzy said. "Okay, seriously, where are we?"

They pulled under the awning, and Darcy smiled, turning to Lizzy. "Welcome to Mohonk Mountain House." She turned the car off and stepped outside. She leaned into the car. "Well, are you coming?" She winked at Lizzy before slamming the door shut and walking toward the valet.

This was going to be harder than she thought. Darcy had brought her A game. And all Lizzy brought was some random trivia about a dead author.

CHAPTER THIRTY-TWO

It was storming outside. That was why they had to pull in here. Never mind that there were dozens of restaurants and casual places on the main street where they came through. No, this was the safest place. There was no telling what was going on down in the town with all this snow.

Darcy continued to convince herself that the fact that she was at one of the most romantic destinations in New York with Elizabeth was totally acceptable. Not only acceptable, it was *necessary*.

She strolled into the lobby and shook the snow off her coat once again. Elizabeth was close behind, shivering. Her thin peacoat was soaked through, and her leather oxfords were also wet with snow. Without the buttons to keep the old raggedy coat closed, it was essentially useless as it hung sopping wet from Elizabeth's frail shoulders.

"Let's go get warm," Darcy said as they crossed the lobby and entered a large dining room.

Inside was a large room with high wooden ceilings and thick stone walls. It had windows on all sides, a large fireplace blazed at the far end, and the view overlooked the frozen lake. Circular tables were set up with linen tablecloths, and a black grand piano was being played in a corner near them.

"Welcome to Mohonk, how many?" a skinny man in a black blazer asked, approaching them.

"Two, please. As close to that fire as you can get us." Darcy motioned toward the roaring flames.

The man nodded and took them to a small round table close to the fire. The place was bustling, so Darcy was glad they could make the accommodation. She slid her coat off and hung it on her chair, and Elizabeth followed suit.

The shoulders of her blazer were wet where the snow had soaked through her coat, and the tips of her hair were brown from the melted snow.

"This place is packed," Darcy said, looking around the busy restaurant.

Elizabeth nodded silently, shivering.

"Are you okay?" Darcy asked, reaching out and feeling her cheek. It was red and cold as ice on contact, but a bolt of heat shot through her hand anyway.

Elizabeth looked at her, her soft eyes glowing from the warmth of the fire, and Darcy almost melted in her seat. "Yeah, I'm fine," Elizabeth said, rubbing her hands together. "Just not used to this much snow."

Darcy sat back. "Took me years to acclimate from Florida. My first winter, all I had was a raincoat and galoshes. I nearly froze to death trekking to and from my office. Then I finally went to Goodwill and bought a used men's coat for ten bucks. I looked like a homeless person, but at least I was warm." She laughed briefly.

"Well, I already look like a homeless person, so maybe I should follow your lead." Elizabeth looked at her hands.

"Trust me, you do *not* look homeless." Darcy's eyes lingered on Elizabeth's face, and she cleared her throat to settle her nerves. Luckily, the server showed up just in time.

"Good afternoon, ladies, what can I get for you?"

"Two coffees, please, and how about some soup?" She looked over at Elizabeth, waiting for an answer.

"Soup sounds good, thank you. Oh, but can I get hot chocolate instead of coffee?"

"You know what?" Darcy said. "Make that two hot chocolates. With marshmallows."

A broad smile spread across Elizabeth's face as they handed their menus to the server.

"Never took you for a hot chocolate woman," Elizabeth said, scooting a few inches closer to Darcy.

"Well, there's a lot you don't know about me." Darcy smiled and watched as crimson spread across Elizabeth's cheeks and down her neck and chest. *Keep it together, Darcy. Do not let your guard down with this woman. She's already hurt you once, and she's still your subordinate.*

Darcy chided herself while pretending to study her fingernails. But without her consent, her eyes drifted back over to Elizabeth, who sat smiling, looking back at her. "What?" Darcy asked, setting her hands down on the table.

"Nothing, I just...I like being here with you," Elizabeth replied frankly.

Her eyes stayed locked on Darcy's, and it took Darcy back to the night they'd spent together. With those eyes on her now, there was no defense strong enough to keep herself from tumbling head over heels. It was like every logical part of her brain shut down, and her heart made all the choices.

"Darcc," Elizabeth said, leaning closer. "I know I messed up with the whole Ana thing, but I swear, it isn't what you're imagining."

Darcy swallowed, and her shoulders tensed as she sat back in her chair.

"Before you do that...that thing that you do where you prickle up and shut me out, can you please just hear me out for a minute?"

The server returned with their hot chocolates, giving Darcy the interlude she needed before deciding if she really wanted to hear what Elizabeth was about to say. She thought of what her therapist would say right now. She'd probably give her a lecture about "listening even if we don't like what we may hear." Or "being optimistic" and "keeping an open mind" or something dumb like that.

But what was the point of having a therapist if she wasn't going to take her advice? "If you insist. But it's not going to change anything between us, Elizabeth." Her voice was soft, even though she tried her best to make it sound distant and curt. She stirred her cocoa, watching the marshmallows dissolve.

"That night, that time we spent together. It meant so much to me. It meant more than you'll ever know. And when I got home that day, all I wanted to do was text you just that. To tell you how much it meant, how much *you* mean to me. But I was afraid."

Darcy continued to study the cocoa. "Afraid of what?"

"I was afraid of scaring you away. Of coming on too strong, too fast. Afraid that maybe I shouldn't be feeling everything I was feeling about you. And not just because of the stupid handbook thing."

Darcy looked up. How did this woman at the age of twenty-four have the courage to say what Darcy had been too afraid to even admit to anyone but her therapist at the age of thirty-eight?

"I went to the show because I thought it was a group of us going. I mean, it was a group, but they all canceled, so it ended up being just me and Ana. It wasn't a date. I'd never have agreed to that."

Darcy nodded suspiciously. "And you just ended up making out by accident?"

"No, that was my fault. I got really drunk, and I…I honestly don't know what happened. I was upset that all I could think about was you. I was convinced that I cared about you more than you cared about me, and I guess I just self-sabotaged."

Darcy stirred the cocoa more. "Did you, I mean, did the two of you…" Why was she asking this? She didn't care. She shouldn't have cared. It shouldn't matter to her if they fucked all day and all night, for heaven's sake.

"No." Elizabeth grabbed her hand. "We did *not* sleep together, Darcy."

Darcy softened at the touch. Elizabeth's eyes were pleading and desperate. It took all Darcy had not to lean across the table and pull her lips into her right then and there. Luckily, the server returned with their soup, and Elizabeth was forced to release her hand.

Darcy cleared her throat and took a slow sip of cocoa. "Well, thank you for telling me that. But it really wasn't necessary. As I said, we're coworkers. You're free to date whomever you want."

They finished up their lunch mostly in silence, but the tension was so thick, Darcy could cut it with a butter knife. It wasn't an uncomfortable tension, like two people who didn't know what to say. No, it was a raw tension, like two people who had *too much* to say. It felt like, at any moment, they would burst into flames from their proximity and set the entire hotel on fire.

Darcy checked her watch. It was close to three, and they had a long drive back. She wasn't sure about the condition of the roads, but she assumed they would be plowed by now. Although the snow had not let up one bit from what she could see out the windows of the restaurant.

"We better get on the road," she said, standing after paying the check.

Elizabeth nodded and slid on her wet coat. It wasn't until they reached the front entrance that Darcy realized just how wrong her assumption had been.

The entire driveway was covered with several feet of snow. It was so heavy, it was stacking up against the walls. The blizzard was still raging, and she couldn't even see the parking lot where her car had been put by the valet. Within seconds, the reality of their situation became unavoidably clear. No one was going anywhere tonight.

Unwilling to admit defeat so easily, Darcy marched over to the concierge. A long line had already formed, and she tapped her finger against the case of her cell phone and waited for the people in front of her to turn around and leave. The look of frustration across their faces gave Darcy a clenching feeling in the pit of her stomach.

"Do you know when we might expect the weather to lighten up?"

The redhead behind the desk looked up from her computer. "I can't say for certain, but I wouldn't expect it to be anytime today. It may even go through the night."

Shit. Darcy pulled out her cell and began searching online. Severe weather alert. Wintery conditions. Shelter in place. Alerts flooded her phone no matter which website she went to. Several people in line began to mutter their annoyance at the holdup in the line.

"Are we stuck here?" Elizabeth asked, a slight shake in her voice.

Darcy stopped scrolling and slid her phone into her bag. "It appears that way." They hesitated as if both were considering the position they were in. Darcy looked at Elizabeth, her clothes and shoes still soaked. "All right, come with me." She turned and walked to the front desk.

After waiting in yet another line, they were finally helped. "Do you have any available rooms for tonight?" Darcy adjusted the black leather bag on her shoulder and pulled out her wallet.

"Oh, boy, let me check, but honestly, I doubt it." The man behind the desk clicked around with his mouse a few times and Darcy dropped her head. "Actually, we do have one, ma'am, it's a one-bedroom suite."

"One? You mean to tell me in this entire massive hotel, you have one room open?"

"I'm very sorry, ma'am, but we are hosting two conferences and a wedding here this week, and they've taken all our regular rooms and suites. And with the storm hitting so quickly, a lot of our day guests are stuck here just like you."

She stroked her forehead, leaning on the tall counter. What choice did they really have? Try to drive back to Manhattan and die? Stay up all night in the lobby? Even getting down to the town was out of the question now with the roads so bad. The line behind her was only getting longer, and she knew if she passed on the last available room, they'd be sitting up all night in the lobby.

Darcy looked at Elizabeth briefly. "Fine," she said firmly. "We'll take the suite."

CHAPTER THIRTY-THREE

E lizabeth's heart raced as she followed Darcy down the long, narrow hall toward the elevator. After it became clear that they were stuck in this magnificent hotel for at least a night, Darcy had taken her to the gift shop where they'd each purchased socks, sweatpants, T-shirts, and sweatshirts, as well as toiletry essentials. She was sure they would look like a walking billboard for the hotel, but it was better than staying in their wet clothes or sleeping naked.

She shook her head as her mind wandered to the idea of them curled up naked in each other's arms, snow falling around them outside.

She was glad Darcy had finally heard her out about the Ana situation, but she didn't seem to be acting much differently. Maybe what she had said was true. It didn't make any difference. There was no going back now. But as they got closer and closer to the room, she couldn't help but feel excitement and optimism at the prospect of being in the same room together for an entire night.

The suite was massive. There was a living room with a gas fireplace that had a large flat-screen TV hanging over it. The fireplace connected to the bedroom on the other side of the stone wall, which meant that the bedroom and the living room both had a roaring fire. The bathroom had a massive Jacuzzi big enough to fit at least four people and a shower with a waterfall showerhead. A huge set of windows overlooked the snow-covered mountains, and Lizzy wished it was snowing a little less so she could see them. The California king bed was covered in Egyptian cotton sheets, and a thick red duvet was spread across it.

God, what she would give to be in that bed with Darcy tonight. But she had a sneaking suspicion she'd be told to sleep on the pullout couch in the living room instead.

Darcy walked into the kitchen and opened the full-size refrigerator.

It was stocked with water, bottles of wine and beer, cheese, fruit, and crackers.

"At least we have snacks?" Lizzy said, shrugging. Darcy had been grumpy ever since she had learned they would be forced to stay in the same room, and Lizzy tried not to let it hurt her feelings. She hung her wet coat in the closet and made her way to the couch, where she tossed the gift shop bags down next to the camera bag. "Do you mind if I get changed?"

Darcy shrugged, pulling out a bottle of wine. "There's plenty of room, that's for sure."

Lizzy nodded, taking the hint. *Change in another room. Got it.* She disappeared into the large bathroom, slipping on the oversized sweatpants and sweatshirt. Her hair looked like a mess from the weather, and she tried her best to detangle the knots that had formed at the nape of her neck, but it was no use. She decided to pull it back into a ponytail. Clearly, her appearance wasn't impacting Darcy either way.

When she stepped out, Darcy was pouring two glasses of wine in the kitchen. She was still wearing her long black boots and fitted pants. Her cream sweater was hanging from her perfect body, and Lizzy regretted getting changed so fast. There was no hope of her ever feeling sexy now. Not when she looked like this, and Darcy looked like *that*.

"Wine?" Darcy said, stepping around the bar and extending a large glass.

Lizzy took it with both hands and sat on the couch. Darcy sat next to her and crossed her legs, staring out the window. Lizzy tried to ignore her heart rate, which elevated as the smell of Darcy's perfume flooded her nose. How did she still look and smell so damn good?

Darcy broke their silence. "I can't believe I didn't bring my laptop. I could be getting so much work done right now."

Lizzy nodded. "Hey, want to look at the photos I took of the house today?"

Darcy took a sip of wine and shrugged, holding out her hand for Lizzy to hand her the camera. Lizzy complied, but as soon as Darcy turned on the camera, a realization hit her. *Oh shit. The photo I took of her outside the house. I didn't get a chance to...*

"What's this?" Darcy said.

Fuck. It was too late. Darcy turned the camera around. The photo of her. Her dark hair swirled gracefully as the snow fell around her perfectly angled face. "Oh, uh, just had to take a test shot, you know?"

"It's the last photo of the day. Wouldn't a test shot be the first?"

Lizzy bit her lip. She was normally so good at thinking on her feet, at coming up with some excuse or some flirty quip. But her mind ran blank. She had taken the photo for herself. Simple as that. There was no getting around it now. "You just looked so beautiful," she finally admitted. Her knees were touching Darcy's thigh on the couch, and the hair on her neck stood on end at their growing proximity. "You always look so beautiful," she went on, keeping their eyes locked.

A slow smile spread to the corners of Darcy's mouth, and a softness flickered into her eyes. She looked just like she did at the Plaza a few weeks ago. Soft, vulnerable, and alive.

Lizzy licked her lips briefly and then looked at Darcy's, slowly inching closer on the couch. She felt herself being drawn in. Her heart began to race faster and faster, and a slow throbbing began to grow between her legs. She touched Darcy's face, and to her surprise, Darcy didn't pull back. Her lips were so close now, Lizzy could almost taste them.

"Elizabeth," Darcy said, her voice low and husky.

But Lizzy didn't wait to hear more. She closed the small space between them and pressed her lips to Darcy's. Fireworks shot off in the room all around them, and Lizzy kissed her again and again, pushing her back onto the sofa and crawling on top.

Darcy quickly sat up, pulling Lizzy's legs on either side so Lizzy was straddling her. Lizzy grabbed a fistful of her hair and pulled gently so her neck was exposed before placing kisses and bites all along her neckline.

Darcy let out a low growl, and she grabbed Lizzy's hips and pulled her closer. "Fuck, I missed this." She moaned into Lizzy's ear, sliding her hand up Lizzy's sweatshirt. Lizzy had taken her bra off in the bathroom, and a look of excitement spread across Darcy's face. She cupped Lizzy's breast before gently pinching her nipple.

Lizzy tossed her head back and whimpered at the contact. "I missed *you*," she whispered into Darcy's ear as she began to rock back and forth on her lap.

Darcy kept her left hand firmly on Lizzy's waist and shoved her free hand down the loose sweatpants. Lizzy had also left her underwear in the bathroom, which made what Darcy was about to do that much easier.

Slowly, Darcy began making large circles around Lizzy's clit, and she bucked and wiggled, inching closer, begging Darcy not to stop. She felt herself begin to quicken with just the light contact.

"I want more of you," Lizzy said as she rubbed her mouth gently against Darcy's ear.

Instantly, Darcy began making harder, faster circles. Lizzy's thighs clenched as she began to move slowly up and down with the contact. Darcy's fingers stopped circling long enough to slide between the slick, wet folds. Lizzy moaned as Darcy's fingers moved in and out of her.

Darcy started off slowly at first, but soon, there was a desperate urgency to her thrusts, and Lizzy began to move faster and faster, bouncing up and down as Darcy's fingers slid in and out. Each time she came down, the pressure inside mounted higher and higher. A bead of sweat trickled down the back of Darcy's neck, and it only pushed her to move harder and faster.

Darcy's free hand lifted Lizzy's sweatshirt, and she began sucking and licking her nipples. Lizzy began to let go, and before she could slow herself down, she was tumbling over the edge.

"I'm coming! Fuck, Darcy. I'm coming," Lizzy screamed, burying her face in Darcy's shoulder before finally releasing on top of her. She stayed like that for a moment, frozen and twitching. Darcy wrapped her arms around her and kissed her cheek, her neck, and her hair.

Lizzy pulled back for a moment, searching Darcy's eyes. Searching for a look of regret or anger or disdain for what they had just done. But all she saw was warmth and happiness staring back at her.

"I missed you too, Elizabeth," Darcy said, pulling Lizzy's lips to hers.

CHAPTER THIRTY-FOUR

Darcy smiled as she felt Elizabeth's warm, naked body lying beside her. She scooted closer, burying her face in her back as she held her. Elizabeth's breathing quickened at the contact, and Darcy kissed the back of her neck and rubbed her hand, whispering for her to stay asleep.

She had no idea what time it was, and frankly, she didn't care. She only knew it was early because the sun hadn't fully risen yet. Last night, they'd barely slept or eaten or done anything but have sex. Somehow, it was even better than the first time they'd been together because this time, Elizabeth had stayed. This time, Darcy got to wake up next to her.

She didn't realize just how much she'd really missed her until their lips had touched yesterday. And then, it was as if she had walked through the back of the wardrobe, and all of Narnia had appeared before her.

In all her life, she had never felt so complete, so content, so alive just being near someone. She thought briefly about how she would explain all this to her therapist in a few days. Or how she would be able to go back to seeing Elizabeth every single day at the office. How it would impact their trial prep.

She closed her eyes tightly, ignoring the flood of unknowns that rushed into her mind.

She kissed Elizabeth's ear again before turning over onto her back. Elizabeth turned next, bringing her bare leg over Darcy's stomach and nuzzling into her neck. Darcy reached around and pulled her close, kissing the top of her head and brushing her hair behind her ear.

Elizabeth leaned up and placed a soft kiss on Darcy's neck before falling back asleep.

❖

A few hours later, they both rose from bed and slipped on their coordinating Mohonk Mountain House sweatshirts and pants. God, Elizabeth looked sexy in those baggy gray things. They hung just off her waist, and Darcy could see the round curve of her butt as she shuffled to the kitchen for a glass of water. Her hair was piled on top of her head in a messy bun, and she rubbed her eyes sleepily, feeling around for a glass.

Darcy sat at the barstool, her head resting in her hand as she watched Elizabeth fill the coffee maker with water and press the on button. She felt like she could do this every single day. Wake up next to Elizabeth and just sit, watching her do menial things. How cute did she look brushing her teeth? What about brushing her hair? Did she bite her lip when she read her mail like she did reading legal briefs?

Elizabeth pulled the hood over her head and turned, smiling a big goofy grin.

"How do you feel?" Darcy asked as Elizabeth rested her elbows on the kitchen counter.

"Hmm...light? Happy? Exhausted?"

Darcy smiled and reached out, grabbing Elizabeth's hand across the bar. "Hope I didn't wear you out last night."

Elizabeth raised an eyebrow over her sleepy eye. "Oh, please, I'm the spring chicken here, remember? It's you I'm worried about. How's your back doing, by the way? Need a walker or anything?"

Darcy swatted at her and laughed. "Are you calling me old?"

Elizabeth jumped back and wiggled her eyebrows playfully. "Sure am. If you get to nag on about how I'm *so* young, then I get to call you old after a night of very active sex."

Darcy crossed her arms, pretending to be angry, but Elizabeth walked around the counter and wrapped her arms around Darcy's neck, kissing her cheek. "We're fighting," Darcy said, playfully pushing her away.

"No, we're not." Elizabeth moved past her arms and planted a kiss on her lips.

They were *not* fighting. Darcy kissed her back and wrapped her arms around Elizabeth's waist, pulling her close. She never wanted to leave this amazing hotel room. She never wanted to go back to work.

She wanted to stay there forever. Just the two of them. No prying eyes or judgmental glares. No questions about whether Darcy had picked Elizabeth for the trial because they were sleeping together. Just the two of them being happy.

But as Darcy stood and walked to the window, she knew her dream could never come true. The snow had stopped, and the roads were fully plowed. It was time to go back to reality. Her phone was already bursting with notifications. She'd emailed Patty last night, telling her about the snow situation. It was really not a big deal that she'd missed a day of work, but the vibrating and dinging coming from her phone was a pressing reminder of how hard reality was about to smack them in the face.

Elizabeth came up behind Darcy and wrapped her arms around her, kissing her shoulder as they looked out the large window together. "Phone blowing up?"

Darcy sighed and nodded, scrolling through the hundreds of emails she had ignored since yesterday afternoon.

"How about," Elizabeth said, turning Darcy around so she could face her, "we just put this on silent for a few more hours?"

Darcy stopped scrolling. "What did you have in mind?"

Elizabeth shook her head, seemingly picking up on the implications of Darcy's remark. "While *that* sounds amazing, I had something else in mind. What if we just…spent the day together?"

"What? Up here?"

Elizabeth nodded. "Yeah. What if we just walked around the hotel or went shopping on Main Street? Heck, what if we built a big-ass snowman right there on the lawn?"

Darcy thought about it for a moment. She really should have been getting back to the city. She'd already lost a full day of work and trial prep yesterday, and now she was about to lose another one. She ran through the options in her mind, then looked at Elizabeth. Her pleading eyes were full and soft.

"Fuck it," Darcy said, tossing her phone onto the couch. "I'm all yours."

CHAPTER THIRTY-FIVE

Lizzy couldn't remember a time when she had more fun with one person. And she had done some pretty stupid shit as a teenager. She and Darcy spent the afternoon doing exactly what Lizzy had suggested. They started off by racing outside and having a snowman-building competition that turned into Darcy ruining Lizzy's snowman by stealing his stick arms and tossing them into the woods.

"Sabotage!" Lizzy hollered as Darcy bolted across the massive lawn, giggling the entire way.

That adventure eventually evolved into a snowball fight that Darcy seemed very unprepared for. She might have been taller, but Lizzy had played softball in high school, and her aim was impeccable. The battle went on for what felt like ages, and Darcy only conceded when Lizzy tackled her and shoved snow down the front of her shirt.

After that, they were both shivering and soaking wet, so they came back up to the room and took a long, hot shower together. If Lizzy thought Darcy's body was amazing the previous night, it was nothing compared to seeing and feeling it with hot water trickling down it. She'd never really been a big fan of shower sex, but after this, she might have to amend that rule.

Then, when it was time to check out, they drove Darcy's car down to New Paltz and had lunch at a brewery she liked. Lizzy laughed as Darcy tossed back two blueberry beers in a row. "So much for your palate for fancy-ass red wine."

Darcy simply shrugged. "As I said, there's a lot you don't know about me."

A sadness grew over Lizzy when the server brought the check because she knew it meant they would be heading back to the city. But, much to her surprise, Darcy grabbed her hand, and they spent another two hours visiting every shop. Darcy bought several books at a local bookstore, and Lizzy picked up a few homemade candles at a quaint, yoga-style shop.

But perhaps the most moving moment came when they walked into a clothing store. Darcy hunted in the racks while Lizzy aimlessly wandered. She couldn't afford anything in the store. It was all name-brand and way over her budget.

"Here," Darcy said, holding up a long, navy blue coat. "Try this on."

"Okay, but I definitely can't afford this," Lizzy whispered, sliding her arms into the sleeves. The fit was perfect. The coat was double-breasted with gold buttons, and it hit around midcalf. It was made of pure merino wool and had a wide lapel that extended to her belly button. Darcy made Lizzy look at herself in the mirror, and she leaned over her shoulder, smiling.

"God, you look sexy in that thing," Darcy whispered while watching Lizzy's eyes.

A tingle ran all the way down the back of Lizzy's neck, through her spinal cord. She reached down and checked the tag.

Eight hundred and fifty dollars.

"Holy shit, okay, wow. I'm just gonna take this off. Nice and slowly." Lizzy began unbuttoning the coat and sliding it off her arms as gently as possible.

"Oh, don't be absurd," Darcy said, helping Lizzy take off the coat and throwing it over her arm. "Do you like the coat, yes or no?"

"Of course, but I—"

"Great. We'll take it." She handed the clerk the coat and looked back at Lizzy. "Want anything else?" Her eyes were wide and carefree.

Lizzy shook her head and tried to protest, but it was no use. Before she could even utter another word, the coat was purchased, and Lizzy was wearing it out the door. "Darce, you really shouldn't have done that. I can buy my own coat."

Darcy shrugged. "I know that. But I wanted to see you in *this* coat. It was purely selfish motives, I assure you. Plus, I owed you, considering I ripped the buttons off your old one." She shot Lizzy a wink and kissed her cheek.

They walked around a bit more, and Lizzy had to admit she was significantly warmer. Not only that, but she felt like some gap had been closed between her and Darcy. Darcy was back in her black pants, boots, and coat while Lizzy was back in her brown oxfords and blue blazer. This new coat made them look like…equals. For the first time, she didn't feel like Darcy's subordinate. She felt like her partner. Maybe even her girlfriend. She couldn't believe an expensive coat could do all that, but sure enough, it did.

"We better be getting back," Darcy said, exhaling a long sigh that sent steam pouring from her mouth. The sun was starting to set on their beautiful day in the mountains.

Reluctantly, Lizzy agreed, and they began their dark drive home. This time, there was no stuffy classical music or jazz. The only music that played was Britney Spears and the Backstreet Boys, which they both knew every single word to. But for the most part, they just talked.

Darcy told Lizzy about growing up in Florida and her life with her father before he'd gotten sick. She talked about how they would go on historical field trips and how much that impacted her love of history. She told Lizzy about doing moot court in law school at Stetson and how she wished she could go back and just relax a little bit more. She talked about how she loved the city, but sometimes missed living so close to a real beach.

Lizzy spoke about her mom back home in Virginia and how she just wanted to make her proud and how that was one of the reasons she had been so driven to succeed for so long. She told her about law school at UVA and how happy living there had made her and how she missed the mountains and hiking and being outside in nature.

"Looks like we both made compromises to get what we want," Darcy said at the end of their conversation.

Lizzy looked at her fingernails. "Darce? What happens now? I mean, tomorrow, when we get back to work, what…how do I act around you?"

Darcy bit her lip and inhaled slowly. "I can't say I haven't been thinking about that all day myself." She paused. "What do *you* want to happen?"

Lizzy was taken aback by the question. She'd never imagined she'd have any say in how this relationship—or whatever it was they were in—would proceed. When they'd first started sleeping together, Darcy had made it very clear they were *not* in a relationship and never would be. But now it was almost as if she was leaving the door ajar for some change in that agreement.

"I don't know," Lizzy said. "I mean, I know what I *don't* want."

"What's that?" Darcy said turning to face her briefly.

"I don't want people thinking I'm dating Ana. I don't want Micah Willis talking about how great your ass looks in pencil skirts."

Darcy gave a look of surprise, but Lizzy just continued: "I don't want Patty babysitting me on our morning meetings. I don't want to have to go all the way to the Village to have dinner with you. And I don't want you getting fired because of me or this trial."

Darcy frowned. "Who told you about that?"

"No one. I overheard Dick what's-his-name talking to you when I was going into your office last week. That's why I've been working so hard to make sure we win this thing."

Darcy placed a hand on Lizzy's thigh and gave it a soft, reassuring squeeze. "Darling, I have way too much dirt on the partners for that to ever happen. Dating you, well, that might be sufficient grounds for termination." The words hung heavy in the air between them, but Lizzy rested her hand on Darcy's, and she was happy when instead of pulling away, Darcy laced their fingers.

"What do you mean? What dirt?"

Darcy tilted her head. "Oh, you know, like the fact that Paul had an affair with his secretary for all of 2019, or that Dick cheats on his income taxes to hide an entire apartment he has in the East Village. Or maybe that I've seen the little folder Mark has on his work computer that he thinks no one knows is full of porn. The men in this profession are repugnant creatures. I've made it a habit to keep track of all of their…propensities over the years."

Lizzy's jaw dropped.

"Trust me, I'm not getting fired. Not over the trial anyway." She shot Lizzy a sideways glance. "You continue to be my sole liability at this firm."

"Holy shit, Darce. You're…you're a shark."

Darcy laughed. "I've been called worse, but thank you."

"God, I fucking love—" The next word cut short in her throat, and she swallowed hard catching herself. "*That.* I love that. I mean, love that you did that." *Keep it together, Taylor.*

A slow crease began to form at the corner of Darcy's mouth. "I'm glad. That you love that about me, I mean. It intimidates a lot of people."

Lizzy stroked her hand. "You don't scare me, Darcy."

"Maybe I should." Darcy shot her a stern look, but soon, her demeanor broke, and they both burst out laughing.

They finished the rest of the drive holding hands, even when Darcy started to navigate the streets of Manhattan to get to Lizzy's apartment.

Lizzy realized they'd never really addressed the issue of what exactly was going to happen at the office tomorrow, but maybe that was okay. Maybe they should both just see what happened. Act normal and hope for the best.

Act normal but don't rip her clothes off like you'll want to, Lizzy told herself as the car came to a slow roll in front of her apartment.

Darcy put the car in park. "Thank you," she said, smiling softly. "For today, for yesterday…for last night." Her face turned red, and she looked down. "It was really special to me."

Lizzy kissed her on the lips slowly. She pulled back a few inches and asked if Darcy wanted to come upstairs. It was a risk, inviting a woman as powerful and successful and rich as Darcy into her shared apartment with three roommates. But she took it anyway.

"I can't tonight," Darcy replied, brushing Lizzy's cheek with the back of her hand. "It's late."

Lizzy bit her lip and leaned in for one more kiss. "If I had a dollar for every time you've said that to me…"

Darcy let out a low moan as their final kiss ended, sending heat radiating down Lizzy's spine. Man, she really wished Darcy was coming inside now. She stepped out of the car and gave Darcy a wink before turning and walking into her building. She knew Darcy was watching her leave, but she refused to turn, not wanting to give her the satisfaction.

CHAPTER THIRTY-SIX

D arcy shifted awkwardly on the soft couch. Would she ever get used to how plush this thing was? Her lanky blond therapist sat across from her scribbling notes, just like last week. Darcy wasn't thrilled that every Friday night seemed to be filled with a therapy session now, but she knew it was worth it.

"So," Danielle said setting her pen down and smiling. "How was your week?"

Darcy inhaled deeply. What a simple, loaded question. How was her week? *Let's see.* Tuesday, she'd spent the day touring the home of one of her favorite authors, the same home she was trying to save from being torn down. Oh yeah, and she'd toured it with the woman she'd been desperately trying *not* to fall for. Oh, and did she mention they'd stayed at a romantic resort having sex all night? Ah, and she couldn't forget the part where the next day they'd walked hand in hand around a quaint, snow-covered town, kissing and playing in the snow like schoolgirls.

"The week was interesting," Darcy said vaguely.

"What made it interesting?" Danielle clicked her pen.

Darcy bit her cheek. What was the point of paying for a therapist if she wasn't going to open up to her? "Well, Elizabeth and I went to New Paltz for work. We got snowed in with the storm, and we...we had to stay at a hotel."

Danielle smiled and nodded. "And how was that?"

Darcy fidgeted with her nails before finally slamming her hand on her lap. "It was incredible. Amazing, really. Not just the sex. I mean, the sex was amazing. I've never known someone who just knows my body so well so soon. But more than that, the entire thing was like magic. We talked and laughed, and the next day, we walked around town and made stupid snowmen and giggled, and I was just so…"

"Happy?" Danielle chimed in.

Darcy sighed and nodded. "Yes. I was happy."

"This sounds great, Darcy. If you were so happy a few days ago, why do you seem so unhappy now?"

She shrugged and sighed again. "Because I keep fucking it up."

Danielle scribbled some notes and nodded. "What makes you say that?"

"Before she got out of my car Wednesday, she asked me how things would be when we got back to work on Thursday. I couldn't answer her. When Thursday came around, I just…froze. I acted like nothing had happened between us. Like the entire wonderful experience hadn't happened."

She paused before continuing. "It was so different when it was just the two of us. Up there, away from everything and everyone, it was great. But at work, I don't know, it's different. The stakes are so high for both of us. Me with my career being the best it's ever been, and hers just starting out. Besides that, people expect things of me there. There are always eyes on me, waiting for me to fail or make the slightest misstep. And then she asked me to have dinner with her tonight, and I was vague and told her I had plans, but I didn't tell her I was coming here again. I could see the hurt in her eyes, but I just…I can't stop these walls from coming up with her."

Writing what seemed like an entire novel, Danielle finally finished and looked up. "These are all good reasons not to be with someone, but something tells me your career, as much as you value it, isn't the biggest driving force here. Tell me more about your mother and father and why you felt like they left you."

Darcy attempted to avoid the topic. "My mom left when I was little, and my dad died. Like I said last week."

Danielle nodded. "Do you blame yourself for any of that?"

She shrugged, tears beginning to form behind her eyes. "No, of course not. That would be ridiculous. I was a child when my mother left. What could I have done about it?" She bit her lip to fight back the sting of the rising swell.

"I don't know." Danielle continued, "Maybe deep down, you think that you're alone because of something you've done. Maybe you think you're not worthy of having someone who sticks around?" She sat back and rested her hands on her lap. "But that's all conjecture, of course."

Darcy avoided eye contact and studied her fingernails. She didn't want to talk about this anymore.

"Fear of abandonment is a very real thing that a lot of people struggle with, Darcy. Has Elizabeth given you any reason to think she would leave you?"

Darcy let out a soft laugh. "Yeah, actually. She made out with a woman the day after we had sex a few weeks ago. I mean, we'd said no strings, so she wasn't breaking any rules technically, but—"

"But it hurt you."

Darcy's shoulders dropped. "Yes. Yes, it did."

"Have you communicated all this? Your fear of abandonment? The hurt her actions caused you? Your hesitation?"

Darcy shook her head. "I mean, I told her I was her boss and how it was a violation of firm policy, so it couldn't really go anywhere. It wasn't even supposed to go as far as it has. Like I told you last time, Byron & Browning allows no room for misinterpretation on this topic. We would both lose our jobs on the spot if there was even a whisper of impropriety on my part."

"But I'm sure you're not the first person to have romantic feelings for a subordinate in your firm."

She thought about the dirt she had on Paul and his secretary. She was certain he wasn't the only partner at the firm to cross that line. But was that really the standard she was holding herself to? Paul and his secretary? Or Mark or any of the other male chauvinists she worked with, for that matter? She was better than that. She had to be better than that.

"Have you ever had a true, raw, honest conversation with this woman aout how you feel?"

Darcy stared at her fingernails again. "No, I haven't."

Danielle scribbled again. "Well, then, that's your homework for the week. Talk to her. Be vulnerable. See how it goes."

As Darcy left Chinatown that night, a sinking feeling began to creep into the pit of her stomach. She was nervous about this little homework assignment. She was nervous as hell.

CHAPTER THIRTY-SEVEN

Lizzy slammed her hand down, punching holes in the stacks of papers. The trial was next week, and the binders were the final crucial piece of work. Darcy was speaking with all their expert witnesses on Monday. The trial calendar had been set, all disclosures had been exchanged, records had been reviewed and organized, and exhibits had been prepared. It was all coming together.

Lizzy could have just waited to do this tomorrow morning, but she couldn't stand to be in her apartment today, so she'd come to the office. She hiked up her Adidas joggers as she reached for another stack of papers. All of the trial materials had been moved to Darcy's office Friday morning so there was one place for everything. That was where she was now, papers and binders spread out in large stacks across the huge, carpeted floor. It was creepy being there all alone. The cleaning crew had come through earlier this morning and let her in Darcy's office once she'd showed her ID badge and explained she needed documents in there. She'd chatted with them for a bit, but other than that, she was the only one on the floor.

She looked at the sprawling glass desk and sighed. She missed Darcy. She wished she was there, organizing these papers with her. The last few days at work, she'd been polite. Not cold or harsh like after the Ana incident, but she wasn't the same person she had been at Mohonk. She was professional and polished. Not warm and soft. Lizzy liked all sides of Darcy, but there was a sharp sting to the contrast after they had spent such a wonderful time together upstate.

She'd asked her to dinner Friday night, hoping that getting her away from the office would give them a chance to actually talk. To figure things out together. But Darcy had said she had plans again, and the growing seed of insecurity had sent Lizzy spiraling.

She'd barely slept Friday night, and Saturday, she'd ridden her bike all the way down the West Side Highway and back to get some of her energy out, but still, she'd felt restless. Today, she'd woken up and decided to come to the office to work and clear her mind. Unfortunately, Darcy's office smelled like her perfume, and it just made Lizzy miss her more.

"Whatever," she said, slamming the heavy-duty hole punch.

She reached over, pulled out her phone, and opened Spotify. Fletcher's "Serial Heartbreaker" started playing, and she turned the volume all the way up, bobbing her head to the music as she made her way through the large stacks.

She was so focused on *not* thinking about Darcy, she was halfway through screaming the chorus to the song when the sound of someone clearing their throat caught her ear.

"Jesus!" She jumped up and swung around.

"You have a habit of sneaking into my office, you know that?" Darcy stood holding a cup from Starbucks, her black coat open over a pair of tight black leggings and a dark green Stetson Law hoodie. Her hair was hidden beneath a navy blue Yankees cap, a few loose strands popping out from beneath the messy bun in the back. Lizzy had never seen her dressed so casually out in public, and if it was possible, she looked even sexier than when she was in her heels and expensive dresses.

Lizzy focused on controlling her breathing and making words as Darcy stood stoically by the door. "I...I didn't know you'd be here," Lizzy stammered, pausing her music.

"Ditto," Darcy said, shifting her weight.

They stood in awkward silence for a moment, both staring, both seemingly not sure what to say to ease the tension.

"This doesn't have to be weird, you know," Lizzy said.

Darcy shrugged. "Who said it was weird?"

Lizzy crossed her arms. "Yeah, you're right. No tension here *whatsoever.*"

With a low laugh, Darcy's shoulders visibly relaxed. "Okay, fine. It's awkward, and you're right. It doesn't need to be. We're both here. Let's work on this trial. What are you doing now?"

"Finishing up the binders." Lizzy motioned to the papers that were spread everywhere. "Just didn't feel like being home today, so I came here."

Darcy nodded, looking down. "Neither did I." She walked to her desk and set the coffee down before sliding off her coat and tossing it onto one of the empty chairs. She picked up the cup and took a deep sip before handing it to Lizzy."Want some?"

She nodded and took it. "You sure you want to share? I mean, I may have cooties or something."

"If you do have any communicable disease, I'm pretty sure I already got it when you sat on my face last week."

Lizzy choked and covered her mouth to keep the liquid from spewing all over the office.

Darcy laughed, taking back the cup. "Cat got your tongue, Ms. Taylor?" A flirtatious grin spread across her face, and Lizzy wiped her mouth.

"No, but my neck is pretty sore from all this emotional whiplash."

Darcy frowned and looked down. "I'm sorry about that."

Lizzy shrugged. "It is what it is, Darce. People can't know about us, or we'd get fired. I get it." *But I hate it.*

"It's not that…it's not that simple," Darcy said, her voice shaking.

"Then what is it?" Lizzy crossed her arms.

Darcy bit her lip. She looked like there was something she wanted to say. Something serious. Lizzy wished she could grab her and pull whatever it was she wasn't saying out of her, but all she could do was be patient and wait.

"Why don't we get some work done for now, okay?"

Lizzy's heart sank. Darcy sat on the floor across from her and started punching holes in the papers. This type of work was beneath her. She hadn't come in to the office on a Sunday morning to put holes in pieces of paper. She'd come in to finish a motion in limine or work on the jury instructions, if anything. But still, she had chosen to sit with Lizzy and do this menial work. The gesture wasn't lost on her, and she smiled softly as they worked in silence.

Eventually, the binders were finished, and they moved to Darcy's desk to go over the trial schedule for the next week. Jury selection started Tuesday. It was unlikely they would get a jury on the first day, so testimony likely wouldn't start until Thursday, possibly even Friday.

Since Cohen Construction had brought the lawsuit, they'd get to put on witnesses first and present their evidence for why the house should be torn down. So far, they had a very expensive economist who would likely testify about the economic boom the new apartment complex would provide, an environmentalist who would testify about carbon emissions being offset somewhere in Brazil, and the owner of the company, who would testify about the number of people he would be employing both during construction and after the complex was built.

Then it was Darcy and Lizzy's turn to call witnesses. The historian they'd met at the Meadows, Molly, would talk about the author and the number of visitors each year and the positive economic impact the house had on the local community. An architect would testify about the historical significance of the house from a structural standpoint, as it was one of the first Victorian homes in the area. Finally, a social studies professor at Harvard would testify about the relevance of the author in modern society.

Lizzy was nervous. They had worked so hard and invested so much in this trial. What if it was all for nothing? What if the promise she'd made to Molly wouldn't happen? What if no one ever learned about Margaret Liventhrop and Judith Leven's true relationship? Or worse, what if no one even cared? She wondered if Darcy was nervous too, but if she was, she wasn't showing it.

After they walked through the complete schedule for the next two weeks and the final things that needed to be done tomorrow, Darcy reached across the glass desk and grabbed Lizzy's hand. Lizzy's heart sped up at the contact, and she bit her lip.

"I'm glad you'll be with me, Elizabeth," Darcy said, her eyes warm and soft.

"Me too, Darce," Lizzy said smiling back across the desk. "We're gonna win this thing."

"Hell, yeah, we are."

They worked in silence for most of the day before ordering Chinese food. Lizzy loved seeing Darcy like this: hair back, baseball hat, leggings, and hoodie, just eating Chinese out of boxes and working in her massive corner office that overlooked all of Manhattan.

"Who is this, anyway?" Darcy asked as Lizzy sang under her breath.

"This?" Lizzy held up her phone. "Don't tell me you've never heard of Fletcher."

Darcy pursed her lips. "Can't say it rings a bell. Is it a band?"

Lizzy's mouth dropped in shock. "Oh, come on! She's, like, lesbian royalty. She's super talented, super hot, and her entire album is basically a big 'fuck you' to her ex. God, Darce, are you even gay?"

Darcy let out a low laugh and shook her head. "I don't know, maybe I should have sex with a man to find out?"

"How about you just *not* do that? Ever. Thanks."

Darcy threw her head back and laughed as Lizzy writhed inwardly at the mental image.

"I have a better idea," Lizzy continued. "How about we conduct our own little experiment? Say…at your place tonight?"

A slow smile spread across Darcy's face. "While that sounds like a pretty fun experiment, the night before a trial probably isn't the best time to conduct it, wouldn't you agree?"

Lizzy crossed her legs. "*Technically*, our trial doesn't start until Tuesday. Tomorrow is just an ordinary day at the office."

Darcy bit her lip and sat back. "You present a compelling argument." She tapped the pen on her lower lip, and Lizzy stared anxiously, awaiting her decision. "Still, I don't think it's wise."

Lizzy's shoulders deflated, but her confidence didn't wane. She stood and walked around the other side. Darcy turned and uncrossed her legs. Lizzy sat on her lap and wrapped her arms around her neck. She cupped Darcy's face and looked into her eyes, tilted her baseball cap off her head, and kissed her lips, slowly and softly, savoring each sweet second of the contact. Darcy wrapped her arms around Lizzy's waist, leaning up into the kiss more and more.

Sooner than she would have liked, Lizzy pulled away and rested her forehead against Darcy's. "I've wanted to do that since I got out of your car last week."

Darcy smiled, kissing the soft spot on Lizzy's neck that made her wild. "So why didn't you?" she whispered between kisses.

"Because someone was playing ice queen with me again. Seriously, I'm gonna need a neck brace from all this back and forth pretty soon."

Darcy stopped kissing her and frowned. "I know I haven't been fair to you. I know this entire situation has been messed up from the start. And I'm sorry for that, Elizabeth."

Lizzy sat back slightly. She could tell that Darcy was being serious right now. She wasn't flirting or playing or making a joke. She really meant what she'd just said. This was it. The vulnerability and honesty Lizzy had been looking for earlier in the day. "It's not your fault," she said gently. "You're being cautious. I get it. The whole Ana thing didn't help, I know."

Darcy brushed a strand of Lizzy's hair behind her ear and stroked her cheek. "It's not just the Ana thing. I mean, yes, that stung. I won't deny it. But even before then, I wasn't being fair to you. I've never been fair to you. You deserve someone who's ready to dive headfirst into love with you. Someone who will send your favorite flowers to the office just because, or hell, someone who even knows what your favorite flower is. You deserve someone who has enough mental headspace to take you on nice dates. You deserve so much more than I'm giving you."

"Hey, hey," Lizzy said, stroking her cheeks with both hands. "Where is this coming from? No one's rushing you here, okay? Darce, you can take all the time you need. I'm not going anywhere."

"But you *should*. You *should* go somewhere. You *should* be dating Ana or someone closer to your own age. You *should* be going to happy hours and flirting with cute single women. You *should* be coming to work late and hungover from getting laid the night before. You *should* be doing all of these things, and you're not because of me. Because of this." She shifted to move, and Lizzy stood.

"Darce, what's gotten into you?" She had never seen her so rattled. If anything, Darcy was a picture of poise, even in the most chaotic or stressul of moments. It worried Lizzy to see her this way.

"Nothing. I'm sorry, I just…I don't think I'm the best person for you to be with. Last week was amazing. Every time with you has been amazing, but where is this even going? I'm your boss. We can never be together out in the open. Even if I do have blackmail on my male cohorts, they keep those things secret. And you…you deserve more than to be my secret."

Lizzy took a step and grabbed Darcy's hands. "Hey, take a step back, okay? You're stressed. I'm stressed. We have a lot on our plate right now with this trial. For now, why don't we focus on that and only that? We, whatever we are or may one day be, we can figure all of that out after we win this thing, okay?"

Darcy let out a long breath and stroked the back of Lizzy's hands. "You're right. Shit. How are you so wise for someone so—"

"If you make one more comment about my age, so help me," Lizzy said, kissing her firmly on the lips. "I'm a grown-ass woman, Darce. It's time you start seeing me as one."

She smiled and nodded. "Yes ma'am," she said, leaning down and kissing her.

"Oh, and by the way?" Lizzy added between kisses. "My favorite flowers are red roses."

"Duly noted."

CHAPTER THIRTY-EIGHT

B reak a leg tomorrow, Darcy," Paul said from across the large conference room table.

"Thanks, Paul." She wasn't sure if he was actually wishing her luck or literally wishing she'd go break a leg. It was always hard to tell with him.

"Yeah, good luck," Richard said, leaning back, propping his round hands on his protruding stomach. "Remember our deal."

She rolled her eyes. "Oh, please, Dick. If losing trials was a fireable offense, you'd have been sacked ten years ago. When was the last time you brought home a verdict?"

He adjusted nervously in his seat and shifted his beady eyes around the room. The rest of the men went silent.

"Right, well, that about does it for the day. Let's adjourn," Mark said, standing and shutting his folder.

Darcy packed her bag quickly and made a beeline for the exit. God, she hated these weekly partner meetings. She'd always loathed them, but lately, they were becoming almost unbearable. She couldn't remember a time when she had been more miserable in her career.

Walking back to her corner office, she sighed. She tried to remember why it was she'd become a lawyer all those years ago. Her dad. The money. It was all so logical back then. But now, here she was at the age of thirty-eight. All of her life goals and dreams were accomplished. And she was so unhappy, she could spit. Sure, there were other law firms, but at the end of the day it wasn't Byron & Browning she was outgrowing. It was the entire field of law.

This trial was the only thing that brought her any joy in her job right now, and it wasn't just because she was working on it with Elizabeth. She cared about this case. She cared about saving this house, about Molly, about Margaret Liventhrop. Hell, she even cared about Judith Levens, and she knew nothing about the woman other than the fact that she might have been gay a hundred years ago.

"All set for tomorrow?" Patty asked, following Darcy into her office.

She dropped the papers on her desk and sighed. "Believe so."

Patty tilted her head. "Are you nervous or something?"

Please, she didn't get nervous for trials anymore. She barely got nervous about anything. Except for having an honest conversation about her feelings for Elizabeth. That scared the shit out of her. Trial? No problem.

"Patty, do you ever wonder…I mean, if you had to go back and do something different, something big, something like your career, would you do it?"

Patty shifted her weight. "You mean, if I had to go back and not have this dream job?" She motioned around the room dramatically and chuckled. "Hell, yeah, I'd do it differently. Don't get me wrong, you've helped me so much in this place, and I appreciate it. Working for you is better than working for anyone else. But I wouldn't exactly call this a dream job."

Darcy nodded and smiled. "That's understandable."

Patty sat and crossed her legs. "Why do you ask? You thinking about not being a lawyer anymore?"

Darcy shrugged. "I don't know. It's just, lately, I've been wondering why I'm doing it, you know? I mean, whose life am I even impacting here? Aside from this trial, what difference does my work actually make?"

Patty nodded in thought. "Well, my mama always told me to shoot for the moon. Even if you miss, you'll land among the stars."

Darcy bit her cheek. "Yeah, well, what about the people who actually do hit the moon, but they're disappointed with what it's like when they get there?"

"Then get back on the rocket ship. Go to Mars, Venus, and hell, come back and visit Earth for a while. You're not stuck anywhere until you stop trying, honey." She reached across the desk and patted Darcy's hands a few times. "You deserve happiness, Darcy Hammond. Not just inside the office, either."

Darcy rolled her neck. "What do you mean?"

"I mean, I've known you your entire career. I've watched you as an eager associate, as a budding of counsel, and now as a kick-ass partner. I've seen you win arguments, trials, and motions. I was with you when you moved into this big fancy office. And even after all of those amazing achievements, I've never seen you as happy as you have been since a certain blonde entered your life."

Darcy's eyes shot up.

"Oh, relax, relax. No one else knows or suspects anything. My point is, be happy, Darcy. For once in your life, just let yourself be happy. Even if it means getting back on the rocket ship and leaving the moon in the rearview mirror. There are plenty of planets still left to explore."

Darcy bit her thumbnail. Patty was right. She knew she was right.

Patty stood slowly and winked. "I know you'll do what's right for you," she said turning and leaving the office.

Darcy nodded to herself. She knew what she needed to do. She knew the steps she had to take. But she'd been a resident on the moon for a long time now. She had a beautiful castle on the moon. It was her home, her dream. She wasn't sure if she was ready to explore deep space just yet.

She shook her head and focused on her computer screen. She didn't have time to think of space travel right now. She had a trial tomorrow. An important trial. Maybe the most important trial of her life.

CHAPTER THIRTY-NINE

Lizzy pulled the collar of her new navy blue coat up high around her neck. It was a cold, early spring day in New York, and the wind whipping down the streets made a tunnel that smacked her across the face. She was glad she didn't have to worry about dragging the exhibits and binders downtown today. Darcy had requested one of the paralegals do that, along with someone from IT who would be setting up everything once they got their courtroom assignment.

As she ascended the granite steps to the beautiful courthouse, Lizzy fished her wallet out of her pocket and flashed her attorney ID badge to the security guard standing at the golden revolving door. She smiled broadly as she and Darcy walked past the line of potential jurors all lining the steps at 60 Centre Street in downtown Manhattan.

She had seen this building before. Heck, she and her mother had seen it once a week for most of her life on *Law & Order: SVU*. They used the front of the building for their photos and the little "dun dun" intro part. The indoor scenes were shot mostly at Surrogate's Court a few blocks away.

As they made their way into the building, she couldn't resist tossing her head back and staring up at the painted rotunda. "Wow," she whispered, soaking it all in.

She was here. She'd done it. She really was a freaking lawyer. Boy, would her mom be proud if she could see her right now. Strutting into this massive court building. Flashing her ID badge and walking past the mere mortals. Plus, the fancy new coat didn't hurt her confidence.

"Counselor," Darcy said loudly across the room. "Shall we?" She motioned toward the elevators, smiling.

Lizzy jogged across the circular room, her trusty black heels clacking loudly against the floor. "Sorry," she said, shoving into the tiny elevator.

"First time in court?" Darcy asked.

Lizzy nodded and exhaled slowly.

"Just breathe, Elizabeth," Darcy said, squeezing her hand. "And remember, nobody knows your case better than you do. Got it?"

"Got it."

The doors to the elevator opened, and Lizzy was met with a sea of buzzing. Dozens of lawyers were gathered outside a courtroom, swarming like bees around a hive. Case names were being shouted back and forth as large doors swung open and shut.

"*Jimenez!* Plainitff on the *Jimenez* case! Anybody?" a tall, gray-haired man hollered as he walked past. His tie was half-undone, and he had a coffee stain on his jacket.

Darcy cringed as she slid past. "Must be doing some conferences this morning. Here, we're this way."

"Is it always like this?" Lizzy asked, flabbergasted.

"Sure is," Darcy replied, pushing her way through the sea of lawyers. "Thrilling, isn't it?"

Lizzy looked back and forth. "I always imaged court being more *Law & Order* and less *Lord of the Flies*."

Darcy laughed, pushing open a door. "Well, I think jury selection will be more your speed."

She was right. When they entered the door for jury selection, it was like entering a different world. Only ten or so attorneys were seated in the large, dark courtroom. There was an American flag and the flag of the state of New York on either side of the judge's bench, which sat several feet off the ground. The room was illuminated only by the sunlight that came through the tall windows on the far side of the room, and it smelled like mildew from years of use. Darcy and Lizzy slid into a wooden bench and waited for the judge to enter. About five minutes later, she did, and everyone stood and didn't sit until the judge sat.

When she called their case name, Lizzy followed Darcy up to the table farthest away from the jury box. "Darcy Hammond with Byron & Browning for the defense, Your Honor. This is my colleague, Elizabeth Taylor, she'll be second chairing this trial with me."

Second chairing?

Lizzy had been told she would be *helping* Darcy, meaning setting up exhibits, running the PowerPoint, and flipping through deposition transcripts for impeachment opportunities. Not second chairing. Second chairing meant her name on the record. It meant sitting at counsel table right next to her. It meant she might even get to examine a witness. This was major.

"Welcome, Miss Taylor." The friendly-looking judge smiled at her. "Would you like to put your name in the record?"

She nodded and cleared her throat, leaning closer to the microphone. "Elizabeth Taylor with Byron & Browning." She looked over at Darcy, who tilted her head. "Oh, um, for the defense. Sorry, ma'am. I mean, Your Honor!" Lizzy stepped back and wrung her hands. Her first official statement in court as a lawyer.

Holy shit.

The judge smiled and looked at a piece of paper. "You'll be with Judge Guacommo. He's in Part 33, second floor. Head down to jury selection. If you need any decisions on rulings, there will be a clerk in selection with you. Let him know, and Judge Guacommo will preside over arguments. Understood?"

Darcy nodded, and the tall, dark-haired man standing at the other table nodded as well.

"Hey, Seamus," Darcy said to him as they exited the courtroom.

"Good to see you again, Darcy. I was hoping they'd keep you on this one."

"They couldn't pry it from my cold dead fingers." She winked.

He laughed. "I'm glad to see that firm hasn't sucked your spirit out yet. You know, if you're ever looking to switch it up, I'd be glad to put in a good word."

She tossed her head back. "Oh, please, Seamus. You and I both know they could never afford me."

He bobbed his head, still laughing, and they all squished onto the elevator together.

"Seamus, this is Elizabeth. She's second chairing this trial with me. Seamus Finnegan, Elizabeth Taylor."

She stuck out her hand. "Elizabeth Taylor," he said. "And here I thought a name like Seamus Finnegan was bad. I think you've got me beat!" He laughed in a friendly way as he shook her hand.

"Oh, I don't know about that one," she quipped back, sending a look of pride along Darcy's poised face.

"Better watch out for this one, Seamus," Darcy said, shooting Lizzy a sideways glance. "She's got claws."

He laughed, seemingly unaware of the sexual undertone. "Well, this is going to be a fun trial. I can't wait, truly. I'm gonna use the little boys' room, but I'll see you both inside." He turned left as they exited the elevator away from them.

Darcy walked in the opposite direction toward a large brown door with a sign that read Part 33. "Seamus is a nice guy," she said, throwing open the door and allowing Lizzy to walk through. "But he's a schmoozer. Juries eat him up, so keep your guard up and be ready to kick me if there's an objection you think I should make."

Lizzy bit her lip, following Darcy inside. The courtroom looked similar to the one upstairs but with more light and about half the size of the gallery. She and Darcy were currently the only ones in the room.

"Hey, wait a minute," Lizzy said, grabbing Darcy's arm. "What was that up there?"

Darcy looked confused. "What do you mean?"

"Second chairing? You never…I mean, I thought I was just…"

Darcy sighed. "You're rambling."

Lizzy exhaled. "You never told me I was going to be your second chair. I thought I was just helping with technology and stuff like that."

Darcy shrugged. "Well, if I'd told you, you'd have been up worried for the last three weeks instead of preparing and focusing. Now you know. You're gonna be fine." She turned and swung the little wooden door that separated the gallery from the well of the courtroom, the area where the lawyer's tables, the jury box, and the judge's bench all were.

"Darcy," Lizzy said, still frozen. "I'm scared."

Darcy set her bag at the table farthest from the jury, the one designated for defense attorneys, and walked back. She remained in the well of the courtroom and rested her hand on the wooden wall separating them. "Do you know why you took a bar exam, Elizabeth?"

That caught Lizzy off guard. She had never thought about it before. "Because you have to pass it to become a lawyer?"

"That's right. And do you know where the term 'bar' comes from?"

Lizzy shook her head.

Darcy slid her hand along the wooden wall. "This," she said, patting it with her long fingers. "This is the bar. This is what separates us from them." She motioned toward the empty seats in the gallery. "You see this little wooden door? They don't get to come past here. Not without special permission. Being a lawyer means you have the right to swing open this door. To walk through it. To stand in this well. To argue before this jury. You have that right, Elizabeth. You have that honor, that privilege." She stepped back and crossed her arms. "You told me to start seeing you like the grown woman you are. Well, it's time for you to start seeing yourself as the lawyer you are. Are you ready?"

Lizzy clenched her fists. She stared at the short wooden door. Without hesitation, she took four large strides, put her hand on the door, and shoved it open, passing through the bar. She exhaled deeply, releasing the tension in her hands. "Fuck, yeah, I'm ready."

CHAPTER FORTY

Darcy tossed back the bourbon and set the glass on the bar. What a week and a half it had been. Trials always took it out of her, and she knew this one would be no different, but there was something about this trial in particular that seemed to be completely draining her.

They'd finally picked a jury by last Thursday morning, and rather than give them the afternoon off like they'd asked, Judge Guacommo had instructed them to do their openings that afternoon. She and Seamus were both uneasy about the idea, but when the judge spoke, the lawyers obeyed. They wrapped up that day at close to five. On Friday, Seamus had put his first two witnesses on, and Darcy had crossed them both.

The construction company's economist wasn't too tough to crack. He showed no emotion whatsoever, and she could tell the jury hated him right away. The CEO of Concord Construction was up next, and he was, unfortunately, very likable. She had spent most of the day going back and forth with him on the witness stand, and they had to break for the weekend before she could finish the cross.

She'd canceled therapy Friday because she was way too stressed to talk about her feelings. Plus, she hadn't exactly finished her emotional homework assignment yet, and she wanted to avoid further inquiry.

By Wednesday, the plaintiff had wrapped up all of their witnesses and rested their case. The judge had mercy on them and let them go home at three thirty, no doubt seeing the fatigue in everyone's eyes.

And so here she sat on Wednesday night at the Ainsworth, nursing her second drink, trying to get herself ready for tomorrow's testimony. She didn't usually drink in the middle of the week, but when on trial, it was hard to know what time of day it was, let alone what day of the week it was.

"Hey, you," Elizabeth said softly as she slid into the empty seat next to her. She had stacks of transcripts under her arms that she slammed on the bar.

Darcy flinched slightly. "Hey." She smiled and tilted her head to the bartender, who came over to take Elizabeth's order.

"I'll have what she's having," Elizabeth said, motioning, but Darcy shook her head. "*Or* I'll just have a margarita."

Darcy nodded and took another deep swig of bourbon.

"It's funny, you know, us being here like this," Elizabeth said, scooting closer. "The last time we were here, I was sitting way down there, and I saw you come in. My heart nearly dropped, and I just *had* to come over here to talk to you."

"If I recall correctly, Ana was all over you, and you used that horrible Emily Dickinson quote to try to win me over." Darcy laughed. "I also recall you asking me to come home with you after only a few seconds."

Elizabeth blushed. "I mean, can you blame me? Have you *seen* you?"

Darcy shook her head and winked. "Yeah, well. I guess the pickup line wasn't so bad after all."

"Why did you come here that night, anyway? From what I heard, you weren't much of a social joiner."

"I came here to see you, idiot."

Elizabeth swatted playfully at her arm. "Nuh-uh, no way. I'm not buying it."

"Believe whatever you want, but I thought you were hot the second I saw you in the conference room. I asked Patty where the happy hour was, and I came here that night hoping to see you. Thought it might help me get over my little crush if I saw you flirting with people your own age."

"Did it work?"

"No," Darcy said. "Just made me want you that much more."

The bartender slid Elizabeth's margarita toward her, breaking her eye lock with Darcy as she took a sip.

"So," Darcy said, letting out a long sigh. "We have Molly on for testimony tomorrow, right?"

Lizzy nodded, turning her attention to the stack of binders and transcripts. "Mm-hmm, first thing tomorrow. She's our strongest witness, in my opinion. I mean, you remember how she captivated us when we were at the house, right? The woman is a font of knowledge, and I just know if she can make the jury feel what I felt that day, we've got this thing in the bag."

"Sounds like you feel very passionately about this?"

"Duh."

Darcy clinked their glasses. "Good." She took a sip. "Because I want you doing her direct examination tomorrow."

"What? No, that...no. You're joking. I can't. What? I—"

"You're rambling again," Darcy said gently.

"I am *not* ready for this. I haven't even been admitted for a year. I barely know the rules of evidence."

Darcy shifted topics. "Do you know why I considered going home with you that first night?"

Elizabeth stammered,"N...no?"

Darcy shook her head. "Because in thirty-eight years, I had never met anyone with that level of confidence. I mean, you saw me from across the room, you beelined for me, and you propositioned me, knowing I was your boss. Knowing that I could report you and have you fired for even making the suggestion. That boldness, that assertiveness. It's captivating, Elizabeth. It's palpable."

She blushed.

"You can captivate that jury tomorrow. Make them feel what you feel about this case. Lead Molly down the path you want, and she'll follow you. And so will the jury."

"But, Darcy, I—"

"I'd never ask you to do something you couldn't do. Think about it. If tomorrow morning comes and you really don't think you can do it, I'll step in. But remember, nobody knows your case like you do. Not even me."

Elizabeth took three big pulls on her drink, nearly emptying the glass.

Darcy checked her watch. "We better get going soon. It's late."

Elizabeth rolled her eyes. "Yeah, yeah, I've heard that one a few times before."

CHAPTER FORTY-ONE

L izzy's leg bounced ferociously under the counsel table.
  Darcy rested a hand on her bouncing knee, and instantly, it soothed her. Darcy leaned over and whispered, "Are you ready?"

Lizzy took a deep gulp and swallowed hard. She looked over her shoulder into the gallery. Molly from the Meadows was sitting in the first row. She waved innocently at Lizzy as they made eye contact, and Lizzy nodded and smiled back. "I'm ready."

"All rise," the court officer yelled, and Judge Guacommo entered the room.

"Counsel, are we ready to continue with testimony this morning?"

Darcy nudged Lizzy under the table, and she shot up. "We are, Your Honor." Her voice cracked at the end, but she cleared her throat and stood firm, crossing her hands behind her back.

"We are," Seamus said from the other table, a smooth smile on his face.

"Very well, you may bring in the jury."

Lizzy sat and clenched her fist, shaking it out and taking deep breaths. Her heart was beating faster than she could ever remember it beating, and she felt like she might pass out or faint or both. Darcy grabbed her hand.

"Elizabeth," she said, looking her firmly in the eyes. "You've got this." Her eyes were piercing but somehow warm, and Lizzy felt her heart rate even.

"All rise," the court officer shouted again, and everyone, even the judge, stood as the jury filed in one by one.

"You may call your next witness, Ms. Taylor." Judge Guacommo smiled at her.

"Defendant calls Molly Rosenburg, Your Honor."

Molly stood from the front row, and the judge motioned for her to enter the well. Her wide hips swayed as she walked across the room while wringing her hands. Her cheeks were red, likely from nerves, and she was wearing a simple gray pantsuit with a black silk scarf tied loosely around her neck. She looked presentable but not intimidating, just as Darcy had instructed her last week.

Molly raised her right hand as she was sworn in by the court officer, and Lizzy collected her notes, hands shaking. "Ms. Rosenburg, please tell the jury a little about yourself," she said, turning to the jury as she spoke, just like she'd learned in law school and just like she'd watched Darcy do all last week.

"I'm the historian at the Meadows, the home of Margaret Liventhrop."

Lizzy cleared her throat. "And what are your job duties, generally speaking?"

Molly shifted in her seat. "Well, I work at the museum five days a week. I greet guests, I give tours, but I also oversee research grants, internships, and other educational programs that go on at the property."

Lizzy bit her lip. She needed her to mention her recent historical research into the author. "And that work also entails conducting historical research, correct?"

"Objection." Seamus stood. "Leading."

Shit. She knew she should have phrased it differently. She tried not to let his objection rattle her, and she looked back to Darcy, who gave her a reassuring head nod.

"Rephrase, Ms. Taylor," the judge said casually.

Come on, Taylor, keep it together. "What, if anything else, does your work as a historian entail?" she said, shooting Seamus a smile.

Several members of the jury chuckled softly.

Catching on, Molly quickly took the answer in stride. "I conduct historical research about Miss Liventhrop."

"Would those studies include learning about Miss Liventhrop's social and personal life?"

Molly nodded. "Yes, most certainly. In fact, we've made some major developments in that area in recent years."

Lizzy breathed a sigh of relief, keeping her shoulders back, trying to stand as tall as Darcy had all last week as she seemed to float around the room. "What developments are you referring to?"

Molly smiled wide. "Well, we've recently learned that Miss

Liventhrop may have had a romantic relationship with a woman by the name of Judith Levens."

"Objection, Your Honor, relevance? What difference does it make if the author had a girlfriend?"

Judge Guacommo raised his eyebrows, and the jury shifted uncomfortably.

"Permission to approach?" Lizzy felt her voice catch slightly in the back of her throat as she choked out the words.

The judge sighed and waved them up to the bench. Darcy remained seated.

"Your Honor, all respect to Mr. Finnegan, but this is our defense to present. We believe Miss Liventhrop's sexuality is very relevant to the defense of this lawsuit and the preservation of the house as a whole."

The judge sighed heavily, shaking his head. "I'll allow it. Mr. Finnegan, relax. You'll have your turn to cross this witness."

Molly went on to explain to the jury all about her recent discoveries regarding the relationship between Judith and Margaret. She told the story almost as if she was standing in the house itself. Several members of the jury nodded and murmured under their breath, leaning forward in their chairs.

It was working.

"Tell me, Ms. Rosenburg, if one were to, say, go visit the Meadows, is this the type of thing they could expect to learn about?"

Molly shook her head. "Oh, we're not quite there yet, but we're making incredible strides. In fact, this coming June, we have an entire event planned to celebrate Pride Month at the Meadows. We can't wait to share this new knowledge with the public and really open the eyes of so many of her fans who only know Margaret by the words she put on paper."

Lizzy frowned, turning to the jury. "I suppose it would be hard to host a Pride event there if Mr. Finnegan's client demolishes the house in May, wouldn't it?"

"Objection!"

"Withdrawn." Lizzy looked over at Darcy, who gave her an approving nod.

When Lizzy finished her questions, which took up most of the morning, Seamus cross-examined her, but she held her ground even better than Lizzy could have expected. For the duration of the afternoon, she sat, nodded, and smiled at the jury, answering every question with a "yes, sir" or an "I believe you are mistaken."

Darcy scribbled notes to Lizzy on Post-its and kicked her under the table when she wanted her to stand and object. Unfortunately, one time, when Darcy was just crossing her leg and bumped Lizzy's, sending Lizzy leaping out of her seat and shouting, "Objection!" with no grounds to state. She looked to Darcy for help, but Darcy stared blankly back at her.

"Uh, relevance?" she said, and the judge, not surprisingly, over-ruled it.

Aside from that brief lapse, the afternoon cross-examination went well. For every snarky leading comment or question Seamus presented her, Molly came back with a polite, poised response. In the end, he ended up looking like a bigot who was beating up a cute little librarian. It went exactly as Lizzy had hoped.

When the judge told Molly she could return to her seat and released them for the day, Lizzy let out a deep sigh of relief. She breathed a double sigh when the judge said they'd be starting after lunch tomorrow because he had to hear motions in the morning.

As they rose for the jury to leave, Lizzy pinched her arm to remind herself that this was all real. This was happening. She'd done it. She'd gone to trial after being admitted for less than six months—heck, she'd barely been admitted three months—and she'd just directed her first witness. There was no way this was real. Things like this didn't happen to people like her. Things like this happened to people like Micah or Cho or even Jackson, but not her. She wasn't born into the same level of privilege that they were. She wasn't a graduate of some Ivy League school. She couldn't even make summa cum laude, for heaven's sake. None of her friends from law school would believe her. What would her mom say?

I bet she'll be proud of me now. Lizzy watched the jurors file out of the courtroom.

Seamus came over to their table after the judge left. "Good job today, counselor," he said sincerely, shaking her hand.

It was nice to see that not all attorneys in New York were scum-bags like the ones back at Byron & Browning. Some people could be decent human beings and just represent scumbags like Cohen Construction.

She and Darcy talked to Molly briefly in the hallway and thanked her for being such an amazing witness. "You did great," Darcy said in a matter-of-fact tone.

Molly gave Lizzy a hug. "Thank you for doing all of this." She looked at Darcy and then at Lizzy again. "It's funny, you know. When I first met you two at the house a few weeks ago and I watched how you interacted, I sensed something special about you both. And then, when I was reading to prepare myself for my testimony today, it hit me."

Lizzy tilted her head. "What's that?"

Molly hesitated a moment. "You remind me a bit of Judith and Margaret."

Darcy's shoulders tightened at the comparison, and Lizzy let out a low chuckle.

"I know it sounds crazy, but it's just…Margaret was always so set in her ways. She was so determined to be a successful author. She holed herself up in that big beautiful home her father built for her and shut out the world. And then one day, here comes Judith. Well, she was anything but reserved. She was, by all accounts, a free spirit. And we can see the shift in Margaret the longer she lived with Judith. She softened her edges. And, well, I see such a similar dynamic between you. It's really something special and powerful, if I do say so myself."

Darcy looked down and cleared her throat, shifting back and forth on her pointy-toed heels. Lizzy blushed and bit her lip.

"I've made you uncomfortable. Oh, ignore me. Too much time with books, not enough time with people, you know how that goes. Well, thank you both so much for doing this. I know it means a lot to all of us at the Meadows, and I know it would mean a heck of a lot to Margaret Liventhrop."

Darcy's eyes shot up, and a look of pride spread across her face. "Thank you, Molly. That means more to me than you know," she said, shaking Molly's hand.

Molly made her way down the hall, her heavy thighs making her pant legs swish as she walked.

"So," Lizzy said nervously. "What did you think? About the testimony, not her Judith-Margaret comparison. I already know you'll overanalyze that one to its death later."

Darcy took half a step toward her and glanced down the long hall, no doubt to ensure they were alone, before leaning over and kissing her on the lips. "I think you better come over to my place tonight," she whispered.

CHAPTER FORTY-TWO

Darcy poured herself a second glass of wine and handed Elizabeth another beer. She'd told herself they would remain platonic throughout this trial, but going to trial with someone was a bit like going to boot camp with them. It was impossible not to form some kind of trauma bond, and that, compounded with their already chemical connection, was too much for Darcy to ignore.

She had spent more time with Elizabeth preparing for this trial than she had with any other human in a very long time. And what she'd found out was that the more time she spent with her, the more she fell for her.

And then there was today. As if Darcy wasn't already teetering on being unstable around Elizabeth, sitting there, watching her lead a direct examination in front of a jury had sent Darcy over the edge. The way she'd handled Seamus's objections, the way she'd spoken to the judge, the passion she'd displayed when Molly spoke. It was all way too sexy, but more than that, it was just really fucking endearing.

For the first time since she'd known Elizabeth, Darcy didn't want to rip her clothes off the second she got the chance. Instead, she poured herself a glass of wine and opened a beer. Instead of the wild, amazing sex Elizabeth was no doubt expecting, they'd spent the last several hours eating bread and cheese from Darcy's fridge and talking.

"Elizabeth, you were so amazing today," Darcy said. "You should be so proud of yourself. Most of counsels I know wouldn't be able to handle a direct that well. You were poised and confident, and the jury loved you."

Elizabeth blushed. "Thanks, Darce. I couldn't have done it without you."

Darcy shrugged. "True."

Elizabeth swatted at her and rolled her eyes. "I wonder what my mom's gonna say."

"Have you told her yet?"

"No. I mean, I told her I was on a big trial, but not that I was doing any of the questioning. I don't know, most times, I think she just likes getting to tell people that her daughter is a lawyer at a big firm in New York. Doesn't seem like she actually cares about what I do or if I enjoy doing it, you know?"

Darcy nodded. "It means a lot to you, her approval."

"I wish it didn't. I wish I could be one of those people who just says, 'fuck you, world,' and lives in a van or something crazy like that. But the truth is, I do care. I care a lot. I just want her to be proud of me for who I am. Not who she's always *wanted* me to be."

Darcy swirled the wine, contemplating what to say. She and Elizabeth had talked briefly about her family on the way back from Mohonk. She knew there was history there. But this was the first time they were getting into the weeds about what the issue really was. And doing something to please others was an area Darcy was all too familiar with. "Well, I'm sure she's going to be thrilled, and even if she's not, ignore her. Because what you did today made a difference. Did you see Molly's face? Did you see how much all your hard work meant to her?"

Lizzy nodded, smiling. "Yeah, it felt really good."

"Good," Darcy said firmly. "Hang on to that feeling, Elizabeth. This is a hard career, and we don't get many feelings of validation or moral pats on the back. Today was a victory, no matter how this trial turns out. Enjoy it."

Elizabeth took a deep swig of beer. "Okay, but did you see the look on the judge's face when I jumped up with that random objection?" She laughed between sips.

"Darling, we all saw that moment." Darcy snickered, walking to the other side of the island and wrapping her arms around Elizabeth.

"Okay, well, it's not my fault someone's pointy stilettoes were jabbing me every five seconds. I think I'm going to have puncture wounds down here," she said, leaning back on the barstool and lifting her leg in the air.

Darcy grabbed hold of it. Elizabeth's leg was bare, and she was still wearing her pencil skirt from the trial. "Not that I'm complaining," Darcy said, nibbling Elizabeth's exposed calf before lowering her leg to the ground, "but what *are* you still doing in these clothes?"

"What are you suggesting, Ms. Hammond?"

"Actually," she said, slowly backing toward her bed, "I was thinking maybe tonight, you could wear something for me?" She bent, and Elizabeth's eyes followed when she leaned back on her stool as if to not lose the view.

Darcy stood, holding a pair of gray sweatpants and her green Stetson hoodie she had dug out from beneath her bed.

Elizabeth tossed her head back and laughed. "Oh wow, *super* kinky. I mean, that's some real NSFW material, Darce."

Darcy laughed, walking back toward the kitchen. "What? You were expecting me to whip out my strap-on?"

Lizzy blushed and stood, walking closer. "*Hoping* would be a more appropriate word," she said, sliding her arms around Darcy's neck.

"Hmm," Darcy said, kissing her gently. "That is an interesting idea." She placed another kiss on her neck. "But maybe next time." She paused. "If you're good."

Elizabeth made a pouting face and looked at the clothes still in Darcy's hand. "I can wear those for you, if you want. But I just figured since it's getting late, I'd probably be heading out soon."

"Or…" Darcy said, unable to hide the disappointment in her voice. She hesitated a moment. "You could stay here tonight."

Elizabeth tilted her head and took half a step back. "Isn't that kind of…a couple thing?"

Darcy exhaled slightly. "I don't know about all of that. All I know is…I want you to stay." She grabbed Elizabeth's hands and gently stroked the backs.

A smile spread across Elizabeth's face. "All right," she said, planting another kiss on Darcy's lips.

"Yeah?" Darcy replied, her voice elevating from excitement. "You'll stay?"

"Yes," she whispered, planting a gentle kiss on Darcy's cheek. "I'll stay."

CHAPTER FORTY-THREE

I s it always this nerve-racking?" Lizzy asked, pacing in the hallway. Darcy was seated on one of the wooden benches outside the courtroom, casually scrolling through her phone. "Waiting for a verdict? Yes. Yes, it is."

It had been nearly four hours since they'd sent the jury out. Lizzy was trying to remember if it was a good or a bad thing when a jury took a long time. But what was a long time? The trial had lasted two full weeks, so was four hours a lot of time? Or not enough? What if they didn't even render a verdict today? What if it took days? What if she spent days in this hallway pacing, only for a verdict that granted Cohen Construction the right to demolish the house and build their stupid apartment complex? What if it was all for nothing? What if she let Molly and Darcy and her mom and everyone else she'd ever known down?

Her mind spiraled as she marched back and forth, her heels clicking with every step on the old marble floor. "Well, what the fuck, Darce, you don't look stressed at all!"

Darcy kept her head tucked toward her phone. "First of all, when have you ever known me to look stressed, even when I am?"

Fair point.

"Second, it doesn't do any good to march up and down the hall like some protestor. You'll just give yourself blisters and a stomach ulcer. We did our best. It's in their hands now. Now, come and sit down." She motioned to the open seat next to her and continued to scroll.

Lizzy sighed dramatically and plopped next to her. "What are you looking at?" she asked, pulling out her own phone for a distraction.

Darcy shrugged. "Just…grad schools."

Lizzy's eyebrows shot up. "Grad schools? For what? Being king of the world at B and B not enough for you?"

Darcy cringed. "Queen," she corrected, "and I never said that. I'm just scrolling. You asked, I answered. The end."

"Is that something you think about? Going back to grad school?"

Darcy let out a low sigh. "All the time."

Lizzy thought back to the day they'd spent at the Meadows. She remembered the excitement on Darcy's face as they'd toured the old house, how alive she'd seemed listening to Molly go on about the history of the author, the house. Everything about it had drawn Darcy in that day.

"Then you should do it, Darce," Lizzy said.

She laughed. "Yeah, okay. I'll jump right on that." She closed her screen and dropped her phone in her purse. "As soon as we go win this trial." She stood and adjusted her bag on her shoulder.

Lizzy looked up at her, confused.

"Seamus just texted me," Darcy said. "The jury is back."

CHAPTER FORTY-FOUR

So," Danielle began, "it's been two weeks since we last saw each other. Tell me a bit about what's been going on with you."

Darcy adjusted in her seat. "Well, Elizabeth and I finished our trial together."

Danielle smiled. "How did it go?"

Darcy paused and looked down. "We won," she proclaimed, smiling and lifting her head. "I don't think we would have if not for Elizabeth. She led the most amazing direct exam of our client's historian. I mean, you should have seen her. She was poised and professional but relatable and sharp and quick. The jury loved her, and I mean, who could blame them, really?"

"You seem very happy, Darcy. That's wonderful. How are things going outside of work for you two?"

"Well," Darcy said, wringing her hands, "we're going out tomorrow night. On a date, actually."

Danielle nodded. "She asked you out again?"

"Actually, I asked her."

Danielle set down her pen and smiled wide. "I see. Well, this is quite a development. How are you feeling about all of this?"

Darcy wrung her hands again. "Nervous? Excited? Terrified? Anxious? All of the above?"

"Those are perfectly normal feelings to have when entering—or potentially entering—a new relationship. What makes you the most scared about it?"

Darcy reflected a moment, looking at the neon lights echoing loudly outside the small window. "I guess, that whole abandonment thing we talked about last time. Maybe that she'll get to know me and realize I'm not just this polished powerhouse like I am at the office.

And when she learns the true me, she won't like it. She'll find someone better, and I'll be left alone. Hurt."

More nods. "Do you think *she's* just the woman you see every day at the office?"

Darcy laughed. "God, no. She's an onion. She's a flirt and a nerd and a goofball and a big kid and a wise old sage, and she likes the most random music, and one minute, we're going back and forth in some banter about my favorite author, and the next, she's sweeping me off my feet or throwing snowballs at me. She's got so many layers, I can't begin to unravel them all."

"Exactly," Danielle said. "No person is just one person at the end of the day. We all have layers. We all take twists and turns, and we are all walking contradictions in one way or another. But finding someone who accepts all those layers and who wants to know those layers is what matters."

Now it was Darcy's turn to nod.

"Do you like all those things you just described about Elizabeth?"

Darcy smiled wide. "I love all those things."

"Good. And I bet odds are, she feels the same about you. But you'll never know unless you're willing to put yourself out there. And it sounds like this first date is a great place to start. I'm proud of you, Darcy."

"Thanks, Doc."

"I'm not a doctor, but you're welcome." Danielle smiled warmly. "Oh, where are you going on your date?"

"Oh, it's somewhere pretty special, don't you worry."

CHAPTER FORTY-FIVE

Lizzy flipped her hair from one side to the other. She'd spent the last half hour curling it, but now no matter what she did to it, it just didn't look as good as she wanted. She sighed, giving up, and walked across the small living room to grab her shoes. After tearing apart half her wardrobe, she'd finally landed on a pair of black oxfords with black jeans and a new, loose-fitting double-breasted gray blazer she'd bought on sale. Her new navy coat didn't match, so she'd been forced to wear her black peacoat, but luckily, she had sewn some new buttons onto it so it didn't look quite as bad as it once did.

She jumped when she heard the downstairs buzzer and raced to the door, her smooth shoes sliding on the hardwood floor.

"*Damn,*" Amina said as Lizzy pressed the button, opening the downstairs door. "Someone has a hot date."

Lizzy blushed. "Actually, yeah, I do."

Amina's jaw dropped. "Oh my God, is she coming up here? Do I get to meet her?"

"Oh God, please, no. No, go hide or cook or jump in a bath or something!" Lizzy motioned frantically toward Amina, who just laughed.

"Easy, killer, why so nervous?"

Lizzy ran her fingers through her hair. "I don't know, I just, I really like her, and I need to not mess this up."

"Mess it up?" Amina said, crossing her arms. "Woman, I know we haven't been BFFs forever, but I can tell you right now, you're a catch. Anyone who doesn't see that is an idiot. Don't be nervous." She flipped her hand toward the door. "*She* should be nervous."

Lizzy smiled and gave her a hug. She'd needed those little words of encouragement more than she'd realized. Winning their trial had shot her confidence through the roof as far as work went, but it also meant she and Darcy wouldn't be spending nearly as much time together. What if Darcy lost interest?

She had been thrilled when Darcy had asked her out on an actual date, and she'd spent the entire day shopping to find the perfect outfit, difficult considering Darcy refused to tell her where they were going.

Every time Lizzy had asked, all Darcy would say was "Somewhere" or "Nowhere." Her stubbornness had continued to drive Lizzy wild in all the right ways. But what if this was just more of Darcy's emotional whiplash? It felt different, Darcy asking her out and all, but what if it was just more games? Lizzy wasn't sure she could do round three with all this.

Amina gave her a wink as she walked back into her room, and Lizzy jumped again when she heard the soft knock on the front door. She inhaled slowly and checked herself in the mirror one more time before casually walking down the long hall to open the heavy door.

"Wow," Lizzy said when she saw Darcy on the other side.

She was wearing men's charcoal gray dress pants that somehow still hung off her hips in a feminine way, and black oxfords that almost matched Lizzy's. It must have been true what they said about lesbians dressing alike after a while. She had a silky white collared shirt buttoned all the way up beneath a loose-fitting black blazer. This was all underneath her long black coat, which was completely open, allowing Lizzy a full view of the splendor that was Darcy Hammond.

To top it all off, she was holding a bouquet of a dozen long-stemmed red roses.

"You remembered," Lizzy said, blushing and taking the flowers.

"I told you, just depends on what I need to remember." Darcy winked and leaned over, kissing her on the cheek.

The smell of her familiar perfume flooded Lizzy's nose and made her heart pitter-patter. "Well, uh, please, come in," she said, looking around the small apartment nervously. "I'm just gonna, uh, put these in some water, and then we can go."

Darcy entered the apartment, her commanding presence halving its already small size. Luckily, she wasn't wearing heels, or she might have hit her head on the ceiling, she stood so tall and proud. She walked around the small space slowly before peeking inside Lizzy's room. "Yours?" she asked, looking toward the kitchen.

Lizzy nodded. "Yup, that's, um, that's my room." Her hands shook as she filled the vase. She couldn't believe Darcy was actually there. In her apartment. Picking her up for a date.

"May I?" Darcy asked as she crossed the threshold, not stopping to wait for permission.

Lizzy cut off the water and set the roses on the round kitchen table before beelining back to her room. "It's not much. I mean, I haven't really lived here long, and I don't have much, and I mean—"

"You're rambling," Darcy said, lifting a photo from the small glass desk along the wall. "Is this your mom?"

"Yeah, that's us at my law school graduation. I mean, you could have guessed that part from the Thomas Moore hat, I'm sure, but, yeah, that's, um, that's us."

"She's beautiful. I can see the resemblance."

Lizzy picked at her fingernails. "Thanks."

Darcy walked around the rest of the room in a few strides, a smile on her flawless face. When she'd completed her observations, she stopped and looked at Lizzy.

"What?" Lizzy said, dropping her hands and smiling.

Darcy shrugged. "Nothing. I just like seeing where you live." She took a few steps closer, filling the remaining space, and leaned down, kissing her softly.

A slow warmth spread through Lizzy's heart, and she leaned up, wrapping her arms around Darcy's waist, drawing her in closer. Within seconds, she felt the desire to push Darcy onto her simple, full-size bed and rip her expensive clothes off, but Darcy pulled away, and the opportunity was sadly wasted.

"We better get going," Darcy whispered, planting another kiss on Lizzy's lips. "We don't want to be late."

Lizzy nodded, leaning up for one more kiss before grabbing her coat.

"Oh God, not that thing again," Darcy said.

"Excuse me, I sewed new buttons on just for you. Plus, I can't wear my navy one. It clashes with black."

"Well, we'll just have to get you a black one, won't we?" Darcy said, sauntering out of the apartment.

"You wanna start off our first date with a fight, Ms. Hammond?" Lizzy said playfully as they walked down the wide staircase.

"Only if it ends in me winning."

After they got downstairs, Lizzy pulled out her phone to call an

Uber but quickly saw it wouldn't be necessary. A black Mercedes was already waiting for them with a man standing beside it in a black suit.

"Welcome back, Ms. Hammond," he said as he opened the door.

"You ordered a car?" Lizzy said, sliding across the seat after Darcy.

Darcy shrugged. "Of course. It's a date, isn't it?"

Lizzy laughed. "I'm glad I didn't plan this. I'd have taken us for hot dogs and a walk around Central Park."

Darcy grabbed her hand. "You can plan the next one. I love a good street hot dog. I just wish New York had yellow mustard instead of that brown Dijon shit."

"Yes," Lizzy said, intertwining their fingers. "I asked a guy for just *regular* mustard one time, and he said, 'This is regular mustard,' and gave me that brown stuff. What is that?"

Darcy sighed. "New York can't get everything right, I suppose."

They spent the rest of the ride chatting while Lizzy looked at the buildings zooming past down the West Side Highway. To her right, she could see the path where she rode her bike pretty often now, and on her left was the sea of skyscrapers she now called her home.

She remembered the first time she'd ridden her bike down that path. The day she'd run into Darcy in the coffee shop in Brooklyn. She'd thought Darcy had hated her then. She never would have guessed that a little over a month later, they'd be on their way to a romantic dinner or movie or whatever the heck it was they were doing.

She shifted closer and smiled. She couldn't remember a time when she was this happy.

The car turned down Twenty-Fifth Street after a few more moments and pulled up to a building where a sign read, *Somewhere-Nowhere. The Renaissance Hotel.*

Remembering Darcy's responses about their plans for the evening, she rolled her eyes. "Clever girl," she said as Darcy pointed up at the sign.

She smiled victoriously and grabbed Lizzy's hand as they walked inside.

The elevator took them all the way to the top, where a two-story rooftop bar and restaurant awaited them. Lizzy was met with the sound of jazz echoing from a live band and couples swing dancing on the small floor in the center of the room. After they checked their coats, a woman showed them to their seats on the second floor by the window that looked over the dance floor.

From their seat, Lizzy could see the Empire State Building and the Chrysler Tower peeking its long, elegant neck out amongst the other skyscrapers.

"I feel like I'm in *The Great Gatsby*," Lizzy said, soaking it all in.

"Good," Darcy replied lifting the menu. "That's the idea."

"Have you ever been here before?"

"Nope. Felt like a good time to try something new, ya know?"

Lizzy blushed. "Agreed."

CHAPTER FORTY-SIX

Darcy bounced her foot to the music. It was a gorgeous place, she had to admit, and she was glad she'd brought Elizabeth there. She was also glad to learn their interests in common did include *The Great Gatsby* and the Roaring Twenties in general, or else this would have been a major flop.

After they had a few drinks and ordered dinner, Darcy leaned across the table. "Want to dance?" she asked, tilting her head to the dance floor beneath them.

Elizabeth hesitated for a moment and then smiled. "Duh."

Darcy reached out her hand, and they walked down the winding staircase to the dance floor. The band was swinging, and Darcy grabbed Elizabeth and spun her out and pulled her in as soon as their feet touched the hardwood floor.

A low giggle escaped from Elizabeth's mouth, and Darcy pulled her close as they swayed back and forth.

"This is amazing, Darce," Elizabeth shouted over the music.

"I'm glad you like it," Darcy replied, placing a kiss on her cheek. "You deserve a night out on the town after your big trial win."

Crimson spread across Elizabeth's face. "You mean *our* trial win. Darce, I still can't believe we won. We saved the house. Like, we actually did it!"

Darcy smiled proudly. "Yes, yes we did. What did Molly say when you called her?" She spun Elizabeth out again and watched as she twirled gracefully back into her arms.

"She was over the moon, of course. Thanks for letting me be the one to call her."

"Of course. She was your witness, after all."

"I'm going to miss it," Elizabeth said, a hint of sadness in her voice.

"What? Being on trial?"

Elizabeth shrugged. "Well, maybe not the trial part. That was the most stressed out I've ever been. But the prep time was nice." She shot a flirtatious grin up at Darcy.

Darcy threw her head back and laughed. "I'm not dying, you know. We work twenty-five feet away from each other." She pulled Elizabeth closer. "Besides, I'm hoping this won't be our last date?"

Elizabeth bit her lip and looked down for a moment before lifting her eyes. "Definitely not."

❖

Darcy leaned back in her seat as the server removed their plates. Dinner had been amazing; the company was more amazing. Elizabeth's eyes were sparkling, and even with the beautiful view outside, Darcy couldn't look anywhere else.

"So," Elizabeth said, setting her napkin on the table. "What's next?"

Darcy laughed. "Oh, I'm sorry, are you expecting more than this?" She motioned to the room.

"Expecting? No." She leaned closer. "Hoping? Yes."

Darcy tapped her finger gently on her chin. "Well, I *was* going to ask if you wanted to come back to my place, but since you're wanting something more exciting—"

"No!" she said, grabbing Darcy's hand. "No, your place sounds great. I'm ready now. Are you ready? Because I'm ready."

Darcy laughed. "Easy, tiger. Let me pay the check."

"I'm sorry, but if you had to look at what I've looked at all night, you'd be ready to get the fuck out of here too." She crossed her arms. "I mean, God, you look incredible."

Darcy felt her heart swell, and she cleared her throat. "Thank you. My view hasn't been bad, either, by the way. I just have a little more self-control than you."

"Must come with old age."

Darcy swatted at her. "Just wait till we get home. You'll regret that."

Home.

She hadn't meant to let the word slip out like that. It was their first real date; they were far from the living together phase. But it felt right, and Elizabeth didn't seem to notice or care, so she didn't draw attention to the faux pax.

The walk back to Darcy's apartment was short, only a few blocks, admittedly one of the reasons she'd selected that place for their date. She didn't have quite as much self-control as she'd let on, and by the time they reached the loft, Darcy's heart felt like it was about to burst, and the dull throb of desire already pulsed between her legs.

She and Elizabeth had had sex more times than she could count by now, but there was something different about tonight. The air felt lighter, the music felt louder, and the city felt brighter. Tonight felt significant, like it was their first time.

"Beer?" Darcy offered as she took Elizabeth's coat and hung it.

"No, thanks." Elizabeth walked over and picked out a record.

Darcy waited and listened as Etta James began to echo through the dimly lit room. She paused by the coat closet, staring. Elizabeth had been in this apartment several times now, even as recently as last week, but there was something about the way she looked in it tonight that sent tingling sensations through Darcy's skin. She looked comfortable there. Familiar.

"Come here," Elizabeth said, crooking a finger.

Darcy strutted across the room.

Elizabeth took her hands, slowly kissing the smooth backs of them. She slid one arm around Darcy's neck, and their eyes remained locked for several seconds. As if they were having a conversation, but no words were being spoken.

They started kissing, steady and intentional, soaking in each touch of their lips. Darcy opened her mouth, allowing Elizabeth's tongue to explore her, the warmth filling the inside of her mouth. She moved her hands beneath Elizabeth's blazer and slid it off as Elizabeth did the same for her.

Elizabeth stopped kissing Darcy and led her to her own bed. They stood there for a moment, kissing again, as they slowly began undressing each other. Elizabeth unbuttoned Darcy's shirt inch by inch, placing soft kisses along Darcy's neck and down to her stomach. Darcy slid Elizabeth's shirt over her head and wrapped her arms around Elizabeth's neck, feeling their bare skin pressed together.

Darcy sat on the end of the bed, and Elizabeth placed one leg on each side of her, straddling her. Her curls tumbled around Darcy's face, and she pulled her closer, until there was nothing between them but their pants and bras.

Darcy stood, picking Elizabeth up with her, impressing even herself with her strength. She laid Elizabeth gently on the bed, kissing her neck, moving her hand beneath her bra before removing it entirely.

Elizabeth followed suit, and soon, they were both topless, rubbing against each other slowly and intentionally. Elizabeth lifted her hips for Darcy to remove her pants and underwear, and Darcy stood at the end of the bed removing her own as Elizabeth lifted up on her arms, watching.

"You are so beautiful," Elizabeth said.

Darcy returned to the bed, placing one leg between Elizabeth's as she kissed her deeply, their mutual excitement for each other becoming readily apparent as Darcy began to move her hips. She listened as Elizabeth's breath grew shorter and faster, and Darcy felt herself begin to build alongside her. She stopped, sliding a hand between Elizabeth's legs. She was met with a smooth wetness that told her just how ready Elizabeth was.

Elizabeth slid a hand between Darcy's legs and let out a low gasp at the instant pleasure the contact produced. Soon, they were moving together in a steady rhythm, climbing higher and higher. Darcy told herself to breathe, trying to make the moment last as long as possible, but it was futile. She opened her eyes and looked at Elizabeth's warm eyes staring back at her.

"Darcy," Elizabeth said, her voice pleading.

At the sound of her name, Darcy tumbled over the edge, releasing not only her orgasm but a flood of emotion into Elizabeth's hand. Elizabeth began shaking, gripping Darcy's back, pulling her closer, their foreheads pressed together as she too unraveled.

Darcy let her body drop onto Elizabeth's, panting heavily. Elizabeth wrapped her arms around her, smoothing her hair. She kissed Darcy's forehead, and Darcy could feel her smile. She couldn't remember a time when she'd felt this way. So connected, so in sync with another person. After a few minutes, they were both sound asleep, their hands and legs still entwined.

CHAPTER FORTY-SEVEN

N ot bad, Eight," Micah Willis said from the doorway to her office. Lizzy's head snapped up. "Huh?"

She'd been lost in thought of her night with Darcy ever since it had happened. They'd spent the rest of Saturday night in each other's arms, waking up to kiss and touch throughout the entire night. And when she'd woken up Sunday, Darcy's arms were still wrapped tightly around her.

They'd spent all day Sunday in Darcy's apartment, not wanting to leave the happy little love shack. She'd slipped into one of Darcy's button-downs to wear in between sex sessions, and it had been so long, it had hit her halfway down her thighs. Perks of dating a tall woman. Darcy had made oat pancakes for breakfast, and they'd ordered Thai for dinner.

Darcy had asked her to stay again last night and told her she could borrow something to wear to work today.

"Um, I think maybe we're not the same size, Darce," Lizzy had said, displaying the length of the dress shirt.

Darcy had laughed and pulled her back into bed, but eventually, Lizzy had to go home.

And so, there she sat, daydreaming, not working on this post-trial memo, not even responding to the *New Paltz Gazette* email requesting she and Darcy be interviewed about the trial victory and the preservation of the Meadows.

Micah's voice snapped her back to reality: "Nice work on winning that trial."

"Oh, right. Thanks," she said, sitting up.

"Is Darcy Hammond as good at trial as they all say? I mean, she's super hot, so juries must love that, right? Did she do the whole bend and snip thing?"

Lizzy rolled her eyes. "It's bend and *snap*, dumbass. And Darcy doesn't need to rely on her looks to be an amazing trial attorney. Which she is, by the way."

He held up his hands in surrender. "All right, all right, damn, just making conversation."

She shook her head as he walked across the hall to his own office. A few seconds later, another knock on her door made her jump.

"Hey, stranger." Jackson's friendly face poked in. "Just wanted to say congrats on the big W! Are you glad to be done? I heard you got to direct a witness. I can't believe it. You must have been so scared. What was it like?"

She laughed, trying to keep up. "How about I tell you over lunch sometime this week?"

He pushed his glasses up. "You got it," he said, bobbing his head and leaving.

It was her first day back in the office since the verdict, and everyone on the floor was buzzing with the big news. Any verdict was big for the firm, but this one had attracted a lot of press, both upstate and in the city. The Defense Bar was about to announce it in this month's journal, and they would be sharing headshots of both Darcy and Lizzy.

It was only nine a.m., and she'd been accosted by "congratulations" and "way to go" for the last hour. Ana had dropped by and given her a celebratory hug that had lingered a bit too long, but she'd let it slide. Cho had stopped scrolling through her phone and said, "Glad you didn't embarrass yourself," when she'd walked in this morning, and now she was having lunch with Jackson.

Lizzy dropped her head to her desk. She was exhausted. On top of the constant congratulatory speeches, plus coming off the trial workload for the last month, she hadn't exactly slept much that weekend. She needed a break.

Her mind started to drift back to Saturday night when there was another knock on her office door. "What?" she snapped.

"Bad time?" Darcy stood bearing two cups of Starbucks, her long camel coat still buttoned and a pair of long navy blue pants and matching heels extending elegantly beneath it. She didn't look tired at all. Of course not. She looked absolutely friggin' perfect as always.

"No, never a bad time for you," Lizzy said, perking up.

Darcy set the coffee cup on her desk.

Lizzy brought the warm liquid to her lips, and inhaled. "Just getting in?" Lizzy asked, checking the clock. Darcy was never here any later than seven thirty on the dot.

"Yeah, took a personal morning," she said, smiling.

There was a warmth to her face that Lizzy had never seen before. She not only *didn't* look tired, but she looked refreshed. Lightened, even. Like a burden had been taken off her shoulders, and she was now weightless.

"Why don't you come down to my office for a second?"

"All right," Lizzy said, grabbing the coffee and following Darcy down the long hall.

Once they were safely inside with the door shut, Darcy took off her coat, throwing it around the back of her chair. "It really is a gorgeous view, isn't it?" Darcy said, staring out the windows. "You know, I used to imagine this view when I was your age. The moment when I'd be able to stand in my own corner office, looking down on the world. The view from the top, I'd call it."

"It's gorgeous," Lizzy said, but she wasn't looking out. She was staring straight at Darcy.

Darcy exhaled slowly, still facing the large windows. "I used to think this is all that mattered. That if I climbed my way to the top, there would be happiness waiting for me there. But the truth is, all that was waiting for me was this big empty office." She paused for a moment. "Until you."

Her voice was quiet; even with the door closed, there were precautions to take.

"Elizabeth, meeting you has been the best thing that's ever happened to me." She had tears in her eyes.

"Hey," Lizzy said, extending her arms. "Are you okay?"

Darcy wiped her eyes and smiled. "I've never been better."

Lizzy kissed her softly on the lips.

"How would you like to get away with me for a long weekend? I always go up to Vermont this time of year. Do some skiing. You could learn to snowboard. I bet you'd be great at it. The resort has a fireplace and all these cute little shops."

Lizzy planted another kiss on Darcy's lips. "You had me at Vermont." Darcy could have said North Dakota, and Lizzy would have gone. She was so in love, she'd follow her to the ends of the earth.

"Great," Darcy said stepping back. "Now, if you'll excuse me, Ms. Taylor, I have a meeting with the partners at nine thirty. There's something important I have to do."

"I'm here for you, Darce. No matter what," Lizzy whispered and squeezed her hand.

"I believe you mean that," Darcy said, her voice still low and hushed.

"I very much do."

VIEW FROM THE TOP

CHAPTER FORTY-EIGHT

Darcy walked down the long, familiar hall to the large conference room at the other end of the floor. The rest of the partners were already seated at the massive, rectangular table, laughing and chatting. The sound of their voices made the hair on the back of her neck stand on end, and she gritted her teeth.

"Congratulations, Darcy," Paul said, leaning back in his chair and smiling.

The men gathered around the table all muttered half-hearted congratulations. They didn't care about her winning this trial, and she knew it.

"Our very own Joan of Arc, gentleman," Mark said.

A brief, forced round of applause echoed around the room as Darcy took her usual seat at the table.

"Hey, Darce, how does it feel? I mean, thanks to you and that junior, an old, dilapidated house gets to sit there and be…old and dilapidated." Richard folded his hands, a smug grin on his face.

"Richard, there's no need to bully," Paul added, his face scrunching up. "Darcy won our firm a lot of good publicity last week. This trial was a means to an end."

"And Elizabeth," Darcy said, her voice cold and distant. "If not for Elizabeth, we wouldn't have won the trial at all."

Mark shifted in his seat. "Uh, who?"

Darcy glared. "Elizabeth Taylor. You know, the junior associate who was on the trial with me? The one who worked her fingers to the bone for a month? The one who did the direct exam of our star witness?"

"Oh, the junior, yes, yes of course," Mark rested his hands on his belly and nodded. "She'll be given due recognition in our firm newsletter at the end of the month, I assure you. You both will!" He clapped and sat forward.

"Well, are we going to sit here and kiss Darcy's perfectly formed ass all morning, or are we going to start talking business?" Richard said. There was a soft collective chuckle from the four men as they leaned forward and looked at the folders in front of them.

Darcy slammed her eyes shut, focusing on each inhale. She felt her heart begin to beat harder inside her chest.

"Yes, well, this week, we have a very big client dinner being hosted at the Mandarin. Darcy, uh, Ms. Kirkpatrick will be there, so perhaps you could..."

"Throw on a dress and flirt with the old dyke," Richard boomed, laughing.

The others joined in the laughter, except for Paul, whose face grew red as he shook his head. "Richard, that is quite enough. Are you looking for a lawsuit?" he whispered through gritted teeth.

"Sorry, Darcy, you know I'm just busting your balls, right?" Richard said, feigning innocence.

Darcy unclenched her jaw and flashed a steely smile across the table. She turned her chair and stared out the window of the conference room. She could feel eyes on the back of her neck as she stood. Crossing her arms, she let out a long, loud sigh. Still, the men sat silently, watching her. "It really is a beautiful view, isn't it?"

There were mumbles behind her. Paul said, "Uh, why, yes, yes, beautiful view."

She heard a few snickers now. Without turning, she uncrossed her arms. "It's a pity it's wasted on morons like you."

The muttering stopped, and the room grew silent.

She took a steady inhale. "I quit," she said, the words echoing off the windows.

She turned. The men sat with their mouths hanging open, looks of sheer confusion spread across their faces.

"I'm sorry, Darcy, what did you—"

"You heard me, Mark. I quit."

They all exchanged glances. Paul spoke up. "I...you must be joking. You're tired. You've had a long trial, why don't you take your Vermont trip a few days early? Clear your head for a bit before you make some emotional, rash decision."

Emotional and rash. Two words only a woman would be described as when making such a powerful statement. The sentence only served to solidify her decision.

"No, Paul, I quit. And in case you're thinking of screwing me over, I want you to know that I've recorded this entire meeting on my phone. And, yes, I will be filing a lawsuit. Maybe even bringing up some other information I know about all of you during my deposition testimony." Darcy pulled out her cell phone, showing the still ongoing recording in progress. New York was a one-party consent state when it came to audio recordings of in-person meetings, and they all knew it. She had them over a barrel now.

"I...well, this..." Richard stood, his fat face shaking with his mouth still hanging open.

"You're rambling, Dick. And honestly, I don't think anybody here is interested in anything else you have to say." She held up the cell phone one more time. "I think we've all heard enough." With that, she walked out of the room, the men frozen in place.

She strutted down the hall to her office. She wouldn't have much time to gather anything. The partners were likely already calling HR, legal, and building security to have her escorted out.

Patty came into her office only seconds after she walked through the door. "Everything all right?" she asked, a concerned look on her face.

"Well, I just quit my job," Darcy said, collecting anything important she wanted to take with her.

"What?" Patty nearly screamed. "Are you serious?"

"Sure am," Darcy said, smiling. "Patty, I'm getting back on the spaceship and getting the hell off this cold, dark planet."

Patty smiled warmly, a few tears trickling down her face. "Oh, thank God, Darcy," she said, wrapping her arms around Darcy. She grabbed her face, smiling through tears. "I am so proud of you, honey."

Darcy felt her eyes begin to well. "Thanks, Patty. But I hate that I'm leaving you like this. Will you be okay?"

Patty waved. "Are you kidding? I'm sixty-four. I've been riding this wave until I can retire in a few years. I told myself I'd stick it out as long as you were here, but the truth is, I've been ready to leave for a long time."

"Oh, Patty, I don't want to cost you your career."

"Darcy, you've just given me years back of my life. Now, tell me what you need me to pack for you."

Darcy looked around. Her diplomas and admission documents were on the wall, so clearly those, and she had a bookshelf with some legal books that were hers, but other than that, the office was pretty sparse. "Can you just wrap up my diplomas and books and stuff? Bring them by my place later next week? We'll have wine and dinner."

Patty gave her a big hug. "Sounds like a plan."

Darcy grabbed her coat from the back of her chair and slid it on. She walked to the bookshelf, removing the single personal photograph from it. It was a picture of her and her dad outside a Southern plantation in South Carolina. She smiled, tucking it into her bag.

Walking over to the door, she looked over her shoulder one last time. She smiled at the beautiful skyline, turned, and shut the door behind her.

CHAPTER FORTY-NINE

Micah's head popped into Lizzy's office, and she took out her headphones. "Hey, Eight, there's drama going down with your woman."

"For the last time, Micah, Ana is not my woman."

"What? No, not Ana. Darcy Hammond. The whole floor is buzzing, you gotta get out here."

What the hell is he talking about? Lizzy threw her headphones on her desk and ran out into the hall. People were sticking their heads out of their offices, and loud whispers and murmurs echoed through the floor.

Ana walked up to Lizzy. "Oh my gosh, have you heard what just happened?"

Panic spread through Lizzy's heart. Was Darcy okay? Was she hurt? "No, what the hell?"

Ana shifted closer and looked over her shoulder. "Apparently, Darcy Hammond just walked into the weekly partner meeting and quit. Right there on the spot. Like, full mic drop and everything."

Lizzy's jaw dropped. She knew there was something different about Darcy this morning, and this must have been it. She had been so reckless, kissing in her office like that. She must have been planning this for a while.

Lizzy couldn't believe it. Darcy had finally done it. She had been so unhappy for so long, and holy shit, she did it. Lizzy started looking up and down the hall, trying to find her. She looked to the area where her office was, and just as she did, Darcy swung open the door and walked out, Patty closely behind her.

God, she looked fabulous. She strutted with her head high and her camel coat open and flowing around her like Superwoman's friggin' cape. She had her sunglasses on her head, her long locks flowing in loose curls behind her. She had a look that exuded confidence. She knew everyone was staring at her. She knew it, and she fucking loved it. She had clearly been waiting for this moment for a long time, and wow, was it glorious to watch.

As Darcy walked past, she gave Lizzy a quick wink before proceeding out the two glass doors, the ampersand between the two *B*s swinging back and forth before finally coming to a rest behind her.

The entire office was abuzz, and Ana finally had to tell everyone to get back to work, but it was no use. The name on everyone's lips was Darcy Hammond.

Lizzy felt a sense of excitement and sadness knowing that the woman she loved was no longer at the end of the hall. She was trying to not be too bummed when she entered her tiny little office and noticed a note stuck beneath her mouse pad.

Dinner at my place?

Lizzy smiled widely as she tucked the note into the pocket of her jacket and unlocked her phone. *See you at 7. I'll bring shitty wine.*

"Hey, Lizzy, think I can pick your brain about something?" Jackson asked, popping around the corner.

"Totally." She smiled. "Fire away."

CHAPTER FIFTY

One year later

L izzy exhaled deeply; her breath billowed and hung around her head like smoke in the cold New York air. She lifted her right hand to block the sun as it reflected from the simple, ten-story brick building and onto her face. *Morris & Morris, PC*, the wooden sign hanging over the door read.

She pulled the black cashmere double-breasted coat tighter around her face. It had been a Christmas present from Darcy, who after almost a year of pleading had finally won the battle of the new coat.

After Darcy had left the firm, news about their trial had continued to spread. Lizzy and Darcy had been invited up to the Meadows last June for the big Pride event Molly had testified about. At Molly's insistence, Darcy had given a little speech about how grateful they both were to be able to represent such an important landmark.

Over the last few months, Lizzy had received so many job offers, she hadn't known what to do with herself. She could have gone to any white-shoe firm just like Byron & Browning and made twice her salary, but taking a page from Darcy's playbook, she'd decided to try a different route.

She'd selected a small immigration firm in the East Village over the glass-covered, monogrammed environment of Byron & Browning. She would still be making a good salary here; in fact, it was more than enough to pay their mortgage and utilities, but unlike at B&B, Lizzy felt like she could actually make a difference at this firm. Like she could impact people's day-to-day lives, not just help the rich people get richer.

Her phone buzzed, and she fished it out of her pocket.

Darcy: *Good luck today, babe. You got this!*

Lizzy smiled wide and texted back: *Good luck to *you* today. Have a great first day at school. Make lots of friends and listen to your elders.*

Darcy: *You'll pay for that when you get home later, counselor.* She ended with a winking emoji.

Lizzy blushed and slid her phone back into her pocket.

Darcy was beginning her first day of graduate school today at CUNY. She had decided to get her master's in history, focusing on Civil War era America, in the hope of becoming a college professor. After studying for and crushing the GRE, she was finally ready to start her new journey in life.

Lizzy couldn't be happier for her.

Apparently, Darcy's little threat to Byron & Browning on her way out had proved to be successful, because she'd received a certified letter stating that she would be getting a very generous severance package for "all her years of hard work at the firm," even though Darcy had been the one to quit.

That severance package had paid for Darcy's entire tuition, and she would be debt free when she graduated in two short years. Not only that, they used the rest of the money to place a down payment on an objectively overpriced condo in Williamsburg.

Darcy had said good-bye to her Soho loft around the same time Lizzy had said good-bye to having three roommates in West Harlem, although she and Amina still hung out and had dinner all the time. Lizzy had offered to move into the loft so Darcy could keep it, but Darcy said she wanted a place they could call theirs, and Brooklyn just felt like the right fit.

Lizzy exhaled again. She remembered this time last year, when she had been looking at the tall glass tower that was Byron & Browning. She'd had no idea what was waiting for her in that building. It was so high up to her then, she couldn't even see the top. But once she did get there, she'd realized that the view was simply that: a view. Pretty, yes, but just a view. It didn't bring happiness or satisfaction or fulfillment. It didn't make her any better a lawyer, and it certainly didn't make her any better a person. No view from a glass building could give her that.

Smiling, she took a few steps forward, pulling open the single door and stepping into the warmth of the new building. As she walked to the elevator and pushed the up button, she smiled. Her new office was on the tenth floor. She wondered what her new view would be like from there, all the way at the top.

About the Author

Morgan Adams currently lives in Boston, Massachusetts, with her beautiful wife and their three fur babies. She was raised in Florida and moved to New York City shortly after attending law school in Virginia. In all, she has lived in six different states. A product of the many places she has lived, Morgan enjoys a wide array of hobbies, including exploring historical homes, hiking, scuba diving, traveling, rowing, and volunteering in her local community.

Books Available From Bold Strokes Books

All This Time by Sage Donnell. Erin and Jodi share a complicated past, but a very different present. Will they ever be able to make a future together work? (978-1-63679-622-2)

Crossing Bridges by Chelsey Lynford. When a one-night stand between a snowboard instructor and a business executive becomes more, one has to overcome her past, while the other must let go of her planned future. (978-1-63679-646-8)

Dancing Toward Stardust by Julia Underwood. Age has nothing to do with becoming the person you were meant to be, taking a chance, and finding love. (978-1-63679-588-1)

Evacuation to Love by CA Popovich. As a hurricane rips through Florida, so too are Joanne and Shanna's lives upended. It'll take a force of nature to show them the love it takes to rebuild. (978-1-63679-493-8)

Lean in to Love by Catherine Lane. Will badly behaving celebrities, erotic sex tapes, and steamy scandals prevent Rory and Ellis from leaning in to love? (978-1-63679-582-9)

The Romance Lovers Book Club by MA Binfield and Toni Logan. After their book club reads a romance about an American tourist falling in love with an English princess, Harper and her best friend, Alice, book an impulsive trip to London hoping they'll both fall for the women of their dreams. (978-1-63679-501-0)

Searching for Someday by Renee Roman. For loner Rayne Thomas, her only goal for working out is to build her confidence, but Maggie Flanders has another idea, and neither is prepared for the outcome. (978-1-63679-568-3)

Truly Home by J.J. Hale. Ruth and Olivia discover home is more than a four-letter word. (978-1-63679-579-9)

View from the Top by Morgan Adams. When it comes to love, sometimes the higher you climb, the harder you fall. (978-1-63679-604-8)

Blood Rage by Illeandra Young. A stolen artifact, a family in the dark, an entire city on edge. Can SPEAR agent Danika Karson juggle all three over a weekend with the "in-laws" while an unknown, malevolent entity lies in wait upon her very skin? (978-1-63679-539-3)

Ghost Town by R.E. Ward. Blair Wyndon and Leif Henderson are set to prove ghosts exist when the mystery suddenly turns deadly. Someone or something else is in Masonville, and if they don't find a way to escape, they might never leave. (978-1-63679-523-2)

Good Christian Girls by Elizabeth Bradshaw. In this heartfelt coming of age lesbian romance, Lacey and Jo help each other untangle who they are from who everyone says they're supposed to be. (978-1-63679-555-3)

Guide Us Home by CF Frizzell and Jesse J. Thoma. When acquisition of an abandoned lighthouse pits ambitious competitors Nancy and Sam against each other, it takes a WWII tale of two brave women to make them see the light. (978-1-63679-533-1)

Lost Harbor by Kimberly Cooper Griffin. For Alice and Bridget's love to survive, they must find a way to reconcile the most important passions in their lives—devotion to the church and each other. (978-1-63679-463-1)

Never a Bridesmaid by Spencer Greene. As her sister's wedding gets closer, Jessica finds that her hatred for the maid of honor is a bit more complicated than she thought. Could it be something more than hatred? (978-1-63679-559-1)

The Rewind by Nicole Stiling. For police detective Cami Lyons and crime reporter Alicia Flynn, some choices break hearts. Others leave a body count. (978-1-63679-572-0)

Turning Point by Cathy Dunnell. When Asha and her former high school bully Jody struggle to deny their growing attraction, can they move forward without going back? (978-1-63679-549-2)

When Tomorrow Comes by D. Jackson Leigh. Teague Maxwell, convinced she will die before she turns 41, hires animal rescue owner Baye Cobb to rehome her extensive menagerie. (978-1-63679-557-7)

You Had Me at Merlot by Melissa Brayden. Leighton and Jamie have all the ingredients to turn their attraction into love, but it's a recipe for disaster.(978-1-63679-543-0)

Appalachian Awakening by Nance Sparks. The more Amber's and Leslie's paths cross, the more this hike of a lifetime begins to look like a love of a lifetime. (978-1-63679-527-0)

Dreamer by Kris Bryant. When life seems to be too good to be true and love is within reach, Sawyer and Macey discover the truth about the town of Ladybug Junction, and the cold light of reality tests the hearts of these dreamers. (978-1-63679-378-8)

Eyes on Her by Eden Darry. When increasingly violent acts of sabotage threaten to derail the opening of her glamping business, Callie Pope is sure her ex, Jules, has something to do with it. But Jules is dead…isn't she? (978-1-63679-214-9)

Letters from Sarah by Joy Argento. A simple mistake brought them together, but Sarah must release past love to create a future with Lindsey she never dreamed possible. (978-1-63679-509-6)

Lost in the Wild by Kadyan. When their plane crash-lands, Allison and Mike face hunger, cold, a terrifying encounter with a bear, and feelings for each other neither expects. (978-1-63679-545-4)

Not Just Friends by Jordan Meadows. A tragedy leaves Jen struggling to figure out who she is and what is important to her. (978-1-63679-517-1)

Of Auras and Shadows by Jennifer Karter. Eryn and Rina's unexpected love may be exactly what the Community needs to heal the rot that comes not from the fetid Dark Lands that surround the Community but from within. (978-1-63679-541-6)

The Secret Duchess by Jane Walsh. A determined widow defies a duke and falls in love with a fashionable spinster in a fight for her rightful home. (978-1-63679-519-5)

Winter's Spell by Ursula Klein. When former college roommates reunite at a wedding in Provincetown, sparks fly, but can they find true love when evil sirens and trickster mermaids get in the way? (978-1-63679-503-4)

Coasting and Crashing by Ana Hartnett. Life comes easy to Emma Wilson until Lake Palmer shows up at Alder University and derails her every plan. (978-1-63679-511-9)

Every Beat of Her Heart by KC Richardson. Piper and Gillian have their own fears about falling in love, but will they be able to overcome those feelings once they learn each other's secrets? (978-1-63679-515-7)

Fire in the Sky by Radclyffe and Julie Cannon. Two women from different worlds have nothing in common and every reason to wish they'd never met—except for the attraction neither can deny. (978-1-63679-561-4)

Grave Consequences by Sandra Barret. A decade after necromancy became licensed and legalized, can Tamar and Maddy overcome the lingering prejudice against their kind and their growing attraction to each other to uncover a plot that threatens both their lives? (978-1-63679-467-9)

Haunted by Myth by Barbara Ann Wright. When ghost-hunter Chloe seeks an answer to the current spectral epidemic, all clues point to one very famous face: Helen of Troy, whose motives are more complicated than history suggests and whose charms few can resist. (978-1-63679-461-7)

Invisible by Anna Larner. When medical school dropout Phoebe Frink falls for the shy costume shop assistant Violet Unwin, everything about their love feels certain, but can the same be said about their future? (978-1-63679-469-3)

Like They Do in the Movies by Nan Campbell. Celebrity gossip writer Fran Underhill becomes Chelsea Cartwright's personal assistant with the aim of taking the popular actress down, but neither of them anticipates the clash of their attraction. (978-1-63679-525-6)

Limelight by Gun Brooke. Liberty Bell and Palmer Elliston loathe each other. They clash every week on the hottest new TV show, until Liberty starts to sing and the impossible happens. (978-1-63679-192-0)

Playing with Matches by Georgia Beers. To help save Cori's store and help Liz survive her ex's wedding, they strike a deal: a fake relationship, but just for one week. There's no way this will turn into the real deal. (978-1-63679-507-2)